A Kingdom's Possession

Nicole J. Persun

Booktrope Editions
Seattle WA, 2011

Copyright 2011 Nicole J. Persun

This work is licensed under a Creative Commons Attribution-Noncommercial-No Derivative Works 3.0 Unported License.

Attribution — You must attribute the work in the manner specified by the author or licensor (but not in any way that suggests that they endorse you or your use of the work).

Noncommercial — You may not use this work for commercial purposes.

No Derivative Works — You may not alter, transform, or build upon this work.

Inquiries about additional permissions should be directed to: info@libertary.com

Edited by: Katie Flanagan

Cover Design: Sean Dailey
Verv Creative / vervcreative.com

Cover Photo: Natalie Norvell

ISBN 978-1-935961-22-2

Library of Congress Control Number: 2011912153

Dedication

This book could be dedicated to so many, but it remains with my mother Catherine for her support, and my father Terry for his guidance.

Chapter 1

Max

I pressed the keys harder into the palm of my hand so they didn't clank together. The sound of my feet scrambling over the cobblestones and my quick breaths became matted and still. Rain pounded on the doors of the taverns like drunken men. And just as ale would wash away their troubles, the downpour washed away the salty grime of the seaside capital. It amazed me that anyone could sleep on such a night, but yet the buildings seemed empty.

The storm created a haze of everything; it masked the detail and smudged the shadows. The sleeping city became a blur of bulky shapes and shades of gray while inns' lanterns flickered in the rain.

I knew the main streets and alleyways of Alice like the wind knew the ocean. Even blinded by the storm, I could find my way. Scrambling, panting, sweating, slipping, I wiped the rainwater from my eyes with a sleeve, looked back, and saw nothing.

The cobblestones were frozen and slick under my bare feet. Numb toes suddenly stumbled and sent me forward, slamming my hands against the gritty ground. I shut my eyes against the fall, suppressing a whimper. Cursing quietly, I slapped a wet hand to my chest, felt the small round pendant still clasped around my neck and my heart beating wildly behind it. I looked back once more, and again, saw nothing but gray.

My eyes swept the area and right away I noticed the keys. They had slipped from my fingers with the fall. I snatched them up and unlocked the metal cuff around my ankle with haste. The hinges squeaked as I pried them open, clattered when I set the contraption on the stones. I rubbed my ankle and examined the rawness in the dim light. Fresh blood dappled my fingers and my right foot, but easily washed away with the rain. I would heal.

I ran a finger over the words etched into the metal and whispered them slowly to myself, "Property of the Red Eye Tavern. Return Accordingly." I spat on it and threw it down the road into the darkness. The resonance of metal hitting stone echoed behind me, but I had already started running, keys still in hand.

Rounding a tight bend, I cut into a small alley, stopped and listened. There were no sounds of footsteps, no cracks of laughter or hushed conversation in the mess of weather. Silence spread its cloak across the town, all except for the rush of the ocean and the hiss of wind and rain. I let my glances skirt the slim road and delve cautiously into the shadows, but they could detect no movement.

Yet something was wrong. A strange sensation shuttered through my body. My muscles began to tighten and jerk outside my control. A profound dizziness took me. My breaths became slow and shallow and my hands gripped at my thin clothes as if someone else was grabbing me. Cold hands fumbled as my mind spun out of control in an instant.

I clutched my head, but it would not stop pulsing. Whispers came into my brain, not from the outside world but from a place deep inside my body. Its vibration rattled my bones, hummed like a thousand flies swarming around hot, raw meat. I flinched and sunk down to the ground.

The clouds above me were parting abruptly, revealing a moon that fit perfectly in the little line of sky the tall alley walls allowed me to see. It looked like the open mouth of a god, ready to envelope me in tongue and teeth.

"Who's there?" My voice sounded distant, simple. "What's happening? What's happening?"

The rain subsided as my consciousness fell over a ledge into a deep lake of disorder. I was sinking fast into a depth that made me quiver. It felt as though someone was climbing inside of me through a hole between my breasts, liquid was being poured into my ribcage, voices roared from above the surface. That liquid was sorrow, thin and red like the finest Delan wine. It pooled into my heart like a spilled glass on the floor of an empty room. My body was a cage, my breath poison, my blood pain. *Something* lingered within as if I could help it. The entity wanted my service, was now inside me demanding it.

I would not give in. I clawed at my chest to get it out, pulled at my hair before the pressure blew open my skull. I screamed, shattering the final walls that held back the spill of its helplessness. And then all was silent but the sound of rain hitting the cobblestones.

With eyes wide, I looked around. The dark colors and shapes of night were all around me; the walls of the alley, the rain drops, my clothing, and the keys, now with a stain of dark scarlet where my hand had started to bleed from a tight grip. My chest felt heavy, but there was nothing to explain the terrible sensation I had just experienced. Everything looked the same.

Rising to my feet, I placed a shaky hand on my stomach and felt it clench with sickness. I rested my back against the wall and lifted my face to the rain falling from above. It cooled my cheeks and urged my head back farther with the weight of my hair. My stomach twisted and I kept looking up toward the unforgiving sky. But soon I had no choice. I buckled over, fell to my hands and knees, and vomited. Tears rolled down my cheeks, lingered at my chin, fell to the ground. A cough escaped my mouth in place of a whimper and my fingers dug into the grit of the cold road. A wave of terror and shock broke over me, pushed the tears to the surface and mixed them with the storm. I sucked in air desperately, spat, vomited again. That sour, wretched smell filled the air and I wiped my mouth on my sleeve. The rain was already washing it away, a diluted yellow-orange that followed the little creases in the stone road down the alley to where the ground met the buildings beyond. I stayed shrunken over for a long time. It was the sudden feeling that I was not alone that made me look up.

At the open end of the alley a tall dark figure walked by. My heart leaped inside my chest and in one fluid movement I stood and flattened against the wall. I held my breath as he made his way down the alley. My hands shook. And he was at my side in seven even steps.

The cloaked man raised a hand and I immediately turned my head to avoid a beating. I waited a moment, felt the sickness still holding on but fear slowly overcoming it in the pit of my stomach. When the violence never came, I looked up at his face. He tipped his hat upward until I could see the tight smile on his lips, the gentle, yet pointed nose. His eyes were still a mystery.

"Out for a walk?" he said through a perfectly shaped grin. He had an accent that I didn't recognize, but it was so fluid, his voice so deep, that I almost wanted to hear more. Almost.

I didn't answer.

"Here, you look cold." He shrugged off his jacket and offered it to me. I sidestepped to avoid his touch.

"I don't know you," I mumbled.

"But you could know me, if you wanted to," he said, shrugging back into his coat. "My name is Johnny." He bowed his head. The man was lanky, but stood confidently; broad shoulders set back to present a chest that was strong, but not burley like a blacksmith or sailor. His fingers, curled around his long sleeves, were undoubtedly matched by hands that were big and callused. But he was still modest, his voice didn't overpower, he didn't hit me like most men did when they saw a slave, or a girl swallowed in the privacy of a dark alley. I couldn't begin to guess what type of man he was. It was hard to know what to expect and that's what disturbed me the most.

"Just...be on your way. I don't *want* to know you," I said a little louder.

"I'm flattered by that," he said with a twist of his lips. They parted into a warm smile and it startled me, coming from a stranger. "And fine, I will be on my way," he said, waving his hand through the air. I flinched. "But you, you'll catch a chill in this storm soon if you don't go home." He paused. "If you have a home." I could see his head tip as if his eyes had traveled down to my pendant, to the keys in my bleeding hand, down to my bloody ankle, and to the ground where my vomit was mixing with the rain and dirt. He looked back up, but this time his eyes peeked out from under the rim of his hat. Little glimpses of light flickered against his dark irises, making me nervous. "That cuff back there, the slave tag, was that yours?" he asked gently.

Rain splashed around my feet and struck my face like an angry hand when I ran. I could hear the man speak to me as I left him behind in that alley, but I never found out what he said.

* Johnny *

It seemed the trees framing the road were all competing to present the deepest, richest shade of autumn colors. And no matter how many hues of gold they presented, their leaves could not match the magnificence of the palace they led to. The structure stood proud and tall on top of a high bluff that overlooked the wild sea and the rolling fields that rested behind its city. Alice, the most powerful of the Four Kingdoms, showed off her prosperity to every ship that entered her port; the snapping flags on her terraces and the high, rosy towers left a regal scent in the air.

I stood at the bottom of the hill, looking up along the road through the arbor of trees to the top, where an overly detailed gate marked the entrance of the noble beast. This was a city that worshipped power, but I had decided long ago that that was solely because power was all Alice held. There was no substance to the kingdom, just a mighty giant, breathing in exports and gold and excreting bad tempers and vanity.

I missed my own palace on autumn days like this. The trees there would look as though they had been painted by the boldest of artists. Retreating storm clouds would match the walls of the Second Kingdom's fortress, the only difference being that the strong stones would hold a glow in the sun, where the clouds would not. Unlike the First Kingdom, Valta was tough and kindly, her green flags waving proudly over the city she watched. Unlike the First Kingdom, Valta was without her heir to the throne.

Without me.

My reason to flee Valta's island in the night some five years ago was simple: her people deserved a king who was devoted to their wellbeing and to their kingdom. And I, simply, was not. She had been my responsibility from the time I was born. But even my younger twin, forced to fend off my father's criticism alone after I left, could not be traditionally accepted as Heir to the Valtan Throne. Selfish as it seemed to all of my family, it was right that I fled.

I turned and went back down the road, away from the long entrance to the castle and toward the port of Alice. Everything was cast in yellows and golds; the cobble stones, the buildings, the water, the boats. Voices bustled along the currents of sea air that ran alongside the shore. It was hard not to drown in them. The crowds rocked as one in a swell of heat and sweat.

Ships carrying exports from Dela, the most fertile of all the Cavail Islands, sailed into port with loads of everything imaginable; grains, fruits, vegetables, meats, eggs, ale, the finest wine in the nation, and of course, flowers and extracts fresh from the island's Fertile Hills. The working sailors were hard to avoid on the busy street as they heaved barrels and bags of grain into the permanent shops along the port.

As I walked through the lines of seaside tents and shops, carefully weaving through the streams of people, vendors called out their offers. I knew which products were good and finally, in the center of the port, I came across the best vendor there. I smiled as I walked up, knowing exactly what I wanted before I even reached the booth.

"Fine day," I commented to the woman calling out deals behind the makeshift counter. She turned my way in a big, sweeping motion and grinned cheek to cheek.

"Johnny, what can I do for you today? The usual?"

I tipped my hat to shade my eyes from the sun. The stiff wool was still damp from my walk in the rain the night before. My jaw tightened at the thought of the slave tag, still tucked deep into my knapsack. The girl had undoubtedly escaped from it.

Despite the warmth of the day, I shivered. "Six apples today, Meg. And do you still have a jar of that sweet lavender honey?"

"Why sure I do," she said as she handed me the apples. I stuffed them into my bag. "Saved a jar just for you," she said, and held out the delicacy.

"I thank you kindly," I said, gently putting the jar into my bag.

"Any extra service I can do for you, handsome?" she asked lightly. It always surprised me when she said that; *handsome*, as if it were a respectable thing for her to say to a young man who could easily be her son.

"That's all for today," I said, and passed her the proper number of coins.

"Can I expect I'll be seeing you the next day the Delan tents are in town?"

"I'll be back for more of that honey, Meg." I walked away.

"I'll take care to save some, real special, just for you, Johnny," she said over the noise of the crowd, but I was lost in the swarm before the last word had been tossed from her tongue.

The walk back to the Gold Town Inn and Stables was fairly short from the main stretch of port shops. Though I was a prince in title and in blood, I was merely a stable hand to the city of Alice.

With an extended effort, I slid the stable doors open. Hung on long metal rungs along the top of the doorway, the sun soon flooded the stables with afternoon sunlight. A horse whinnied and shifted in its stall while another kicked at its door in restlessness. The barn smelled of ripe apples, straw, and horse manure, but it was familiar. A small tack and feed room with a cot in the corner had remained my home for years. It was nothing like the Valtan Palace, but it was my current stay nonetheless.

I threw some hay into each of the attended guest stalls and sneezed from the dust. Snatching an apple from my bag, I strolled to the end of the barn and offered it to the Inn Keeper's horse. She took it gently from my hand and made sure to lick the excess juice from my fingers once she was done with the fruit. I patted the palomino's shoulder and then went about my barn tasks.

Hours later, my arms tired from cleaning out the stalls and my hands from polishing leather, I closed the doors of the stables for the night. The sun had already slipped below the hills behind Alice, and the sky was welcoming another set of storm clouds. With them came a deep, sea-misty fog and a thin rain that was so sharp, it pierced through my clothing.

I strolled along the waterfront in the quiet of the late evening until all light had left the sky. Ships bumped up against old wooden docks; water caressed their sides. They swayed in rhythm with each other, like dancers in a ballroom. Music moving them in sync with one another so carelessly and gracefully even the darkest night could not hide their rosy cheeks and shiny brows, the way the water helped them waltz.

The salty air quivered over my lips and whispered along the sea.

Deeper into the city, the tavern lights glowed like lost fireflies. They were a sorry comfort for a young man, missing his kingdom, thinking of a mysterious girl. But a barmaid would serve ale to anyone, if he had the right wink and an extra penny. And that was a lure too strong for resistance tonight.

I made my way through a crowd of thick, clingy fog to a waterfront tavern, tipped my hat just over my eyes, and stepped through the door.

* Max *

The morning sunlight turned the puddles dappling the road into pools of gold. I knelt beside one, peering into the muddy water to see my reflection. Strands of dark brown, knotty hair stuck to my forehead, dirt smudged my cheeks, the skin around my lips and under my eyes looked puffy. But that is not why I examined myself.

I had developed a rash behind my right ear, raised slightly like a burn. It extended down the side of my neck, was the color of fresh carrots. And the more I studied it, the more it puzzled me. This was no rash; it was too perfect. It swirled in maybe four, maybe five, spirals and in the center of the biggest spiral was the letter *A* nearing the size of my thumbnail. Altogether the mark was the length of my index finger, a stain on my skin like that of blackberry juice or chopped beats.

I stood up and stepped over my reflection and down the road, trying not to worry about the mark or the strange sensations the previous night. I was free. My ankle was swollen and raw, my stomach was empty, and my mouth tasted of vomit, but to walk in the streets with no aim or chore was as golden as the First Kingdom's palace.

I kept close to the walls of the buildings, took back ways and alleys. Everywhere I went I ended up back on the waterfront. Men and women had just started to rise from their city homes and come out to buy from the Delan tents. The moan of tightened lines and old hulls filled the air, as a shout here and a snort there would fill the pockets of empty sound.

I peeked around the corner of a building, trying to listen closer to a conversation. I'd always thought it would be wise to stow away on a ship and live on Dela. Her Fertile Hills would cradle me and I would live out my days with no name or reason. I would be truly *free*. There had been no slaves on Dela or anywhere else for thousands of years, but in Alice, where greed and power could drive anyone to gain anything, it was still accepted as a viable business. It sickened me. Perhaps if I could escape the city, I could escape the chance of becoming a slave once again.

Unfortunately, I could not hear the words of the sailors and men on the docks. Someone was whispering behind me, words toiling in beautiful gibberish through my brain. I spun around, yet there was no one. I looked over my shoulder, no one. I turned in a complete circle to try to find the whisperer, but I was alone in that little alley.

I focused back on the port. Men were moving barrels and sacks of grain, talking and grunting and flexing their thick arms. Women held baskets and coin purses, giggling in groups or flirting with the lazier workers. The vendors in the tents busied themselves with minute tasks; the earlier risers were already calling out their products to the little crowds of customers.

The whispering started again. I shook my head to get rid of it, but that only made it come stronger into my ears, hum through my chest. I fingered my pendant, trying to relax, cool down. The air had gotten hot fast; my back and arms started to sweat.

The voice was that of a young woman's and she was speaking in a language I did not recognize. I had the tense, eerie feeling that this voice came from the sensation I had had the night before. It was the same kind of desperate, demanding force. And the voice was coming from within me, deep in the pit of my stomach, riding out my thought.

I clapped my hands nervously and shook my head, and then she was gone. Perhaps the voice had been only nerves, my mind playing tricks on me. Wiping my nose on my sleeve, I started down the port's main road. I stomped my feet, wiggled my fingers, anything to feel as though I was still in control. I paced for hours. I was safe by the main stretch of port; the owners of the Red Eye Tavern never ventured down that far, especially when the streets were packed with people. I simply kept moving, trying to ignore my own uneasiness.

As the day ripened, so did the swell of people and the stench of their breath and bodies. The warm day was packed with men and women on the shoreline, mingling for products and yelling over the sounds of the rest of the crowd. They were slower than mules, but I paced around them, bumping shoulders and muttering apologies. I wove at a steady pace through the mess of consumers.

I didn't get a worried, edgy feeling again until later that day. There was no more whispering, no more voices or movements from inside as before. This was a feeling like someone was watching me, following me. I swiveled my head casually, catching my followers in the corner of my eye. Two men, burly like fat steers, and they had swords.

It was uncharacteristic for anyone to have that sort of weaponry in such a crowd. This was no festival day, and they were no guards or men of the law. They were Alician *soldiers* and they were after one thing. It was obvious that it was me, but their reason was not so evident.

I turned and walked faster through the crowd, the men on my wake. They bumped and shoved while I sidestepped and wove through the sea of bodies. My pace was faster, didn't draw as much attention.

Quickly, I cut down an alleyway and ran so fast my feet flew over the cobblestones, tense and ready to stumble. But I did not.

The sun was already slipping behind the hills into another day, and the sky was filling with the storm of the night before. Good. I could easily lose the men in a sea fog.

A Kingdom's Possession

I came out the other side of the alley and turned left, heading into the pit of the city to follow a road that would skirt the northern edge and eventually lead back to the port. The men were gaining on my heels, their swords clattering in a chime of threat and violence. I got back to the port and ran through the streets like mad. Delans were packing up their booths, getting ready to return home in the morning. Slaves followed their masters, heads down. Alicians meandered, talking to whoever wanted to listen and buy them drinks later on. None of them paid attention to me, but that had always been the case.

Heading south toward the city's palace, I turned down a small road, thinking to shake the two big men off my tail, but at the other end of the road, another appeared, clad in the same worn and faded leather, with a sword and pulsing muscles. I ducked past him in one bold, swift move and ran. The three of them were catching up, not wearing down like I had anticipated. But then in one small instant, I doubled back, cut down a skinny alley, and ducked into a door to watch them hurry past from the shadows of the dark room.

My head and fingers pulsed in warning. I waited, but the sound of their feet didn't return. I could hear yells coming from down the road, but none that came back to greet me.

When all sounds had closed to silence and the remaining shards of sun were gone from the sky, I stood on stiff, cold legs and looked around. Dim, spotty light touched each and every blocky shape in the room. It smelled of dust and oil, with a faint wisp of grain and manure. I reached down and touched the floor. Blinking, I lifted my hand and let the thick and bristly strands of straw fall through my fingers.

It was a tack and feed room, probably joined to a small stable for some inn. A horse whinnied from behind a door opposite the one I came through. I crouched behind some bales and suppressed a sneeze from the dust. My fingers dug into the straw. A slow whine from the door made my heart thump wildly inside my chest. And then there came the sound of someone's voice, speaking into the dark in a deep, musical whisper.

"I know you're there, come out or I'll make you." What he said wasn't a threat, just a fact.

Rising to my feet, I stepped out from behind the bales. There wasn't much light, but the silhouette of the hat and the sound of his soft and warming voice was enough to trigger my memory.

* Johnny *

Something glinted in the straw when I stepped through the door into my room, ready to surrender to sleep. I could hear breathing, a soft but heavy inhale and exhale, like someone was nervous or tired from running.

Slowly, I let my knapsack slip from my shoulder onto the floor. Then I bent down and hooked a finger through the chain that had caught my eye when I had walked in. I stood tall and breathed lightly, fingering what looked like an amber stone, set in silver and hung beautifully on a chain. I held back a gasp and whispered into the dark. "I know you're there, come out or I'll make you."

It took a moment for her to creep out from behind the bales stacked in the corner, but when she did, she stood straight and waited. I made no further sound, no fast actions.

Carefully, I tucked the pendant into my pocket and walked over to a shelf to get a lantern. "No point in running any longer, you're safe here. You may sit on that bale," I pointed to it with my chin. She made no move to do as I asked at first, but when I turned to get a stool from beside my bed, and placed it in the center of the room, she moved over to the bale in the corner and sat down. Searching for matches, I spoke again, hoping to console her a bit by breaking the uncomfortable silence.

"There's a blanket hanging on the wall over there, you see it? If you're cold, you may use that," I said. Turning toward her once I found a match, I waited for a response. She didn't move or make a sound. "Like I said, you're safe here. Do you want *me* to get the blanket for you?"

She shook her head. "I'm not cold."

I let out a light laugh. "Well I'm sorry. I just assumed you were, by your violent shaking."

She shook her head again. "I'm fine."

I walked over to the stool I had set out, and sat down across from her. Searching her face like it would hold all the answers in the world, I marveled in how perfectly it was shaped. This was a beautiful, intelligent young woman. Brilliant green eyes stared back at me, all but reluctant. She was simply silent.

I shook my head and went about lighting up the room, hoping that my fascination was nothing more than just an interest in a stranger; curiosity in something different.

* Max *

With the flare of the new flame, the man's face was lit into a real form. The little fire danced, cast shadows across his sharp features and turned his dark eyes into pools of black. In the little circle, the obscurity of the night subsided and the light brought on the detail of his shape, his clothing, his face. It made me uncomfortable to think that he could see me just as clearly as I could see him.

His brow was creased in concentration as he tampered with the lantern, but when he looked up his expression relaxed into a contemplative smile. He placed the lantern on the ground between us and returned to his stool. It moaned and creaked when he leaned forward, his elbows on his knees, and spoke to me in a whisper. "Normally my first question would be regarding why you're here, but that is not what I'm wondering now." He tipped his head. "I remember you from last night. What are you doing here?"

I glanced down toward my feet to avoid his eyes.

He wasn't deterred. "Are you going to speak? Or must I sit here in silence and simply wonder?"

I pierced him with my stare and he looked away in one, obvious, weak moment. I knew I had to be strong, assert myself. "I will speak, but I will do nothing more."

"I never asked for more," he said.

I leaned back so my face was obscured by the shadows of the bales behind me.

"So do you have a name?"

After a long moment, I answered. "Yes."

He laughed, snapping the tension in half. His expression gave away nothing but an unmatchable intelligence that stopped my breath in my throat. It intrigued me, and it scared me.

"Well," he waved his hands in a flourish and I flinched. "What is it?"

"My name is Max," I said flatly.

"A boy's name?"

"Is that a problem?"

He shook his head. "No, I would just expect a more suitable name for a lady like yourself. Mine's Johnny, but you already know that."

"A lady like myself? And exactly what is that?" I asked, leaning forward into the light. Johnny shifted in his seat.

"I have something to show you," he said. I shuttered when he stood, but he patted the air with his hands. "I will not hurt you," he assured. Then he strode over to his knapsack and pulled out my slave tag. It was as if I were staring a demon right in the face. I clenched my hands, bracing for what would come next. He settled back in his seat and tossed it onto the ground. It bounced on the hay and landed against my foot. The metal was cold and all too familiar.

"Why did you show me this? I know very well what it is," I said, my voice intentionally bitter.

His lips twisted and his eyes narrowed slightly. "So you wore it once?"

"I never said that."

He frowned. "The keys you had last night, were they not to the lock on this slave tag?"

"Don't say that word." My voice wavered and trailed off and my nails bit into the palms of my hands. Every part of my body was sore, whether it was from an open wound or a tense muscle. And now he was practically beating my freedom, all that I held dear, with the cuff at my feet.

"I didn't mean to offend you," he said. It bothered me that his tone reflected exactly what he had said. He was truly sincere, a trait not common in the city of Alice.

"Why do you have that?" I asked, staring at his face so intently that he looked away.

He tipped his head up and tossed his hat into the corner. "I found it. Is it yours?"

"It does not belong to me," I said.

"But you wore it once?"

"Once," I said, my tone silken.

He walked toward me and knelt down so he was at my level. Looking into my eyes, his voice caressed the air so lightly I could barely hear what he said. "I am sorry, Max. Truly. I know what it is like to live without voice."

I raised an eyebrow and held his stare while reaching down and grabbing the cuff. Without breaking eye contact, I threw the metal ring into the corner. "And how do you know, hmm?"

"I was a prince once, of Valta, the Second Kingdom. But that is in the past." He stepped away and sat back on his stool.

"A *prince*?" I laughed. "Fool. You're comparing the life of a slave to the life of royalty?"

I was surprised when he laughed also. "You don't doubt that I was a prince?"

I nodded at his right shoulder and he glanced down. His shirt was stretched over his shoulder slightly, revealing a scar right where his arm attached to his torso. He quickly settled his sleeve back over the little mark.

"I believe you *are* a prince," I said. "You have a brand."

He glanced at me from the corner of his eye and touched the mark through his shirt. "I have the Royal Brand, yes. So you do not doubt my heritage. Regarding why I am not in my palace and instead living as a stable hand, I will not say," he said urgently.

I shrugged. "Everyone has their secrets, and I did not ask. But you are still wrong. The life of a prince is leisurely and fat. That of a slave…" I trailed off.

"I only meant that both lives are lived under the veil of someone else. Both lives are overpowered by the ones around them."

I spat on the ground, heat rising in my chest. "I recommend you spend some time on the street before you go finding similarities between royalty and trash." I said.

Johnny waved his hands in the air to wipe away the subject. "I apologize," he said.

I shook my head. "Don't."

For a moment, the room was silent. Johnny looked at the floor, and I held my gaze on him. The lantern light flickered.

Heavy fists pounded on the door suddenly, angry and wild, killing the quiet. I slipped behind the bale I had been sitting on and Johnny stood up, alert.

"Who's there?" he asked, his voice loud and deep. I steadied myself as the door burst open and three big men strode into the room. They were the same men who had chased me earlier that day, and I held my breath, waiting for the moment when Johnny would point to the bale I was behind and they'd take me away, somewhere cold and cruel.

But Johnny's voice was not weak. It was cold. "How dare you intrude?"

"A woman. An orange mark behind her ear. Seen her?" The voice that spoke was deep and overpowering, but Johnny seemed to hold his ground. I closed my eyes, bracing for his next words.

"I have not." He said. I could hear the big men shifting around on the straw.

"You sure?" The squeak of leather and the sliding of a blade in its sheath was enough of a warning.

But Johnny's voice didn't waver. "I have seen no women tonight."

I let out my breath, but still I waited. My heart thumped faster and faster in anticipation.

"I'd recommend you leave my stable now, men. There's no need for hostility," he said in a stony voice.

All I could hear after that was their feet shuffling out the door and the lock being twisted behind them. Relief flooded into my veins.

"Come out Max, I need to tell you a story." He was serious.

I stood and crept around the bale to face him. He stepped closer and ran his fingers through my hair, revealing my spiraled mark to the light of the lantern and the darkness of his eyes. I felt cold and

A Kingdom's Possession 21

awkward under his glances. His hand was warm, firm and kind on my neck. I could hardly move, afraid to look uncomfortable under his touch, yet unwilling to bear it much longer.

"What do you need to tell me?" I asked him quietly. All day, I had tried to forget about the strange sensation the night before. If it had caused the orange mark though, caused the men to come after me, then it must have been more than a hallucination or nerves. The whispers inside my head must have been more than just my mind playing tricks on me, too.

"I need to tell you what that mark on your neck means, Max." Johnny's expression was still and warning.

I took his hand from my neck and sat on the bale, motioning for him to sit on his stool. "Then tell me."

Chapter 2

* Johnny *

The way the light flickered across her face made me still. Her full lips were a soft red, crowned by a perfect nose. And staring back at me was a set of green eyes that shined in more brilliance than any royal, hand-cut jewel. Her eyebrows were dark arches, crests that shadowed her features as they creased in waiting. Pale skin glowed like a white sheet, draped over a frame of mere bones. There were streaks on her face where water had cut through dirt.

She had to ask me again to tell her what was going on. I blinked.

Clasping my hands, I tried to run through and remember all the stories I had heard as a young boy. Stories of battles, wars, brave men and women, queens and kings that had saved ancient lands. The Four Kingdoms, bound together by an ancient agreement, torn apart by divine mistakes even worse than the race of man. I could almost hear my father's words, feel the thick woven rug of his study under my hands. My brother and I had listened intently for hours to the stories our father told. Passed down through the royal generations were legends that inspired, taught, warned, and entertained the new princes.

Only one was told in secret, on dark nights when even the cooks and maids were sound in their beds. It was the story of a goddess named Adahlia, known as the Mistake of the Gods because she was so similar to man. Half god, half mortal, she had a duty that no other had to perform. She was sent down to Earth by the other gods every thousand years to enter the body of a woman, as punishment for her imperfection. Only the tortures of life as a mortal could allow her release back to her godly realm. Forced to live the lives of both god and human, whichever form she took, she suffered from fear and isolation.

"Or so I was told," I concluded to Max. Her head tipped downward and I waited.

After a long time, she finally looked up and spoke to me. In a weak voice, she began, "The other night, I had this sensation, one like no other. It was as if someone had torn open my skin. Plucking out my ribs, hands or claws or…" she swallowed, "whatever they were, pulled back layer after layer of flesh." Her hands clamped and unclamped, restless in her lap. "It felt like I was drowning on the inside, filling up with water."

My shoulders slumped. All those years I had taken the story as a myth, all those years…

"If it is this goddess, this *Adahlia* in my body, then it is her voice I hear whispering. It's been on and off all day, torturous. Do you know how to stop her voice?" Max asked.

I shook my head, waiting for her to say more. As if waking up from a nightmare she sat straight. "And this still doesn't explain why the men were after me."

"The mark you have, the swirls trailing down from behind your right ear, my father told me and my brother that it was a mark obtained by a transformation…like magic," I explained.

"Magic? But magic is illegal isn't it?" she asked. "I heard it was illegal once, I never knew there really was such a thing."

"Except for in the Third Kingdom, Bortal."

"Oh," she said. "But the men?"

"Well, that is why the story of Adahlia is so secret," I said. "When the goddess comes down from the heavens, she must have a mortal of royal blood release her back. My father said that in the legend, each of the Four Kingdoms sends out spies to identify and capture the woman that Adahlia embodied, the woman with that mark," I pointed to it with my head. "Then it is up to one member of that royal bloodline to release her. And for that, the Kingdom is rewarded by the goddess in the most generous proportions."

"How do they release her?" Max asked. I stood from my stool and went over to her and, sitting next to her on the bale in the tiny lantern-light, told her the worst part of the story.

"Through death."

* Max *

I woke on the ground behind a bale of hay, under a blanket. I rubbed the dirt from my eyes and let them adjust to the pale, weak morning light. It shined through the cracks in the door, leaving the straw caught in its light-lines to glow jagged and yellow, like splintered wood.

I peered up toward the top of the bale to see Johnny's back to me, his legs draped over the other side with his elbows on his knees, head in hands. I sat up and observed him in the new light. His dark hair was ruffled by his fingers, which were massaging his scalp vigorously. A sharp nose jutted out from his face, leaving a perfect dip into the crest of his lips. His jaw, evenly speckled with dark stubble, clenched when I shifted on the straw.

But he didn't turn to face me. So I stood, lifted one heavy leg at a time over the bale to sit by his side.

I wasn't much for conversations, but I tried to create one nonetheless. "Did you sleep?"

He turned slowly and looked at me with dark, tired eyes.

"I did not," he said.

I looked down to his hands, which were now carefully working to turn an object. He cleared his throat and handed it to me. "I believe this is yours? I found it in the hay last night," he said.

I touched the center of my chest to find it naked; in my other hand was my pendant. An amber stone set in a simple silver setting, it was hung on a strong silver chain. It soaked in every ounce of light in the room and sent it off in every direction it could manage. I clasped it around my neck once more and placed a hand on Johnny's arm, only to pull away awkwardly. I couldn't form a word of thanks.

But he smiled. "How did someone like yourself acquire such a piece of jewelry?" he asked.

I hung on his last word, enjoying the deep musicality of his voice. "I found it," I said.

Johnny leaned forward and swept a large hand over his face.

"I only noticed, after being pushed down onto the ground. The clasp scraped my hand."

"Pushed down?" Johnny asked, his eyes rapt.

I turned to obscure my face, uncomfortable in his stare. "I was walking to the storage building for the inn to get some bread." I said. "It was just around the side, down an alley. And I couldn't really go far, I was young at the time, knew that if I escaped, I'd starve and die out on the streets. A man happened to walk by. He came over, started speaking to me in a thin, quiet voice. He told me to be a good girl, to do as he asked. I refused, so he struck me. I fell into the water and he spit on me, then walked away." I was glad when he didn't ask more about my life as a slave.

Johnny placed his hand on my leg for a moment, then slid it back into his lap. "It suits you," he said.

I twisted my lips, avoiding a smile. "I didn't want to sell it, or to let anyone see it and take it away. It's special to me, I suppose."

"We should get you some food. You look famished."

I shook my head. "I can just be on my way."

"No, you have been recognized now. You must stay with me. I can keep you safe from the spies." I nodded reluctantly. "You can trust me," he said.

* Johnny *

The sun hurt my eyes at first, but they adjusted. I kept a hand on a dagger at my hip, walking casually. No one but a noble spy would recognize Max's mark, and with her mess of dark brown hair waving around her face, it was left completely out of sight. Max shot glances everywhere as we walked down the streets of Alice. She stalked next to me, tattered clothes waving in the gentle wind. Her bare feet were turning red with the cold of the autumn day as they silently carried her over the stone roads.

"You need shoes," I told her.

"I've never had a pair," she said. Her cheeks were rosy and though she was only inches under my height, she looked small wearing my old jacket. She would have to get new clothes too.

First I bought her breakfast. She seemed uneasy, eating in a tavern. But she ate more than I did, not picky about what was put in front of her; whether it was eggs or bread or meat, she ate them all willingly.

In the very northern part of the city, there were shops providing cloaks, shoes, and knives, everything a traveler would need. Being so close to the small northern town of Mala, a place of drifters and wary outcasts, it was a shop to satisfy its location. We hurried out of the old, crumbling brick building with Max in a new pair of boots, holding a black wool cloak.

"Shoes are uncomfortable," she said as we headed down the empty street. An overcast sky had moved in, taunting the earth with the threat of more rain.

"More uncomfortable than rocks poking into your feet?" I asked.

"Yes," she said.

I hoped for even a hint of a smile to sweep across her lips, but one never came. Just a glimpse of those magnificent, sea green eyes.

"And what are those tubes on the inside of them?"

I glanced down at her legs, noticed her black pants tucked into her new boots and only the slight bulges of sheaths on the insides. "Those," I said, rummaging in my bag, "are for these." I pulled out a pair of short, plain daggers and stopped to slide one into each boot. "But you only use them to defend yourself," I said.

"I've never killed a man," she said, starting to walk again.

"Neither have I, but I've gotten close," I said. "Let's hope you never have to."

"I never said I was afraid to, just that I hadn't," she said, her voice plain.

I couldn't help but glance down at her, surprised at her tone. It sounded like she almost *wanted* to.

"I was taught from the moment I was born how to fight." I said. "In Valta, we use bows. That's where I'm most comfortable. It wasn't until I was older that I learned the sword. I never thought I'd have to use one, but it's insisted that all princes of the Four Kingdoms learn how to fight and how to ride. How we are taught, and with what respect of life, varies between the rulers and the personalities of the princes."

Max kept her eyes forward, settled on the gentle decline as we headed back toward the center of the city.

"It depends on the recklessness of the kingdom," I added snidely, looking around. I could vaguely see the Alician Palace, golden and monstrous in the distance, atop her cliff. Flags fluttered in the growing wind.

I could feel my blood burning despite the chill coming into the city. Alice was becoming more and more power hungry. I just hoped my father recognized a growing beast when he saw one.

Max stopped abruptly, grabbing my arm to stop too. In the main part of the city, it was easy to get lost in the crowds of people. Even on a quiet day there were men and women sauntering almost aimlessly from tavern to tavern, house to house, shop to shop.

"What?" I asked. Then I could hear it, the cries of a woman coming from a slim alley between two pubs. A man grunted, laughed. I turned to cross the road toward the alley, when Max stopped me again.

"Not that," she said, just as the woman shrieked with joy. A horse pulling a cart stacked high with chicken cages rushed by us, startling me. "Shh," Max pressed. "Don't turn fast to look, but we're being watched."

* Max *

"Watched?" Johnny repeated dumbly.

"Shh..." I insisted, squeezing his arm. He swiveled his head casually to one side, as if trying to decide where to go next. The wind picked up, making me shiver.

"I see them," he whispered finally.

"What do we do?" I asked, more out of annoyance than fear.

"Walk," he said quietly.

As we started down the road, the goddess began whispering to me again, droning out Johnny's voice, the sound of the ocean, the crowd of people. I clapped my hands over my ears and hummed. It was all I could do to stay on my feet. It seemed like she almost wanted me to collapse.

"Max," Johnny said sharply.

Adahlia's voice cut out and the wind rattled in my ears invasively. Johnny squeezed my wrist and started jogging, weaving through people and buildings and avoiding horse carriages. He was leading me toward the port.

I swung the black cloak over my shoulders and tossed the hood over my head. When I glanced back, three burly men clad in red leather were hurrying after us. Their broadswords swept behind them in a steely wake.

"This way," Johnny said, cutting down an alley

I ran behind him, right on his heels. "Do you have a plan?"

He laughed. "I haven't thought that far ahead."

Turning around a tight bend, we ended up on the road that skirted the port. Docks bobbed in the returning storm and I could feel the first drops of rain starting to fall. When I turned to look again, I couldn't see the men.

"Quick, over here," Johnny said, urging me down a dock littered with barrels and sacks of grain. A huge ship was tethered to the end of the dock. I pulled away from Johnny and craned my neck to see the men who hurried down the road, getting caught in the groups of people. When I turned back to Johnny, he was holding the lid to a large crate. Open.

"Get in," he said.

"What?"

"Get. In," he repeated.

"I can't, I...It's almost filled to the top with sacks of grain," I protested. He threw back the top and easily lifted the sacks out and onto the dock, leaving them on top of others out in the rain.

"Now *get in*," he insisted. "Do you want to die, Max?"

I shook my head quietly and lay down on my side in the crate. Quivering, I watched as he bent beside me.

"Scoot over," he ordered, throwing his bag into the crate. Then he slid in next to me, bending his knees to contort himself in the small space. "Keep your head down," he said. And then he pulled the lid over the both of us.

Our faces were almost touching and I could feel his breath curling over my cheeks. I tipped my head downward and he

stretched so that his head was above mine, my face buried in his chest. I coughed.
"It's close, I know," he said. "Sorry."
"Don't be," I said into his shirt. He was helping me, could have possibly just staved me, but I still could not trust him. I had grown up trusting no one, fearing everything.
"If those men get you, you'll never be free again. That is, until they kill you." His chest vibrated as he spoke, making him seem more powerful and demanding than he really was. To be that near to another human being, especially a man, made me nervous. I sucked in a breath and he touched my cheek. "I wont let them do that, Max. I'll keep you safe," he said.
"Why are you doing this?" I asked. "Why help me?"
"Because," he said quietly, "I just have to."

* Johnny *

But maybe that's not really what it was. Maybe I was helping her because I was a prince, and it was in my blood to keep hold of the goddess, gain the leverage for my kingdom. Maybe it was because I didn't want the rebellious Alice to win her covert battle for power. Maybe it was because I had nothing better to do with myself. Maybe it was just because she needed me, and that's all there was to it.

But I wasn't sure, just yet. "I'm sorry," I said.
"You already said you were sorry," she said. I could feel her body shaking next to me.
"Yes, but I'm sorry you have to be a part of this. It's right that Adahlia is called the Mistake of the Gods. She is a mistake," I breathed.
"We're all mistakes," Max said bitterly, "every damn one of us."

* Max *

It was quiet, until the crate shifted and voices hovered above the wooden panels. It rained harder and harder by the moment, and the layer of grain bags beneath us was starting to swell with water. I shivered.
"Oh, mask me," Johnny swore.
"What is it?" I asked.

"Get these crates onto the ship, before the storm moves in. We sail to Bortal," a rough voice ordered above us. Two men groaned as they lifted a crate and walked it onto the ship. "Quick, sailors. The crated bags must stay dry."

Johnny snorted. "Stay calm," he said, "it looks like we're going for a boat ride."

"This is absurd," I whispered harshly. "We have to get out now. We can't ride this ship off into the—"

"No. We can't go now," Johnny said, then he paused to listen. He held his breath and covered my mouth to keep me from speaking. Heavy footsteps approached from the head of the dock. They stopped near the crate.

Someone answered a question I hadn't heard. "We're not taking passengers, this is a messenger boat headed to Bortal."

Boots shifted on the dock and I could see the tip of a sword wave through the air. I closed my eyes and pushed my face into Johnny's chest again.

"We do not wish to catch a ride to the kingdom north of the Wall, we're merely looking for a girl," another man said, his voice was frustrated, scattered. "She has a birth mark behind the ear. It's orange. Brown hair. She's this high."

"We've not seen a lady like that. Sounds fine though. Is she your whore?" a sailor asked.

Johnny squeezed my shoulder, pulling me closer.

"She's nothing of the like." The man with the sword bellowed. "My sister is all, she escaped, um, her wedding, unsure about the arranged marriage. You know how the women are."

"Ah, only good on their backs, is what I say," the sailor said. The men on the dock laughed. "But we have not seen your sister."

"Very well, we'll be on our way," and with that, the Alician spies left the dock.

I lifted my head a little.

"Afraid of commitment?" Johnny asked.

"I'm too young to marry off," I mumbled.

He laughed quietly and ran a finger over my mark. "I'll keep you safe."

I nodded into his chest.

Hands grabbed the crate we were lying in. "Heave," two men yelled, hoisting the crate into the air. It jostled from side to side and rain leaked through the edges, soaking our clothes.

Once on the boat, the sailors dropped our crate in a dark room that smelled of mold and seawater. I could hear the other crates moaning as the ship shifted from side to side. As soon as the door to the room had been closed and the ship was on its way into the open ocean, Johnny lifted the lid to our container and stood, stretching his arms. The dark shape of his body gave me chills. How could someone so strong and prestigious be so modest and kind?

I stood up and looked around. "What now? Nice plan. We're on a ship to Bortal."

"I didn't plan anything. I'm just trying to keep you safe" Johnny said. "I'm not sure what else we do. Maybe Bortal is the safest place to be, what with fewer spies."

"Maybe," I said, my tone rising. "But how do you know they aren't looking for me there too? Or who knows? Maybe we'll end up dying from some magical incident in the land of ...magic." I waved my hands through the air.

"Bortal is only misunderstood. It has been a kingdom allied with Valta forever," Johnny retorted. "The Third Kingdom was cut off from the rest of Cavail because it was a threat, not because it took action. We'll be fine up there. And as for the spies, they will be looking in Bortal too, but Alice is the kingdom to avoid. Alice will kill you. Chances are, if Bortal gets a hold of you, the kingdom will try to release Adahlia through magic, not through death."

"Maybe you're one of them. Maybe you planned to get me on this ship. Are you going to kill me instead? Are you with another kingdom, out to kill me like the rest? Maybe that's why you told me what was happening, to gain my trust," I said. I could hardly swallow my nerves. Not more than two days ago, I was only a slave. Everything had changed, spun out of control, trapping me in a new kind of slavery, a binding of fear and the unknown.

"I'm not out to get you," Johnny said, hands patting the air.

"Then tell me why you're helping me."

"Shh..." Johnny urged, "they'll hear you. Messenger boats don't deal well with stowaways."

"Check the baggage," a voice commanded from somewhere above us. Footsteps bumped along the deck above and down a set of stairs, ready to enter our room in the very bottom of the boat.

"Hide," Johnny said. I crouched behind a pair of barrels that smelled heavily of stale liquor. Johnny hid in some other shadowy corner of the room.

A man burst through the door and my pendant caught the light of a lantern hung near the stairs beyond our storage room. "There you are, little noise. I see you hiding," the man said slowly. My foot tangled with a thick heavy rope and I struggled to escape its hold; the man crept toward me and snatched my arm before I could stumble out of his reach. I pulled a dagger out of one of my boots and swung it in the direction of his chest, but he caught my wrist and twisted it easily. The movement matched the grin that came to his face. I shrieked in pain and the dagger fell to the floor. The cool steel clattered and shot a shard of glassy lantern light in Johnny's general direction. But as much as I hoped, I could not see him in that dark corner of the room. There were only more crates and barrels, more sacks of grain.

"Let's take you up to the captain now, shall we young lady?" the man snickered. He dragged me up the stairs into the storm on deck.

He strode up to a lean man, standing proud at a large wheel. The man fought to keep a soggy hat on his head, even as the wind threatened to lift it from his tangle of wiry hair.

I spit rainwater out of my mouth and it landed on his shoe. The man squeezing my wrist said, "I found this little gem in the storage room caught in a rope, Captain."

"Why don't we send her over, eh?" another sailor asked, joining the scene.

The fat man holding my arm yanked me up, so that my body turned in the air. "I was thinking she could serve as some entertainment for the crew," the man yelled to the captain. A few nearby sailors laughed and cheered in agreement.

The captain held up his hand and the crew silenced. I was slowly lowered until my feet were on the deck again, but the man still held me with my body stretched upward.

"We will put her in our little brig, that is punishment enough. We can let her off in Bortal, have her die a slower death than drowning and a worse death than by her own hand after the touch of my crew. She will die in the Black Market; she will be choked by the hands of magic," the captain said. Many of the crew grunted in disappointment. "Now take her away."

The man holding my arm dragged me back down the stairs, only to turn and walk me into a room made of steel bars. Before he let me go, he grabbed my waist and thrust his tongue into my mouth. I pushed him away and he grabbed my hair, pulling my head back. "You're lucky I follow the captain's orders, you little whore," he said. Then he shoved my head down and slammed the door. He locked it with a key and grinned at me through the bars. "Stupid little thing, to stow to Bortal," he said with a laugh. Then he turned and went back upstairs.

I crawled over to the corner of the cell and drew my knees to my chest. Closing my eyes, I could feel every inch of my scalp tingling. I spat, the sour taste of onions and beer new and terrible in my mouth. I wanted to heave at the mere smell of that man so close to me, but I did not. I just rested my head down on my knees and kept my eyes closed.

A cool breeze wafted in from the small circular window in the side of the ship. My stomach rumbled and I placed a hand on my mark. It felt hot to the touch, as if I had a fever. And as I stroked the place, whispers came into my brain. Her voice was soft, gentle, and yet there was no way I could trust it. The language rolled off her godly tongue and stroked my mind as the sea would stroke a swimming body. I tried to push her voice out of my head, but it came louder, more forceful. Adahlia spoke clearly, every syllable pronounced as if she wanted me to pay attention, but her language was lost on me.

As the hours moved on, her voice became as regular as the sound of the sea outside my cell. And it was all I could do not to fall asleep to her tormenting.

Chapter 3

* Max *

"You stowaways infest like rats," I heard a voice say as footsteps approached. It must have been hours since I was thrown in the cell. Gray light sifted in through the tiny window and I took a deep breath of salty, dusty air. I had lost track of time while listening to the goddess and dipping in and out of sleep. My limbs were cold and numb.

Two ragged sailors brought Johnny down to the brig and unlocked the door. The hinges squeaked and one of them shoved Johnny onto the ground.

Before going back up to the main deck, the other winked at me. "She's a fine one, don't be too rough," he said to Johnny. They both laughed. Their footsteps were heavy and uneven as they shoved each other back up the stairs.

The ocean rushed outside the little window.

Johnny brought himself to his feet slowly and examined his hands. Beads of bright red blood began to form on his palms. He brushed them off on his pants and turned to face me. He looked bare, standing alone in the middle of the room. Even his eyes looked dull, though they did not lack their original intelligence. His body looked lanky and his jaw was sharp. "Are you alright?" he asked me.

My mouth pursed, ready to speak, but my throat was too dry to utter any words. I shrugged and licked my cracked lips.

"I thought sailors had higher standards than that," Johnny mumbled, looking toward the stairs.

"What do you mean?" I asked hoarsely. My stomach felt acidic, empty.

"He didn't try anything with you did he?" Johnny knelt down beside me. His voice was comforting, but the closeness was not.

"No," I said quietly. "Nothing more than any man would do to a girl my age, although he wanted to. Sailors from Alice have low standards, Johnny."

"I don't understand," he said, twisting so that he was seated with his back against the wall, right next to me.

"Well," I began, "the men in Alice usually don't do more than hit or grope girls my age. It's the older women that are subject to rape. The men here prefer maturity."

Johnny nodded, his expression solemn. "So he didn't?"

I shook my head. "Why would you care anyway?"

"Well, I'm here to keep you safe, aren't I?" he asked.

"You weren't here to do anything up until a day ago," I said, scooting away from him.

Johnny looked me in the eye. "It's been more than a day, Max. We've been on this ship two nights already, haven't you noticed?" he asked.

I moved my legs stiffly and looked at my feet. "She's been keeping me company, Johnny," I said. "Not to sound strange, but Adahlia has been speaking to me again. Whispering things as if I can understand. It's like she wants me to listen to her."

He moved closer and put an arm around my shoulders. I shrank in his embrace, though he did feel warm and strong against me.

We sat there for a moment in silence, and then Johnny stood up abruptly and began to pace the room. "Are you scared?" he asked.

I shrugged. "What do you mean?"

"I mean exactly what I said," he said. He stopped and faced me. I didn't want him to step closer. "Are you scared?"

"I don't know what I am," I said. It was true.

"I don't believe that," he said. "The unknown is a scary thing. I can't imagine what it's like for you."

"Well," I said, beginning to feel uncomfortable, "I've never been on a boat before."

"That's not what I was talking about," Johnny said.

"I know that's not what you were talking about," I mumbled. "I just don't know how I feel about all this. I'm sorry." I shrank against the wall.

His face softened and he bent over, placing his hands on my shoulders. "We're almost to Bortal," he said seriously. "There are creatures and people there that are hard to imagine."

"But I thought you said they were allies to Valta? Doesn't that mean we'll be safe there?" I asked.

"No. Unless we are taken inside the kingdom walls, we are not safe. And believe me, the sailors will not take stowaways into the palace. It doesn't work like that. The king and queen are wary of their own people, let alone anyone from anywhere else."

"Do you know the king and queen?" I asked.

"I've met them before, yes. But we still wont be able to get into the palace. They don't take visitors readily," he said, sitting back down. His hands were placed firmly on the ground by his hips, and I couldn't help but stare at them, unbelieving that they were the hands of a prince.

"Of course," I mumbled.

"We'll have to take refuge in the forest," Johnny said.

Even I knew that was a bad idea. "We can't do that," I said. "I've heard stories about Bortal's Forest. It's full of magical and evil creatures. Things that can turn invisible, and others that play tricks on you." I shifted on the ground, beginning to feel my muscles, sore from stillness.

"There is no other choice. Bortal, as the Third Kingdom, may have good intentions, but Bortal on the streets, in the citizen's perspective, is about trickery and magic. It is safest if we are unseen, and the forest is the most solitary."

I didn't speak, not knowing what to say. Threat was around the corner anywhere I went, so whether it was a spy or an evil creature didn't make a difference.

Johnny reached a hand deep into his pocket and pulled out a piece of bread. "Here, I knew they wouldn't have fed you so I stole some bread while I was in the storage room." I grabbed it out of his hand, his fingers brushing mine.

"Nothing for you?" I asked, taking a bite.

Johnny shook his head. "That's all I grabbed when they found me. But eat, you need it more than I do."

I looked away and finished the bread. Outside, the sky was still enveloped in heavy clouds. A breeze came in through the window and I pulled my cloak closer around my body. My pendant hung perfectly in the center of my chest, and I placed a hand over it, as if to protect it from the chill.

"Being on a ship reminds me of my brother. He was always fond of ocean-travel." Johnny's gaze was distant with the memory.

"You have a brother?"

"Yes, my twin. He's younger by only a few minutes." His lips parted into a warm smile. "I have a sister also. She'll be eleven years old this year."

"Their names?"

"Perido and Sarah," Johnny said.

"Will Perido be king? Now that you're not in the palace?" I asked.

Johnny laughed halfheartedly, shifting in his place on the floor. "I'm not sure. I doubt it. My father doesn't like Perido much; he has been second best since the moment I came out of my mother's womb first. It's tradition that the eldest becomes king, and my father will count on me to come back and take my rightful place. The sad thing is that I have not once wanted the crown, and Perido has wanted the responsibility his whole life. He's more suited for the job too, but all father sees is his sarcasm and his failures. My father does not see a king in Perido, only a prince."

I nodded, trying to understand his situation. "It sounds like you have no choice but to become king." I said.

Johnny's brow creased. "I have a choice. It is not unheard of to reject the crown, only frowned upon." His voice was low.

"Will you ever go back home?"

"No."

* Johnny *

The boat rocked heavily as it hit the dock in the port of Bortal. Max's eyes darted around as three sailors led us out of the brig and into the chaos that bustled on the surface. Men went about their tasks while the captain watched from the helm. The sun poked through the clouds as rain sprinkled the ocean and the deck of the boat.

The vacancy of the port was eerie. Its single dock came out from the base of an ominous cliff; the top was only accessible by a set of old stairs that zigzagged their way to the top. They swayed on warped stilts and the rain made them look slick and gloomy. The sailor behind me nudged me down a ramp from the ship onto the rotting dock. I stepped carefully, looked over at Max. Her lips were pursed with an emotion that was unreadable, and she held her mess of long hair to one side, covering her right ear.

A man in a maroon uniform holding a large scroll pushed past us and led the way down the dock and up the stairs, quickly moving his feet over the slippery planks. The captain followed briskly behind the messenger, a look of authority on his face, but not in his position. The messenger would be the only one here to get into the palace.

Max and I were forced up onto the stairs next, shadowed by two sailors. The rest stayed with the ship, drinking and swearing.

The rain was cold, and as we gained altitude, the wind gained speed. Stepping cautiously, I worked my way up the stairs, just behind Max. The sailors rushed us, mumbling curses to the gods. I swallowed and kept my pace in silence.

When we finally reached the top, I glanced over the edge. The white water rolled below us, and the wind whistled with command. The cliff stood tall over the small messenger boat down below, bobbing in the waves. The sailors pushed Max and me toward the head of a path that lead us away from the stairs. The messenger hurried inland, his feet scuffing the ground as he walked. A thin forest of evergreens bent in the wind, their needles fluttering down as the path went deeper into the wood. Other trees scattered the scene, with long roots that trailed above ground like snakes. Everything was bearded in long pale moss and each cough or snort of the captain and sailors sounded out of place in the silent swaying of trees.

Max lifted her hood and moved toward me. "Is this Bortal's Forest?" she asked.

"No, this is on the outskirts of the palace wall. We should be getting to it soon," I said.

A few minutes later we were walking along a very tall wall. It seemed to loom over the little path like a giant. Vines spilled out of the cracks in the stone and Max pulled her cloak tighter around her body, glancing upward. I followed her eyes and saw at the top of the wall soldiers looking down at us. Clad in Bortal's famous maroon armor, they whispered amongst one another, their eyes following us.

As we rounded a bend in the wall, I noticed a small wooden door crammed into the stone. The messenger raised a hand and our little party stopped. He rapped his knuckles on the door five times, and looked to the soldiers on top, waving his scroll to let them know his authority. One of them disappeared from his lookout and reappeared in the doorway. The messenger followed him inside and closed the door behind them. I could hear heavy locks tumbling into place and imagined that there was a plank hung across the door for extra support. No normal man could breach this fortress, but a wizard probably could, if he were compelled. I could understand the lengths that the royals of Bortal went through to keep all the illegal magic out of their kingdom walls.

The captain turned to our little group and snickered. "You will be free soon, stowaways."

Max looked at me, her eyes rotated up from underneath the rim of her hood. They looked big and thoughtful. "Where are they taking us?"

"To the Black Market, young lady," the captain answered.

Max lowered her head once again, concealing her eyes.

We were led down the path along the wall for nearly an hour before it veered away and into the thin wood. The trees began to thin into buildings, and the pine needle path turned to stone. Everything felt frozen, the small road was completely deserted, but yet there were shops and stores along the street. In the haze of rain, I could see crooked signs hanging above the buildings. An eerie fog still floated close to the ground, left over from the morning.

As we rounded a bend, I looked up at a sign that was hung on a huge arch above the road. I stopped and read it out loud, "Bortal's Black Market Curve."

It was the most famous stretch of road in all of Cavail, and one I had never intended on visiting. At the heart of the Black Market, it served as a main-street for magic. The fact that no one was there was enough to awaken the stale seasickness in the pit of my stomach.

"We leave you here," the captain said, planting his feet. "I give luck to you, though that is useless in the Black Market." He chuckled.

One of the sailors that had been behind us swung my pack onto the ground. I was surprised they had brought it up, though it was of no use to us now. A jar or two of lavender honey and a slave tag would do nothing against a nymph or wizard. The second sailor threw down three daggers; the sound of them hitting the stone was sharp against the silent fog and buildings. I cringed at the noise, and I noticed Max shrink under her cloak.

The captain turned back down the road, followed by the two sailors. I watched them as they disappeared into the mist.

I turned to Max, and she glared at me from under her hood. "Thank you for this, really," she said. "I suppose we wander in this godforsaken place until we reach the tainted woods, and in there, we will meet out demise?"

I laughed quietly in the settling darkness of the town. "On the contrary, I know exactly where to go," I said, picking up my two daggers and handing Max the third. I didn't know how she managed to keep her other one from the sailors. "As a prince, I've studied the roads in and near all the kingdoms, including those of the dismissed Third. We go straight. That will lead us to the one and only path into Bortal's Forest."

"You seem to be in a pretty good mood for a prince who's about to die," Max said quietly.

I shook my head and started down the road. "We have a higher chance of death on these streets, speaking as loud as we are. The safest place to be that is even remotely close to where we are, besides the palace, is that way," I said pointing.

"If the creatures are said to be so terrible in the forest, why don't they leave Bortal's territory and terrorize the rest of Cavail?" Max asked.

"They have their territory and we have ours. There's no need for them to escape, only to defend their forest when others trespass," I said.

"When we trespass?"

"Perhaps," I said. "Let's try not to disturb anything while we're in there."

Without another word, Max shuffled down the road at my side.

When we finally got to the head of the path, I regretted the idea of going inside. A deep, dark wood towered to the sky. It cast a thick, spiny shadow along the cracked street of the Black Market. A screech came out from the depths of the forest and I held my daggers close. Max swayed behind me, her hand placed lightly on my back, between my shoulders. It quivered against my clothing. Without wavering in step, I walked into the woods, Max close behind me. As my eyes adjusted, every shadow and rattling leaf seemed to jump out and attack us. Even the sound of my own footsteps and breathing became unfamiliar in the darkness of vines and trees. The forest moaned in the strange light. There were trees whose roots wrapped around other trees in a messy knot, or slithered along the ground like tentacles waiting to pull at our legs. There were ferns and mushrooms that seemed to whisper. And the fog, still a haze in the forest, muffled everything in white. I kept my head low, with my hood covering my face. Out of the corner of my eye I could see Max do the same. The sound of trees falling over came from a distance, the breaking of twigs and bushes as the giants ripped through the thick forest. Falling, but never reaching the ground, as if they were walking through the underbrush.

Soon we stopped to rest. I adjusted my hood and looked to Max. "So far so good, I guess."

She gathered her hair, guiding it to cascade over her right collarbone to conceal her mark completely, though the hood did that as well. "The goddess will not quiet, it's hard to focus," Max said. She shivered.

"I'm not sure what to tell you. Is there anything I can do?" I asked.

Max's eyes met mine. "Get her out."

"Oh, but she is not ready," a voice said.

My muscles stiffened and my fingers tightened around the daggers. I looked down the path into the dark and saw a very feminine shape approaching. "Who are you?" I demanded, louder than I had expected.

"Keep your voice quiet, do not wake the creatures of the forest," she said. Her voice was like nothing I had ever heard before. It carried through the air like a song, gentle and lulling. But it was also wary, intelligent, and warning.

"Who are you?" I asked again, guiding Max to stand behind me.

"I am Avaline," the woman said. "And your names?"

"Johnny," I said. "And that's Max."

She stopped a fair distance away, but even in the space between us, I could see her in complete detail. She glowed like an ember, still hot from a newly dead fire. Orange and red swirls and intricate patterns were tattooed over her left arm, up along the left side of her neck and face, and down the length of her right leg. A thin, tattered dress fell over her body, barely there in contrast with her bright red hair and pale white skin. Her eyes glittered like amber, and her feet were bare.

"Are you a mystic?" I said, reluctant to move toward her, but drawn all the same. There was a warmth that encompassed her body and the space around her, and it was hard not to fall into it from the cold night air.

The woman cocked her head to examine her detailed hand. Her hair rippled with the movement. "That would depend," she said, "on how you view magic." Holding out her hand, she closed her eyes and her markings began to glow. I could not will my feet to move away as she summoned a spark at the very tip of a white-painted fingernail. The flame danced as if her fingers were its wick, her body its fuel. It traveled along her markings in a fluid pattern as if it were molten liquid. It raged in some places, calmed in others, and began to grow into one steady fire. The flame covered the lines on her body so carefully my eyes could not veer from the sight. She ignited, basked in the fire with a familiarity that was startling and beautiful.

She smiled and opened her eyes, rocking slightly in the warmth. I could feel it blazing against my cheeks. And in an instant, it was gone. Not even a speck of ash on the ground, only the faint smell of smoke in the breeze.

She glanced down at the blackened edges of her flame-colored dress, smoothing out its wrinkles. "Would you consider that magic?" she asked thoughtfully.

"I would," I said. "You wouldn't?"

Avaline examined her hands again. "I would not," she said sadly. "I do not consider my exploiting of the element, my trickery, as magic. This human body does not have the capacity to honor the fire to the extent of magical ability."

"I don't understand," Max said.

I looked into the dark that surrounded our group of three, expecting a pair of eyes or a moving shadow to be staring back from the underbrush. But I could see nothing in the night. I turned back to Avaline.

"You do not have to understand now," she said to Max. "All you have to do is accept my offer in helping you release Adahlia."

"How do you know about the goddess?" I asked.

"Can you make her stop whispering to me?" Max said.

Avaline shook her head slightly. "Each woman she has entered throughout the thousands of years of her existence has found her own way to cope with Adahlia's tormenting. You will learn to do the same, come time." Avaline then turned to address my question, "I keep a close connection with the world and the heavens. Something as significant as Adahlia is something I need to know about. I have been alive for a very long time, but on this thousandth year, the gods have chosen me to guide Adahlia home. I am deeply humbled by this and you must know that I will reach to the very furthest of my ability to help you release her without harming Max."

"How can we know you are true to your word?" I asked.

Avaline shrugged, her dress flickering in the wind. "I will prove myself, if I must."

"And how will you do that?" I asked.

A grin came to her face. "First, I will get you a visit with the king and queen of Bortal. I believe they will be of help on your quest."

"So now we're on a quest?" Max said.

I let out a laugh, "How will you get us council with the king and queen? They do not take visitors."

"We are not ordinary visitors," Avaline seemed to announce to the forest. "We are of great importance to their kingdom and we will be heard."

"That's all very well, but I still do not understand how we will breach the wall," I said.

"I will show you," she said, and she began down the path, back toward the Kingdom of Bortal.

* Max *

I touched Johnny's arm to get his attention. He leaned in close, but I kept my eyes focused on Avaline, who strode through the forest paces ahead of us. "I'm not sure about this."

He lifted his hood and folded his arms, concealing his daggers. "Neither am I, but we can't turn down the possibility that she is trustworthy," he said. "For now, we will follow."

"How did she know Adahlia is in me?" I asked.

"How does she not see herself as magic?" Johnny said, "There is no way to know, but to follow." He straightened and began to pick up his pace to walk beside the mysterious woman.

The goddess whispered; her voice was more raspy and pained as if she were hoarse from speaking so relentlessly. Her language was still lost on me.

"You will see, I promise you," Avaline said to Johnny, mid conversation. Her dress fluttered lightly over her perfect skin. I had never seen a woman more beautiful, or more intimidating. As a creature from Bortal's Forest, it was easy not to trust her.

"How do you know of the Mistake of the Gods? It is passed down through the generations of royalty. I don't see how a woman of the forest could hold such a tightly kept secret," Johnny said to her. His eyes wondered over her body as if he wanted his hands to do the same. But yet he still held the daggers close.

"A king told me a very long time ago. He was of Valta, very kindly, just like his kingdom. But he was also very bullheaded, wary of power and threats that could never be. He is only a memory to me now, but one I hold very dear to my heart," she explained, with pain in her voice. "We should be getting to the Black Market soon, keep your heads and voices low."

As we came out of the forest, we were thrust into a mess of people. The nocturnal urchins of the Black Market bustled and yelled into the night with enthusiasm. Avaline moved forward through the crowds with no hesitation, and I hurried to keep my hand on Johnny's back.

I could hear people laughing and moving in the darkness. It was surprising that there was little light in the Market, though it made sense all the same. This was a place of magic and trickery, all the more suited for the cloak of night. I kept my eyes down, avoiding the little flashes of green or white light that occasionally rippled over my boots. I didn't look up until Johnny turned and touched my shoulder. I could see Avaline clearly, though she was down the road a ways. A haze encompassed her body as if she were burning internally; the thought made me shiver. In comparison, Johnny looked dark and grainy.

"Look, you see that?" he said, so quietly I could barely hear him. The goddess moaned in the back of my head as if in anguish. I ignored her voice like I would one in the physical world, but she still spoke, muted in the background.

"What do I see?" I asked Johnny.

"The robed man over there, watch," I looked over and the silhouette of an old man took form. He held a stick and moved it through the air wildly, muttering slightly louder than the crowd bustling around him. A slender figure stood before him, a ragged boy, shaking and tousled and bracing for something powerful to arrive, it seemed. The tip of the stick began to glow, dull compared to Avaline, but intimidating all the same. The raggedy boy stood back, turned to run, but was caught by the green blast from the old man, and shrank down to the ground dramatically. He screamed, yet no one went to look or react; all the people kept on their way through the Black Market.

The robed man seemed pleased as a mouse scurried away from his feet. It was an abnormal mouse, wobbling through the streets as if it were drunk.

"What just happened?" I asked Johnny, grabbing his arm.

"That boy," he said slowly, stuttering.

Avaline came swiftly to our sides and gathered us to continue down the road. "Do not speak of this, and pay no attention," she said hastily. "Do not worry, it is only temporary. Magic is common on these streets, and little law is enforced. Keep your heads down, or that will be you," she pointed to the mouse, his nose pointed to the sky, smelling humans and avoiding the feet that fell over his head like rain.

As we approached the outskirts of the market I took my hand off of Johnny's arm. Avaline walked at a quick pace, not nervously, but with intention. I did not want to trust her. She was a creature of a forest known for terrible things. Yet, aside from Johnny, she was all I had. And I did not want to be alone.

The kingdom wall came fast on our right, towering so black against the sky that the two seemed to blend. We walked along the wall opposite to the direction we had come.

"We are almost there," Avaline said, her voice soft.

"How will we get in?" Johnny asked.

"You will have to be patient," she said.

She pushed vines and low branches out of her way as she strode with confidence down the overgrown path. Her dress fluttered. When she stopped, she turned to look up to the top of the wall. I followed her eyes.

Above, there were slow, thick shadows of men moving against the sky at the same level as the treetops. I looked back at Avaline and she smiled.

"Do not make a sound," she said. Johnny moved back behind her, pressing into the brush. She went down the path a few more feet and stood in front of a very large doorway. The wooden double doors stretched tall and wide, built right into the stone wall.

I stood with Johnny, watching as Avaline summoned the fire back onto her skin. She began to mutter, moving in the flame as if she were dancing. Johnny grabbed me and pushed me into the brush behind him. Thorns tore at my cloak and I could feel things moving behind me.

But I didn't move.

Avaline raised her arms and the wooden door caught on fire in an instant. Men from above called out orders and warnings, but Avaline kept still. She willed the fire forward, her skin igniting and her dress flapping wildly in the heat. I could feel the blaze pushing against my cheeks. Johnny breathed heavily as he reached to hold my hand behind him. I slid my fingers from his grip and placed his hand on the sheathed dagger on his belt. He pulled it out and held it in front of the both of us, along with the other dagger that had never been put away. He made no move to confront Avaline though. He only watched.

The door began to fall away and a chaos of shouts came from the kingdom within. The fire cracked and hissed as if to respond. Ashes, sparks, and smoke flooded the sky, contorted and hot against the cool night. Avaline lowered her hands as the courtyard beyond the door came into view. The outer edges were still burning in a heavy flame. Fire curled upward, charring the wall above.

Soon the entry was a mere arch, flames shifting as the wood panels fell away from their hinges. Despite the soldiers bustling inside the castle walls, Avaline began to walk inside, her body still ignited and enveloped in flame. Her hair waved wildly as the fire cracked and leaped in all directions.

Johnny began to follow her into the mess of sweaty bodies and clattering armor. I grabbed his arm in an attempt to pull him back into the forest.

He turned.

"What do you think you're doing?" I asked.

"Do you see another choice Max?" His musical voice taunted me. When I didn't answer, he stepped through the burning arch, after the woman who called forth the spitting flames.

Chapter 4

* Johnny *

Men and women hurried out of the way as soldiers rushed out of the gates of the palace, down the stone paths and over the grass to reach the three of us. As soon as I entered the courtyard, two soldiers clad in dark armor seized me and one other rushed past to get Max. I put up little fight against their strong holds, and I hoped she did the same.

Avaline stood in the center of the garden, her pale skin seeming to cool as she waited, her feet planted close together, relaxed on the white stone pathway.

The chaos of the scene began to melt away as a slim robed man came out of the castle, directly in front of Avaline. He walked smoothly, a wooden staff in hand, down the steps and through the courtyard. His robes rippled over the stone and his white beard looked stark against the night.

Three soldiers rushed to Avaline. Two held her arms while the third lay his sword against her neck, just under her jaw line. I could see her cheeks tighten when the blade began to glow. As the robed man stopped in front of her, the soldier dropped his weapon and it clattered, steel against stone. The man in armor swore and shook his hand, as if that would heal the burn.

"Your entrance is noted," the bearded man said. His voice was raspy and quiet, but it was also strong.

Avaline nodded slightly. "As is yours," she said. I couldn't help but notice the tweak in her voice, as if something was not being said.

The man's brow creased. "I expect you wish a council with the king?"

"I wish a council with anyone who will listen," Avaline said.

The soldiers shifted next to her. The old man peered around the courtyard. Everyone had stopped and was looking toward the pale woman with the orange tattoos.

"You also wish for your friends to come inside?" he said, smoothing his robes.

"They are the reason I seek a meeting."

"Very well, I will alert the king and queen at once," the man said, turning to leave.

"They would not like to meet in the morning? When we are all fresh?" Avaline asked.

The man stopped, but did not turn around. "I will ask, but I doubt they will wish you to stay in their home for long," he said. The man continued on into the shadows of the castle.

Avaline turned, despite the soldiers gripping her arms. "A good entrance is all you need," she said lightly to the little crowd of people.

I looked back at the arch, noticing the black marks on the stone and the scattering of ashes on the ground. Coals still smoldered, a glowing red and smoky gray. Wind rustled the tree branches and brought the smell of smoke to my nose. I coughed, glanced at the torches scattered around the yard. They were nothing compared to what Avaline had just created.

All the soldiers straightened as a short man came out of the castle and approached Avaline. "Follow me," he said, and started to go back inside.

"May I have one less soldier to lead me into the palace?" Avaline asked.

The man faced her and straightened, clearing his high-pitched voice. "You will do as you are told."

The soldiers holding Avaline nudged her forward after the small escort, and she moved slowly toward the castle. The guards holding Max and me hauled us forward as well, their armor clattering against the silent air. My arms itched under the tight grip of the soldiers.

Once inside, we were led down a dark hallway. The floor was made of broken marble, and the walls had no paintings. It was the first time I had been in a castle since I left Valta and unlike the

Second Kingdom, the Third was unwelcoming and cold. Though it was clean and simple, there was an eerie echo that made the whole palace feel like a gloomy dream. And with the lack of servants and guards, it was a very lonely place.

This time of year, Valta would have guests and maids and cooks bustling throughout the castle, even through the night. Banquets would be held and men and women would come and go, participating in the feasts and balls.

But Bortal's Kingdom was completely empty; not even a mouse dwelled.

Our escort led us into a small room. By the neatness of the furniture, the thick rug, and the smell of dust, I could tell it had not been entered in a while.

"You will wait here," the man said. The soldiers took their stance outside the door and I could hear it lock into place as the escort closed it behind him.

Avaline lowered herself carefully onto one of the chairs as Max watched her uneasily. "I feel that I have not gained any trust from our break in," Avaline said. I could not tell if she had intended humor or was serious.

Max shook her head and I crossed the room to face the woman. "Who are you to break into a palace? We can't easily trust a woman who burns down a wall and nearly gets us all beheaded."

"But you see that we are not in any danger. I have gotten us council with the king," she said, stroking her hair.

"Do not expect any thanks, you wont get it," I said.

"We are safe though, Johnny," Max said, stepping forward.

"But are you sure of that?" I yelled. Avaline stood and I gripped my dagger, pointed it at her. "We don't know who she is, she came from the Forest of Bortal, and she just burned down a wall."

"Mask me, I do ask for you to lower your voice and your weapon" Avaline said. "I am here to help you. But I need your trust."

"Then I need you to tell me the truth. Who are you?" I said. My cheeks were hot. I should not have been so curious. I should not have followed her so willingly.

Avaline stood, hands at her sides and eyes locked on mine. "I am Avaline. I used to bring change to the living, help those who were passing into the realm of death; I was a re-creator. A very long time ago my body was," she clenched her hands, "altered." Avaline sat in her chair and cleared her throat. "I seldom concern myself with human affairs, but I am held close to the gods as a being and I felt it was time for me to step forward. I am here to help you, and I ask that you do not push me away. I am merely an old woman now, and I cannot spend my power without consequences to my energy."

"You don't look like an old woman," Max said.

Avaline laughed a little. "I am older than you will ever know," she said.

The door swung open then, and three guards strode into the room. The small escort stood in the doorway. "This way," he said. The three men in maroon armor drew their swords and one by one led us at point down the hallway, through two massive doors, and into a large ballroom.

The floor was made of faded dark blue tiles that spun white patterns along the floor, as if it were water. Maroon drapes hung down to the tiles, masking huge windows. The ceiling was painted with many colors, all with a golden hue, each blending with another to depict a scene swollen with jolly people clad in extraordinary outfits. The background was filled with light, yet in one corner, there was a black smudge that seemed to loom over the rest of the scene. It ruined the glorious laughter on the faces of the dancers, and made the picture peculiar and slightly melancholy.

"You may go," a woman's voice said, and I lowered my gaze. The throne was in front of me. There, the king and queen of Bortal sat poised in their empty kingdom. The soldiers and escort left reluctantly, but closed the doors regardless of their pause. The old man from the courtyard stood to the king's right, his frailness more noticeable in the lit room.

I stepped forward and bowed to the royals of the Third Kingdom. They lowered their heads in acknowledgement to the three of us, and I straightened. Max came forward as well, and Avaline passed the both of us to state her purpose. She lifted her thin skirts and bent her knees, bowing her head, then stood tall and brushed her hair back over her shoulders. "We come in peace," she said confidently.

"You burned down our wall," the king said.

"There are few other ways to gather your attention," Avaline said.

The king shrugged. "Indeed, I suppose."

"Your titles," the queen said, waving her hand.

"I am Avaline, Immortal Soul of the Forest," she said. "I live on your ground."

The queen nodded, sent a glance to her husband, then looked to me. "I am," I hesitated, "Johnny. A stable hand from Alice." The old man raised his hand and the king patted the air to silence the motion.

Max raised her chin. "I am Max," she said quietly.

"And your title?" the queen said sweetly, leaning forward.

"Slave."

"Former slave," I said, looking at Max. She shrunk back into the folds of her cloak.

The queen nodded and directed her stare to me again. "Tell me your real title, Jonathan."

Shivers cascaded down my back and I straightened, pushed past Avaline so I was in front. I didn't think they'd recognize me. "King and Queen of Bortal," I started, "I am Prince Jonathan of Valta, heir to the throne of the Second Kingdom."

The queen smiled. "It has been a long time since I've seen you, Johnny."

* Max *

I looked over at Johnny as the queen stood and rushed to embrace him. She pulled away slightly and checked his shoulder for the royal brand. "Just to be sure," she said. The queen looked into the prince's eyes. "Have you been home?"

Johnny shook his head, "I don't plan to go back."

"Oh, but you must. Your mother sends messages to me on the messenger boats; she still loses sleep over her lost boy. And your father expects a king."

"Perido can be king," Johnny said.

The king of Bortal stood. "But that is not in tradition with Valta. Unless you are dead, your brother cannot accept the throne."

Johnny turned to face him. "Then they can consider me part of the earth now. Cold." There was a long silence, the royals all facing each other. It was Avaline that spoke up next.

"That is not why we are here," she said.

The old man stepped forward. "I must agree, let us hear their news, I have other things to attend to."

"Ah, yes, but let us sit more comfortably," the queen said. "I do apologize Jonathan, had we known it was you at our door..."

Johnny shook his head and the old man raised his arms. "Prince or not, it is not wise to break into the castle walls with Avaline herself. The damage is large and unnecessary."

"Air, the years have given you a temper," Avaline said. The whole group directed their eyes to the old man.

"I ask that you please call me by my full name in front of my superiors, old friend," he said to Avaline.

"Storret Airet, I would have expected you to grow old in solitude," she embraced him.

He pulled away and smiled quickly. "You have not aged a bit, Avaline," he said, stroking the hair out of her face.

"A gift and a curse I presume."

The queen stepped forward and placed a hand on Storret Airet's shoulder. "Care to explain this mysterious guest?"

"An old friend, my queen. I apologize for the informality," he said, bowing.

"I do not expect much formality from the palace wizard, yet you act as though I keep you on a ball and chain." She turned to Johnny. "A wizard is scandalous, I know, but I must protect those within the walls from those outside them. The forest at our feet and that market to the west keep us under tight security."

"But why are you prisoners in your own home?" I asked the queen.

"Storret Airet deals with all of our land outside the palace wall, to keep our magical friends in check. We are not prisoners, we still rule as any royals would, just under different regulations and circumstances. In fact, we are quite safe, but security is a cautious and necessary step."

Johnny touched her hand. "I understand."

The queen turned back to Storret Airet. "Not secure enough, I see," she said, motioning to Avaline.

He glanced at the floor. "I apologize, my queen. She is the only being I know of that I am powerless against. Her fire has properties all its own."

She glanced around the room, then motioned to a door opposite the ones we entered through. "Let us meet in the study, it will be more comfortable. There we can discuss what is so urgent."

Avaline smiled at the royals, then squeezed the hand of her longtime friend. "It is quite urgent. I appreciate your flexibility."

The king and queen led the way out into a slim hallway. The wizard came next, his robes brushing over the ground, his feet at the heels of the royals. Avaline spoke to Johnny in hushed tones, walking close, leaving me to walk behind them. I stayed close on their heels though, uncomfortable without Johnny right by my side. We filtered into a smallish room, lit by only a few candles. Avaline let off a glow that brightened it slightly, as if the room were filled with magic. I suppose it was.

* Johnny *

The room reminded me of home. The furniture was made of dark wood, and white candles offered their light from tabletops and shelves. It smelled like dust and stone and stale bread; in Valta it would have been fresh. Two huge windows were covered by Bortalan-red drapes, instead of Valtan-green. There was wax and a seal for letters on the table; no doubt the seal was crafted into a *B* enveloped in a crescent, instead of the four swirls of my kingdom.

There were skins on the floor and large tapestries to hold in the heat of a small fire, flickering in the hearth. As Avaline walked in, the flames became more enthusiastic, dancing and reaching for the tattooed woman.

The king and queen seated themselves in two large chairs, their wizard to the side, on a stool. I sat on a small couch with Max and

Avaline, our bodies all touching, shoulder to shoulder. I could feel the cloak of heat coming from Avaline's skin, the cool outdoor air coming from Max. I watched her hand slide down her leg, to rest on her knee. I looked up to her face. I could see the hesitation as her lips parted, but I smiled back nonetheless.

Avaline adjusted her skirts on the other side of me. "I trust you are familiar with the story of Adahlia?" she asked the royals.

They exchanged glances. "We know the story, but it is a surprise that you know it as well," the queen said.

"Go on," the king said impatiently.

"Max, may I ask that you please show them your mark?" Avaline said.

Max nodded, lifted her hood and pulled the mess of hair off her neck. In the candlelight, her mark was revealed to everyone in the room. Both royals gasped and Storret Airet stood to take a closer look.

"She bears the mark of Adahlia," Avaline said.

"Spies have already been seeking her out. It is a long story, but ultimately that is how we got here, how we met Avaline," I said.

"I have vowed to help them, yes. As the story goes, there is someone who leads the way, someone to hold the torch in the darkness, so to speak. I have reason to believe that there is a way to release Adahlia, and not by the death of Max. I believe that there is a spell written, crafted by an old wizard, that may rid Max's body of the goddess. That spell lies within the Vault," Avaline said. The royals startled and my stomach sunk into my feet.

"The Vault, as in the chamber that supposedly gives Valta her name?" I asked.

"Yes," Avaline said.

"I have searched my palace and never found it. I don't mean to doubt you, but isn't the Vault a myth?"

"I have seen it," Avaline said.

I shook my head. "When? That is not possible."

"That is a story for later."

I looked at Max and her eyes flickered with hope. "So there is a way for me to avoid death from this?" she asked.

Avaline bowed her head. "That is my hope. But the spell would be risky; I can't promise you anything. And if the spell was executed incorrectly, you would suffer from something much worse than death."

Max didn't make a sound as the glitter of hope seemed to drain from her eyes.

"Not to sound greedy on behalf of my royals, but who would cast this spell? It is said that a kingdom must release the goddess, and in return that kingdom will be blessed by the gods," Storret Airet said.

"Alice is rebelling. Do you believe that she is seeking the goddess to win her battle for power?" the queen asked.

"Yes," the king said.

Avaline nodded her head in agreement. "I believe that is the case."

"Johnny, you must go home and tell your parents. I trust that they will understand you and will be able to help. If Avaline is right, you'll need to go to Valta to access the Vault," the queen said.

"Or we could keep her here," the king said. He rose out of his chair. "Bortal has been suppressed for hundreds of years. If we killed this girl now, we'd have an upper hand. We could rise out of our grave, be an important force in Cavail again."

"And have no friends, only enemies. Even with a favor from the gods, Bortal could not stand a chance against the other kingdoms," Storrett Airet said. His eyes were keen on the king.

Everyone else stood in shock. I inched closer to Max. These people were not greedy like the royals in Alice, but under tight security from the rest of the realm, I could see the king's motivation. This was his chance to finally bring his kingdom back from ruin. I could not accept the idea, though. I could not watch Max die knowing there was another way. I didn't know why I was so protective of her, but as my heart pounded, I knew it was genuine.

I swallowed the lump in my throat as the wizard went on, waiting for the conclusion to be made. Waiting for the sign whether I should press into action to escape the palace with Max before she could be killed, or calm my nerves and continue discussing the goddess.

Storrett Airet guided the king back down into his seat. "If we release Adahlia and win this scramble for power, then we lose Valta, our greatest ally. But if we support Valta in this, we'll be better protected. If anything, the Kingdom of Bortal will be better off sticking to Valta's side than being hasty and releasing the goddess now."

"He's right," the queen said to her husband. "I know it's painful, I know what this could mean to us, but we must be careful in our strategies."

The king stared at me from under a creased brow. "Yes," he said finally. "We are best off if we let them carry on with their quest. But know this Jonathan: Your parents, your people in Valta, need to know what we have done tonight. The Second Kingdom needs to know that we, the royals of Bortal, did not act on this opportunity."

"Yes," I said, my voice stiff. "They will not forget you, they never have. Valta is ever loyal to Bortal."

"Will you tell them yourself?" the king asked.

"Why should I?" I asked. "By no means am I willing to go home. And what makes you think my parents will be alright with this? They are very traditional rulers. I can't imagine them letting a strange woman lead us through our own palace in search of a mythical room full of illegal spells and potions."

"They will do anything they can for their kingdom and the safety of their people, just as we would. With Alice as a threat, the most powerful of the kingdoms as it is, they will heed this warning," the queen said.

I shook my head. "And in the case that they don't? I haven't been home for years. They would think I'd lost my mind." I could not imagine my return. Perhaps there would be a way for me to help Avaline break into the Valtan palace and explore the Vault without my parents knowing. We could continue our quest without my return home. But I didn't need to tell the king and queen of Bortal that plan.

"More than your brother?" the queen asked.

I laughed, a little startled by her jest. Many royals knew my brother often acted more like a street urchin than a prince. "No one is more contrary than my brother, yet people forget that he is perfectly sane," I said.

"Before we lose track of the situation," the king said, "may I add that we are dealing with a rogue kingdom? Alice will stop at nothing for power, and that could ruin Cavail. Bortal has no outlet to uncover any information regarding the First Kingdom."

"I'm not sure who would," I said.

The king grinned. "Dela will know. The Fertile Island trades with them regularly; they will know what Alice plans. Go to Dela. See what you can learn. You will ride the next messenger boat out of Bortal and down to the only island that will know what Alice plans."

Avaline rubbed her hands together and they started to glow. "Dela," she said, "I have not been there for many years."

* Max *

The king and queen had two guardsmen show us to a room where we would stay until the next messenger boat came. It had three beds, each dressed with thick red sheets. Johnny laid on one bed, while I sat on another. Avaline was lighting candles and stoking the fire in the hearth with the tips of her fingers. I couldn't help but notice the grin on her face, as if she was possessed by the fire.

I stroked the sheets on the bed, admiring the softness. "I've never slept on a bed," I said.

"No?" Johnny said, walking to sit next to me.

I shook my head. "Always on the floor."

Avaline looked our way. "I prefer the ground, though I don't sleep," she said.

I looked at the floor, then back up at the strange woman. "How old are you, Avaline?"

She glanced away, out the window and into the darkness of the night. "I am well over one thousand years now." Her voice was sorrowful.

Johnny's eyebrows creased. "How is that possible?"

"I am Avaline, Immortal Soul of the Forrest."

"That doesn't explain..." Johnny's voice faded.

"In my heart, I am a phoenix," Avaline said. "When I was old and tired, I built a nest so I could renew myself."

"Rebirth," Johnny said. "Burn alive and in place of your ashes, a new phoenix would rise."

"I was interrupted," she said. "A man turned me into a woman, enslaved me. I thought I would die in this body, but in the change I had not lost my ability to create flame. I did not lose my immortal blood. I have been stuck like this for a long time."

"It must be terrible to be trapped like that," I said.

Avaline sat across from us on Johnny's bed. "It's not horrible."

"What is it like to fly?" Johnny asked.

Avaline looked out the window again. "I don't know how I would explain that."

I followed her gaze. "Have you tried ways to get back into phoenix...form?" I asked.

Avaline tipped her head. "The Vault, yes."

"So it's real? You've seen it?" Johnny asked.

"I've seen it, but it had nothing that could help me. Out of all the vials of potions and out of all the shelves upon shelves of books and scrolls of spells, I found nothing."

"How long ago was this?" Johnny asked.

"Eight hundred years or so, I'd say."

I looked at my feet. "Why are you helping me?"

Avaline smoothed her tattered skirts and focused her purple eyes on me. "Because that is what I do. I protect and aid the world of the living, while connecting with the world of the gods. I am Immortal Soul of the Forest, phoenix or not. I must help, it is my duty."

"What is your excuse?" I asked Johnny.

He didn't answer for a long time. "The thrill, I guess," he said finally. "It could be that it is within my duty as prince to protect my kingdom. The goddess concerns all four kingdoms, Max. Even Dela, though that kingdom holds no title." He paused. "It could also be because I feel an obligation to help people. Granted, it is not my wish to be king, but it is in my blood to help those in need."

"I guess you could say that I am in need," I said. Johnny placed a warm hand on my thigh. I moved away and he pulled his hand back.

"Indeed you could," Avaline said.

* Johnny *

The next morning someone rapped on the door and a moment later, opened it slowly. I lifted my head to see Max sit up straight, reach for the dagger in her boot, still laced tightly over her foot. I planted my bare feet on the ground and rushed to take her weapon, but Avaline was there faster, her pale hands lowering Max's.

"Who's there?" I asked.

"Orders from the royals. They wish me to escort you to their company." The small and non-intimidating man in the doorway rested his hand on the hilt of the sword at his hip.

I reached over my bed to pull on my boots. Max stood, placed a hand over her pendant and swung her cloak over her back. The flames in the hearth went out and Avaline grinned.

"Alright," I said, swinging my pack over my shoulders.

We followed him through a maze of hallways until the man stopped and opened a door. There, the queen was seated in the great hall where we had first met her. The man positioned us in front of her throne, bowed, and left.

"I wish to give you a few things before you go. The boat leaves soon and you have full authorization to board," she said.

"Thank you," I said. She nodded.

"The king and wizard could not attend your farewell, though they send best wishes," the queen said.

I felt a little relieved to know that I would not see the king again. After his brutal proposition, I felt more wary in his home.

The queen turned to grab something to the side of her throne. "Avaline, Storret Airet asked me to give this to you." Avaline stepped forward and spread her hands so the queen could place a thin leather belt in her hands. With it, she also placed a few small bags.

Avaline smiled. "He is a character isn't he?" she said to the queen. "Tell my friend to take care."

The queen nodded. "He has missed you greatly, I can tell." Avaline stepped back and the queen went on. "Johnny, take this scroll to your mother, and send her my love. She is a dear woman and will be happy to see you." I took the scroll. I'd have to give it to Avaline to take to Valta, or possibly send it there, but I would not be returning home.

"Thank you," I said, "for your hospitality and for your counsel. Dela will aid us well, and we will then give message to Valta."

"I thank you in return. Now, Max," she continued. She stepped forward and I moved to the side with Avaline. "I'd like to give you something that was once very special to me. I hope it will bring you strength during your journey." The queen reached into her pocket and handed a small bag to Max, who in turn, opened it very carefully.

"It is just a bell, I know," the queen said, "but I've had it a long time. There is no magic to it, though I have had much luck while it was in my possession. I believe you need it more than I do."

Max looked up from the bell in her hands and smiled at the queen. "Thank you." She rang the little bell once and its sound filled the hall. Sweet music sang for a moment, then vanished.

"Now Johnny," the queen said, standing, "it is not like a queen to take part in informalities...but come here." She wrapped her arms around my body and squeezed tightly. "Take care, Prince Jonathan. Tell Prince Perido that I send him my love," she whispered and pulled away. "I know you've only been to Bortal once in your life before this, and I know you were very young, but your family is quite dear to us."

"Goodbye," I said, bowing. The three of us turned to leave and guards opened the door. We were escorted through the palace and out into the cold northern air. We walked along the interior of the kingdom, through the courtyard and past the stables to a drawbridge that opened as soon as we arrived. One of the guards handed me a scroll, bound in red ribbon.

"Give this to the captain of the ship," he said. I nodded at the man and started down the path toward the port.

Without a guide, it was hard to follow, but we managed, listening for the gulls and walking toward the smell of sea air. When the trees broke into the open, I could hear Avaline's breath catch.

"I have not seen the sea in ages," she said.

"Are you not afraid of the stairs?" I asked, leaning to eye the rickety way down. A small messenger boat tethered to the dock bobbed on the water.

"Height does not bother me Johnny. Remember, I used to travel mainly by air," she said lightly. "It is my human body I worry will fail me. Whether it be drowning or a broken limb. I was never this delicate."

I laughed. "Max are you ready?"

Her eyes were cast down, with her hood pulled up around her face. "As ready as I'll ever be," she said quietly.

Avaline rested a tattooed hand on Max's shoulder. "Do not fret, the goddess will be gone soon. Have you found a way to silence her calls?"

Max shook her head.

"Then come now, Max," Avaline said, guiding her toward the stairs, "listen to the sea birds and the wind instead."

We made our way down the stairs and to the rotten dock, where a portly man greeted us. He wore loose trousers and a puffy white shirt, with a belt around his large stomach that seemed to cinch everything into place.

"We delivered the message from Dela to the king, what more do you ask for? I'd like to get out of this cursed place," the man said.

I handed him the scroll. "For your captain," I said.

"I'm the captain," he said, and snatched the scroll from my hands. His stubby fingers untied the ribbon and he read the contents of the scroll, his mouth moving as he did so. "Alright, Prince, you may board with your women," he said.

The captain turned and clapped his hands. Moments later a slender sailor trotted up. "Fredrick, escort these…um…guests to the guest's quarters," he said.

"Yes sir," the sailor said. "This way." He led us downstairs into the hull of the boat and into a small room with a single bed. "I'm sorry we don't have more room, but I will bring down blankets to make the stay more comfortable for all of you." He tipped his hat and left the room.

I went and sat on the bed. "In a few days, we will see the wonderful crest that is the Fertile Hills."

Avaline smiled. "I have not seen them for hundreds of years," she said.

A bell started to ring and I could hear shouts from above. "Leaving port!" men yelled, and I could feel the boat slipping away from the dock, away from the Third Kingdom. We were on our way to Dela, the most beautiful place in Cavail, and I could only feel doubt churning in my stomach.

Chapter 5

* Max *

The air gave me goose bumps as we walked from the boat, down the ramp to the dock. I let my cloak slide down my shoulders and rested it on my arm.

"There they are," Avaline said.

I tried to smile at her. "The hills?" I looked up from the port and saw a purple crest of slumbering lavender. To the side was another crest, brown with the stubble of harvest.

"I can't wait to see them, after all this time," Avaline said. She fell silent as Johnny strolled up and placed a hand on my back.

"Dela is beautiful. Look around," he whispered to me.

There were old wooden buildings that lined the port, along with stone ones that cast shadows over the docks and ships that were parked and loading vegetables. Big men jostled barrels and sacks of grain around us, some cursing, but most smiling as they walked by. A dirt road led up a grassy hill, out of the port. Modest people pulling carriages walked through the dirt, either to or away from the busy waterside market. People crowded the coastal cobble road, buying things from the stores or socializing with one another. All their faces seemed to glisten in the warm sun, as if it were still summer.

"Let's go," Johnny said as he started up the hill.

We strode around the town's people, each of them giving us a genuine smile. One man, dressed in modest clothing, had two goats pulling a cart of apples. "Best apples in the nation," he said.

Johnny shook his head. "No thanks."

"They're good for the health. Have a few! No charge," the man said, handing Johnny three huge pink apples.

"I appreciate it, good man," Johnny said as we continued up the hill.

"Come back for more, any time," the man yelled back as he led his goats down the hill to the port.

I grinned and took a bite of an apple, watching Johnny put the other two in his bag. "You're not going to have one?" I asked.

Johnny shook his head.

"I heard once that Dela is the best place to be among the islands," I said. I could feel elation in my veins, filling me. It had always wanted to get to Dela, and I was finally here. Perhaps it would be the last place I'd have to visit. Perhaps Dela, with warm weather and jolly people, could keep me safe from slavery and Adahlia. The thought of never being in danger again made my limbs tingle. Certainly Dela was not so perfect, but I had never heard of any crime on the Fertile Island.

"I could agree with that," Avaline said, breaking my train of thought.

I nodded in response and continued up the hill. When we reached the top, the Fertile Hills bent below us in waves of color. To our right sat a small and beautiful castle; to our left, a path led down to a small town, tucked between the hills and the coast of the island. At our feet, the sun kissed grass bowed to the wind. Fall had just recently passed and winter was setting in, but the Fertile Hills looked alive, as if it were spring. The sun broke through the thick clouds, drawing out the last little bit of warmth before the storms came in to stay.

"We head to Laven Soll, down that path," Avaline said.

"Laven Soll?" I asked.

A man passed us with a cow and grinned at us with yellow crooked teeth.

"The Delan spies are in Laven Soll, the southern town. They will know more than the royals about the state of Alice, being the party that watches over all of Dela's affairs," Avaline whispered.

Johnny nodded. "Should we go through the town of Dela Av?" he said, pointing to our left.

"We go through the fields. If we hurry, we can get there by nightfall," Avaline said.

"Does it only take a day?" I asked.

"If we hurry," she said.

We made our way down the small road, getting passed by people with carriages full of produce. Farmers gathered the last of the fall crops in the fields and waved kindly as we walked by. We came to a bridge that arced over a calm river. Fish swam in the water below as we crossed. Morning turned into afternoon turned into evening as we walked through the Fertile Hills.

The sun had just set when we got to the outskirts of Laven Soll. The dirt path transformed into a stone road that was long and straight. Trees lined the road, along with a meek fence that held in a green pasture and grazing cattle. I could see in the distance the flicker of warm lights in cozy homes. To the right stood a sign with the town's name: *Welcome to Laven Soll.*

The fields became scarcer as we went along, and trees started to dapple the land. I could see small livestock pastures woven between the thicker patches of trees, and townhouses became more and more plentiful.

Avaline was explaining the history of Laven Soll to Johnny, and I watched him listening intently. I walked behind the pair. It did not bother me so much, not being a part of the conversation. I felt safer on Dela, not so vulnerable if I was slightly distanced from Johnny, and it gave me a chance to simply observe.

"Don't be a fool," Avaline said to Johnny. The sunlight had almost left the sky, and now Avaline had a slight glow.

"I am not a fool, I just know what I want," he said. "I'm not going back to Valta."

"You're not a fool," I said to Johnny. They both looked at me like I was a fool myself. "What?"

"Nothing," Johnny said. "But it is foolish of me to stay away from my home. It's just something I must do," he explained to Avaline.

"Well I don't think that's foolish," I said.

"Thank you," Johnny said. "That's very nice of you."

"I can be nice."

"I know, I just," he paused and looked at Avaline, "I didn't know you were listening." Johnny smiled at me. It was a warm smile, his lips parted, his cheeks tight. There was a glint in his eye I hadn't seen before.

"Oh," I said.

It was completely dark now, and the candles in the windows of the buildings flickered. A twig snapped, and my eyes darted. Johnny stopped, fingered his dagger and Avaline spun on her bare heels, as if ready for a fight.

Someone grabbed my wrist from behind me, a hand cupping my mouth so I couldn't yell. Another person had his hands on Johnny, one covering his mouth and one on his arm to halt his weapon. Avaline ignited and a third person splashed her with water from a nearby water trough. The flames still covered her body until a cloth was shoved into her mouth, cutting off her oxygen. Her flames died, and she slumped as we were led down a path that shot off from the main road.

The person who had me whispered in my ear, breath smelling of fresh bread. "Do not struggle, we are here to help." It was a woman's voice, strong but feminine, trustworthy, though I did not trust her completely.

I stopped resisting her and she stood behind me, grabbed my shoulders, and guided me on the overgrown trail. Johnny was still being led with a hand over his mouth, another hand on his arm. Avaline had the cloth out of her mouth now, and walked forward willingly.

We followed our captors around huge trees, twisting into a thicket that only let us glimpse at the stars. Fog hung between the branches, concealing the house where we eventually stopped. We were led through the back, candles were lit, and the door shut behind us.

"Now," the woman said as we were seated around a large table. It was crammed into a kitchen that was modest and warm. Besides our captors, there were four other men. "There are things you must know." The woman wore working clothes that fit loosely around her frail figure. Her voice sounded youthful, but the wrinkles around her face told us otherwise. I could see that past the ripples around her lips and brow she had once been a beautiful woman.

The man behind Johnny's seat grunted, placed a teapot on the table and had the man who led Avaline place cups on the table as well. I glanced into the one placed in front of me and could smell the mint leaves in the bottom. When they were done serving us, they sat as well, speaking softly to the other men in the room.

"What is going on?" The reluctance in Johnny's voice was obvious.

"You may go if you please. You must have realized that we didn't take your weapons in our capture. There's no reason to use them now, I assure you," the woman said. "But before you decide to go, I believe you have been looking for us?"

"Who are you?" Johnny asked.

"Drink first, I'm sure you're thirsty. Do not worry, it is only mint. Good when you steep it in water," she said.

"Answer his question," Avaline said.

"Ah, the woman of fire," the woman grinned, "my name is Charlotte Lazuli, assistant to these men...the ah, brains behind their operation." The woman's smile broadened.

"And your men?" I said.

"Oh, well they are the spies of Dela! But that is beside the point. We are here to help you," Charlotte said.

I looked across the table at the man who had led Johnny from the road. His eyes were a steely blue, so cold that I froze when they rested on mine. They lingered a moment, then moved down to my pendant, where they lingered longer. They broke away when Charlotte began to speak again.

"Goddess, the First Kingdom is in turmoil over your untraceable adventures," she said, her eyes just as blue as the man's across from me. My breath caught. "Oh, I feel foolish," the woman said. "What are your names? Please, we are all friends here."

"More or less," the man across from me said.

"Kye, please," Charlotte said. His blue eyes fell to his cup, which he filled again.

"I am Johnny," Johnny said.

Charlotte glanced around the room at the spies. "Your full title? Let me remind you that these are sharp minds. Do not attempt to lie." She ruffled the hair of the man sitting next to her, making him look like a child. He shifted on the bench and ran a big hand over his face.

"I am Prince Jonathan, heir to the Valtan Throne."

Charlotte's eyes went wide. "I asked for you not to lie…" Her words broke when Johnny pulled his shirt to the side to reveal his Royal Brand.

"I see," she said.

"I am Max, no title," I said.

"No? Well then, I guess we move on to the pale one," Charlotte said.

"Avaline, Immortal Soul of the Forest."

"You are a phoenix of Bortal?" Charlotte said, surprised.

Avaline let a small flame arrive on her finger, and she lit a candle that was on the table. "It is a story that is not meant to be shared tonight."

"You are not afraid?" Johnny asked the spies.

Charlotte answered for them. "It takes a lot more than magic to scare us, Jonathan." She glanced at the men huddled around the table. "We are living amongst cowards of one of the purest and most amazing substances in the whole nation. Magic is a curse if used in such a way, but it is also a gift in the right hands. Does magic scare you?" She rested her elbows on the table and laced her fingers together.

I looked at the floor, and the goddess began to speak.

"No," I said aloud, urging her to stop her tormenting.

Charlotte smiled, "You are like me then, Max." The woman's glance sunk to her cup and she reached down and took a small sip. "Anyway, we saw you arrive on a boat this morning. Max must do better at concealing her mark."

I pushed my hair to the right, over the red and orange swirls.

"We were coming to find you," Johnny said. "We hear rumors about Alice, we need answers to report to Valta. We have the goddess and we intend to keep her safe from their killing spree.

Avaline believes that there is a way to release Adahlia without hurting Max."

"I see," Charlotte said. "Yes, Alice is rebelling, as the three other kingdoms should have realized by now. Dela is the minor kingdom, not official by any title, but our words and opinions hold very true in the minds of the real royals. These men before you are spies. They find information, send it on messenger boats from Dela's port, just as the farmers on the Fertile Hills send their crops. We are the giving island in the realm."

"But Alice, what will they do next?" Johnny said impatiently.

"They will find the goddess, release her, and overpower all the other kingdoms until there is only one left. Alice," Kye said.

"But how does the goddess fit in to this? What does she matter to them?" I asked.

"In the story that is passed down among the royals, the goddess will reward the kingdom that releases her," Charlotte said.

"I know that. But reward how?" Johnny asked. He took a sip of his tea and glanced at me.

"Riches, power, good trade. It is all only rumored," one of the men said.

"Rumored?" Johnny repeated.

"Amazing what people will do over a rumor. But Alice believes that if she releases the goddess, she will win her war for power," Charlotte said.

"Truly? Alice believes she can win against three other kingdoms?" Johnny said.

"Four," Kye said, "if you royals would like to include little Dela."

"You know Valta has been pushing for Dela to become an official kingdom. She participates in the realm just as much as the others," Johnny said.

"If not more. But it is Alice who pushes Dela away. Alice wants it all," Kye's voice became harsh, deep. His blue eyes darted around the room and his fists clenched.

"Kye," Charlotte said, raising a hand.

He took a hasty sip of tea and relaxed again.

"You two must be careful. Alice has people all over Cavail searching for Adahlia. Max, keep her concealed."

"I will," I said.

"Thank you for your help," Johnny said.

"You three may stay here tonight, get some safe rest, I'm sure you are all quite tired," Charlotte said. "Where are you headed next?"

Avaline explained briefly, only mentioning the Vault, not our plans to get inside it, nor whether or not I'd be returning home.

"I see," Charlotte said when Avaline was finished. She stood. "Well Kye, show them to a room where they can rest tonight."

Charlotte disappeared among the bulky bodies that stood and filled the kitchen. Kye stood and led us down the hall while the other men went about their own tasks.

"Here it is. Only one bed, but it's comfortable. Big enough for three if you don't mind sharing. The room to your right is a small place to bathe. Should I bring some hot water?" Kye said, his eyes resting on me.

Johnny shook his head, as did Avaline.

"I would," I said.

"Alright then." Kye disappeared down the hall and when he came back, he filled the tub with steaming water.

"Here you are," he said, his eyes resting softly on me. Chills cascaded down my back. "Enjoy your soak." He went to leave, but stopped when I spoke.

"I will."

He turned around to face me. "How did a girl like you get a jewel like that?" He asked.

"I found it," I said.

"It suits you," he said quietly, smiling. His eyes glanced over me before he left, making me feel suddenly awkward.

I closed the door behind me and could feel the room getting steamy from the heat of the water. I undressed slowly, letting my clothes peel off like dead skin. I stood in front of a mirror hung on the wall and looked at myself without them. I wasn't ugly without the fabric. I turned around and gazed at the pink scars that crisscrossed over my back. Some were still raised, giant long welts, while others were flat and smooth, no color left in them. The pain that every lash came with, and my screams in the dark, every memory up until I threw the slave tag down the road, flooded my mind.

I faced the mirror once again, closed my eyes against the tears. I wasn't ugly, but the pale skin draped over my bones, the unnatural curves, the lack of weight, was everything but beautiful.

One foot at a time I slid into the tub. The hot water seeped into my veins, warming my whole body. I combed my tangled hair, letting the water loosen the knots that held the strands in a mat. I rubbed my legs, stomach, chest, face, feeling the dirt float away. Slowly, the water became murky.

Sighing, I heard a little knock on the door.

I straightened when the voice came. "Max?" It was Kye, the deep voice came through the door hushed and soft.

I put an arm over my chest, in case he came in. "Yes?"

But he spoke through the door again. "I have clean clothes for you to have under your own. And towels too, all from my mother."

"I don't need them," I said.

"The towels or the clothes?" Kye asked. I could hear him laugh a little.

"I...I'm not dressed. Will you place them inside the door?" I asked.

"Yes," he said, opening the door slightly. He pushed the garments inside and shut it again. "Was the water hot enough? I can fetch more," he said.

"I'm fine. I'll get dressed," I said.

"Alright, sleep well Max." He waited only a moment before he left. I could hear his footsteps down the hall.

"Thanks," I whispered.

I dressed in the clothes Kye had given me. They were loose, but warm, comfortable for sleeping and to have under the clothes Johnny got me. I placed a hand on my pendant, making sure it was still there. It was warm from the water.

Before I left the room, I glanced at the mirror again. The woman staring back at me was different than the one who had gotten in the tub. She looked brighter somehow. I smiled at the freckles that dusted my face, then left the room.

Johnny was sitting on the bed and Avaline had found a chair in our little room. She sat on the edge of her seat, perched and ready, speaking to Johnny. They both looked up when I entered the room.

"New clothes?" Johnny asked.

I nodded. "They are Charlotte's."

"They look nice," he said.

My face went flush and I was glad when he changed the subject. "You can have the bed. I'm fine with the floor."

"I don't mind the floor," I said. "And what about Avaline?"

"I don't sleep," she said. "Remember?"

Johnny smiled at her, then at me. "You'll take the bed, Max." He ushered me into the room, pulled back the blankets, motioned for me to lie down. "There," he said, when I did.

The candles went out, startling me, but I could see Avaline grin in the newly dark room. Johnny lay down on the floor and sighed.

"Sleep well Max," he said. I craned my head to the little window by my bed. Moonlight filtered in through the lace curtains, quiet and meek.

The goddess did not speak to me that night; I fell asleep right away.

* Johnny *

I woke up when I heard angry hands pounding on the door. Muffled voices called in the dark as Kye rushed in and I sat up startled. Max was still asleep in the bed, her side rising and falling as she breathed peacefully. The room was dark and there was a coolness drifting through the house. It was morning. Early.

"Max, wake up" Avaline said, placing a hand on her shoulder.

Max sat up in her bed, began dressing. "What's going on?"

"Alician spies have found you. They are knocking on our door, demanding the goddess. Mother will take care of the intruders. She asked that we meet with the Delan spies behind the house," Kye said. His blue eyes had a glint of terror in them as they darted around the room.

We followed Kye out the back door into a maze of apple and oak trees. The other men were waiting for us, swords drawn, rushing to surround us and lead us away. A sea of hazy rain filled the air. Not even the shouts of the Alician men could reach us through the fog. The dim morning light cast shadows that leaped; the orchard became denser than what was true.

We ran for a while, through thick dewy grass that bent along our legs. We finally stopped when we got to a great oak, somewhere close to the center of the orchard. The trunk was carved into spirals and patterns, much like the ones that covered Avaline. The branches, some tattooed in the manner the trunk was, hung low to the ground. All of its leaves had fallen and were flat along the base of the tree.

Kye urged us to crouch under the canopy of leaves and branches. Panting, he whispered instructions. "My mother said she'd be here in a moment. She has provisions for your trip up north to the port, so you can travel to Valta." Kye leaned against the tree with his hands on his knees, sucking breath in and out. I ran my fingers over the spirals that covered the wood and tried to calm my breathing as well. The other men shifted, but did not speak.

Avaline touched the tree with her tattooed hand. "This is an old tree," she whispered.

"Yes." Charlotte strode up, her chest heaving, and stopped in front of us under the cover of the oak branches. Her grey and tattered lace dress rippled around her ankles when she stopped. "Marked to ward off bad magic. It was done a long time ago, when Bortal was going through its civil wars."

Charlotte let the sack over her shoulder fall to the wet ground. She nodded to each of the men surrounding, then finally looked at Kye. Her son stared back with the same intensely blue eyes as his mother.

"We must hurry you out of Laven Soll, into the port of Dela. I will lead you through the graveyard," Charlotte said to me. "Kye, get the bag, it's heavy."

Outside the shelter of the branches, Charlotte hurried us along a path that led us farther into the labyrinth of trees. Their boughs hung low in the dreary rain that continued to fall. The Delan spies sheathed their swords to be more swift.

Suddenly, Charlotte stopped. "Do not move," she said. Listening for a moment, everyone was quiet, waiting for the woman to give the next command. "This way," she said, and started to run. Her dress flowed around her feet in a grey storm of lace.

The mist was thick, and all I could see was Max running just a step in front of me. Avaline did not glow, and I could only catch glimpses of her fiery hair beyond Max. The Delan spies behind me were almost silent in the grass.

As the trees began to thin, a new shadow emerged out of the haze. A building, slumping in the rain, no doubt deserted. As we came closer, I could see boards on the windows, a crooked old sign nailed to a nearby tree that said only one word: *Graves*.

In the sloping field beyond the building, gravestones were dappled within the fog. Some were overtaken by weeds, others jutted out from the ground like stone bodies.

"We must cut through the graveyard. I sent the men at our door the opposite way, but they are not ignorant. Some spies may be hidden among the dead down there," Charlotte said.

Avaline's eyes widened. "This place was deserted?"

"Long ago," said Charlotte, glancing at the ground. "Come, we must hurry, beyond this is the road back to the port. They will not follow you once you reach the Fertile Hills. It is too open."

We walked to the right of the building, turning left into the sea of stone. The orchard loomed over the little valley; apple trees bending to the last apples, rotting on their weak branches, the oak boughs twisting and contorting, shielding their fallen leaves from the early morning sky. It was barely light out; the sun had not quite lifted over the hills.

We spread out as we walked through the graveyard. Charlotte's eyes were cast down, her brow frowning as much as the corners of her mouth. Max walked with Avaline, their shoulders brushing with the rise and fall of their bodies so close to each other. The men of Dela remained silent.

"You there." Seven big figures ran toward us, weaving between the graves.

"Alician spies," one of the Delan men grunted. He pulled his sword. The unmistakable sound of ringing steel echoed throughout the buried.

"Hide," Charlotte said, and I grabbed Max's arm and began to run. Avaline followed, weaving through graves until the four of us were hiding amongst the oak and apple trees.

I pulled my dagger and peered around a tree, looking into the battle in the graveyard. The Delan men were fast, but did not overwhelm the men from Alice. One Alician man went down, clutching his stomach as his blood spilled over the graves. It looked gray in the morning light, rather than red.

Four other men were fighting the Delans, but I had lost track of three. Blood surged through my veins as I glanced at shadows. There. A figure darted behind a tree, footsteps shuffled, a twig snapped.

Max screamed as a man ran toward her, sword out, swinging. Another came too, but Avaline cut him off, throwing fire at his flesh until his skin had charred in places, boiled in others. The burnt man fell, but not until his sword had cut Charlotte's shoulder as she had been running to aid Max. The older woman stopped, went to her knees.

The next man came, but it was Kye who took him down, slicing at his wrist. The spy yelled as hand and sword fell to the grass. He gripped what was left of his arm with his other hand.

Kye spun around, his eyes wide as he stood motionless and watched Max struggling with another Alician spy. The man had managed to seize her arms, bending both back until her knees gave, her body coiled and twisting on the ground. He laughed, an eerie sound to join that of the clattering swords distant in the graveyard.

"No, please..." Max cried, but the man laughed more, pulling at her arms until she began to weep. I rushed; blindly thrust my dagger into the man's neck. The point came out the other side, shining bright red with the blood, the upcoming sunlight. He yelped, gurgled, fell. I could not feel guilty, not after seeing the fear and pain on Max's face. Not after hearing the man's laughter.

Max looked up, a hand on her shoulder, eyes wide. Her full lips were parted, her hair was tousled, her green eyes flickered. Kye helped his mother stand, ripped a piece of his shirt to tie around her shoulder where she had been cut. The Delan spies came too, some helping others, but all were more or less whole. We walked to the graveyard in silence, where Avaline had ignited the bodies of those who had not fled.

"Report," Charlotte said once our small wounded group had circled around a grave.

"Four wounded, all minor," one of the spies said.

She nodded. "Max, Johnny, Avaline, are you all okay?"

I glanced at Max. Her eyes shone out from under her hood. They were bloodshot, wet. "Yes, we're fine."

"We must not waste time, I apologize," Avaline said, waving a hand.

Charlotte bowed her head. "We understand your urgency," she said.

"Thank you for your protection, and all of your help," I said.

One of the Delan men handed me the bag Charlotte had brought for us. "Here, food for your trip back north," he said.

"If you follow that path there, through the graves, it leads to the main road of Laven Soll. You'll find your way from there," Charlotte said. "Farewell."

"Yes, take care," Avaline said.

Charlotte rested her attention on Max. "Be safe, dear. You are important in this rebellion."

"We will not forget Dela in this," I said. "Some day, Dela will be called the Fifth Kingdom."

Charlotte grinned and the spies smiled as well. "I hope that to be true," she said.

We walked away, leaving Charlotte and her men behind among the trees and headstones.

Kye rushed, placed a hand on my back before we were out of sight. "Well done, saving Max," he said.

"Anyone could have done it," I whispered.

"I hesitated when I saw the man running toward her. I'm glad that you did not," he said, glancing at her figure disappearing into the dwindling fog with Avaline. "Take care of her," he added.

I nodded. He had been watching her since we had arrived. "I will." His steel blue eyes looked deep into mine before I turned to walk away. I felt the chill of winter creeping down my back, or was it merely his stare? He was serious, but so was I. I shook the hair out of my face and ran to catch up with Avaline and Max.

As soon as we got out of Laven Soll, the thickness of trees broke into open fields and though it was raining, Dela's Fertile Hills were still beautiful. Farmers, still working on their very last harvest despite the rain, waved cheerfully.

The only color left was the lavender, slumbering in its rounds, small and cut and ready for winter. I thought about the lavender honey I had bought in Alice only a few weeks before. The bread I would have spread it on. It amazed me how things had changed.

As we walked, I began to think about home. The last fruits in the orchards behind the Valtan palace would be harvested soon. Apples and pears, apricots and plums, would fill the palace with their scent. Among the smoke from torches and warmth from hearths and ovens, Valta would feel warm and settled. Furs would be brought out from their storage and laid for extra warmth on beds and chairs. Feasts would be rich with honey-bread and caramelized meats. Just the thought of Valta at this time of year made me feel an unwelcome longing for home. Yet after the skirmish in the graveyard, I could see the value in returning to the palace. The shelter of Valta could keep Max safe, and meanwhile we could be working toward solutions, ways for Max to survive the release of the goddess.

"Thank you," Max said, interrupting my thoughts. It was the only thing she had spoken since our parting with the Delan spies.

"For what?" I said. I could see Avaline glance over, but continue to walk in silence.

"For saving me," Max said.

"That's what I'm here for, to protect you," I said.

"I still don't understand why."

"I barely understand myself," I said.

Max smoothed her hair and adjusted her cloak before returning her attention to me. "It was brave," she said.

I nodded. "Don't worry about it."

"I won't."

I cleared my throat. "I am going to have to wish you all the luck when you go to Valta. Even though I am not returning home, I will still support you and Avaline once you explore the Vault."

"You are going, Johnny," Avaline intervened. Her voice was unwavering.

I shook my head. "I can't. You don't understand. I haven't been home in nearly six years. What would they do with me now?" Even as I said it though, I could not help but think of the benefits of my return.

"You'll have to find out," Avaline said. "It is your duty as prince. You must at least properly decline the throne. And Max and I have no way of getting into the palace. You have your mark."

"You could do it the same way as Bortal," I said, smiling.

Avaline laughed a little. "We will be menacing enough when we ask the king to see the Vault. We don't need to storm more castles."

"I can give you a letter to take to my parents," I offered. Avaline began to speak, but I held up my hand to stop her. I sighed.

If I went to Valta, I'd have to face my father, the throne, my duties. I doubted I'd be able to dodge being heir. Father was too traditional to allow me to refuse being king. My only reason for returning home after so long would be Max. It would keep her safe from the Alicians, keep Cavail safe from Alice's rebellion. I could not be so selfish to deny Max her safety. And worse, I could not endanger kingdoms and towns and citizens by not carrying on with our quest to release Adahlia. I could not, as much as I had denied it for six years, stay away from my home and my people any longer. Though I did not find joy in the weight of a kingdom on my shoulders, I could not isolate myself from my family any longer.

I looked at Max, the way she moved, turned her face toward the wind. I could see Dela's castle in the distance, flags waving above her port. It was late in the day, the sky livening with pinks and golds as the sun poked through the clouds in places, ducked beneath boughs of autumn haze.

"You are right, Avaline," I said finally, gathering the courage to make my decision.

"About what?"

I dreaded what I was about to tell her. I had to, though. I had to return home. "I can't avoid the blood that runs through my veins. And going to Valta is the only way to save Max from the goddess," I said. Max was worth it, worth all my duties as prince and heir to the Valtan thrown. I had not realized that until I'd seen the look on her face after I'd saved her. I would do anything to see that look again.

"Noble," Avaline said. "You are doing right by returning home, Johnny."

I nodded. The three of us were arriving at the top of the port. The sun had set and the rain had stopped. Breaks in the clouds revealed stars, but no moon. I sighed again.

I would have to show my mark to a captain to get us all on a boat to Valta, but it didn't bother me now. It was time to re-enter my role as a prince. Avaline and I started down the hill toward the docks.

* Max *

I stopped at the peak of the hill. I was glad Johnny wanted to return home, but I had been thinking hard all day about Adahlia and our quest to release her. It would be much easier to hide, to save Johnny and Avaline the trouble of my situation and simply stay on Dela. I'd always wanted to live on the Fertile Island. I'd always said to myself that I would go to Dela once I was free from slavery, and here I was. Despite the Alician spies in Laven Soll, Dela was the safest place I could be. If I hid, learned from Charlotte and the Delan spies how to remain in hiding, then I could live out the rest of my days without need of going to anymore kingdoms or encountering anymore problems regarding Adahlia. I could simply be with her, suppress Adahlia into the depths of my mind, and live a simple life.

If I left Dela with Johnny and Avaline, went to Valta, how could I ensure my own safety? How could I be sure that the king of Valta wouldn't want to kill me like the king of Bortal? How could I be sure that unlike the king in Bortal, Johnny's father would follow through with it?

Of all the risks, Dela seemed safest.

* Johnny *

"Wait," Max said quietly. I went to her, back up the hill.

Her eyes were wet, greener than I had ever seen them before. "What is it?" I asked.

Her lips were tight, her nose red from dripping. She breathed deep, her breath coming out in a cloud. "Maybe you can go, but I can't."

"What do you mean?" I asked.

"I can't go to Valta. I want to stay on Dela. I can hide my mark, no one will know. Charlotte can watch over me, and I can be safe that way," she said.

"This is absurd," Avaline said harshly, marching back up the hill.

I spun around. "Meet us by the docks." She went to argue. "Please."

She turned and walked down the hill, her body glowing red.

"What are you saying Max?" I asked. "That we stay here?"

"You and Avaline will leave me here, Johnny. You have to go home, and take Avaline with you. Tell your parents about Alice, but don't mention me. Forget me. I will finally get to be free here, and no one will ever know about Adahlia." She wiped her eyes.

I raised my hands. "What makes you think you can hide?"

"I've done it my entire life."

"I can't let you stay here," I said.

"You have to. Help your father suppress Alice. Fulfill your duty as a prince. Go."

I shook my head, looked out into the distance. There, in the rise and fall of waves of fields, I saw a man and woman. His gaze was unwavering, hers seemed determined and motherly in the falling light.

Only slightly comforted, I took another deep breath. "I will see you again, Max," I said, my eyes still on the pair in the distance.

"I can't promise you that," she said, her eyes now dry.

"Promise me you'll stay safe," I said. I wasn't sure if she knew that Kye and Charlotte had followed us here, but I knew that they would watch over her. They would keep her safe, if she failed to do so on her own.

She nodded, reaching for her pocket. She handed me a ring with two keys on it. "Here."

"What is it?"

"This unlocked my tag that night you found me," she said.

"Why are you giving this to me?" I asked, studying the rough metal.

She placed a hand on my shoulder. Her green eyes held me. "So you remember that I am free."

"Not of the goddess," I protested.

"It's nice to know that someone cares," she said.

"It's nice to know that someone doesn't," I whispered. She laughed, a sweet musical sound. Rare but beautiful.

I would miss it. I turned and left, met Avaline at the bottom of the hill. My head hung. I could not imagine being without Max.

She touched my arm. "She's staying," Avaline said. It was not a question.

I nodded. "Yes. I saw Kye and Charlotte among the hills. They'll watch over her," I said.

Avaline squeezed, released my arm. "Leave her then, Johnny. She'll be safe with them."

I looked into Avaline's big eyes. They were darkened by the cover of the impending night.

My heart suddenly filled with doubt. "We need her, don't we? This rebellion is stoked by Adahlia, we can't leave her here, not now."

Avaline shook her head. "I know. When we find our answer, we'll come back and find Max."

I looked out over the water and east, toward Valta. "Alright," I said. "Let's hurry then."

Chapter 6

* Johnny *

Leaving her had been a mistake. It had been six months since I had returned to Valta and still I could not forget her. Still I could not stop worrying. Avaline and I had searched the castle as best we could, but it was like a maze, and the Vault was nowhere to be found.

I closed the book I had been trying to read and looked around. My eyes were bloodshot, no doubt. I ran a hand over my face, opened the leather bound book again, studied the watermarks, the wrinkles, the wear. Some letters were impossible to read, but I knew the story of Banilgar by heart. The queen of Bortal had been kind to give me a copy.

Avaline lay on my bed, resting, but never asleep. The candle she had lit for me hours ago had turned into a lump of wax on the table. I picked at it, blew it out. The sun would be up soon anyway; I could already see the curtains turning from the gray of nighttime to their true color: Valtan green. The same noble colors spread across my bed in silk and velvet.

Winter had been cold and dark, long compared to most seasons. The spring, though already a month old, was just now waking the flowers from their slumber. The Valtan gardens were sprouting new leaves, were dappled by flower buds. I stood to look out the window over the courtyards. The sun, though still behind the horizon, lit the sky enough to remind me of the night that dwindled. I had not slept, and was not even tempted by the quietness of the castle to go to my bed now.

I turned away from the window. Avaline had sat in my chair. She was thumbing through the book, candle relit.

"Perido knows this story by heart," she said. She placed the book on the table next to the candle. "Or so he claims." She looked up at me, smiled.

As soon as I had returned home, my playful younger twin brother had insisted on going for rides with me, reading Banilgar, catching up. He stayed in my room often, as did Avaline, so they had become very close.

"He does. We both do," I said, sitting on the bed.

Avaline studied her fingernails, went to her belt strewn over the chest at the end of my bed and retrieved a small vial and a brush. She returned to my chair, opened it, and began painting white liquid onto her nails.

"What is that?" I asked, though it was not the first time she had done it since our arrival at the castle.

"Dragon's blood and lily nectar," she said. "It has strong healing powers. Reminds me of my own."

"There are no dragons," I said.

Avaline grinned. "You're right, there are no dragons *now*, but dragons did live at one point in time. Storret Airet gave me this vial. Perhaps it's the last of their blood. He knows the importance it holds to me."

I nodded, lay back on the bed. Avaline went about her painting and soon I had fallen asleep.

I woke to a soft knock on my door. I opened my eyes to daylight, threw the hot sheets off my body and placed my feet on the floor. Sweat drenched, I shivered, trying to remember what I had dreamt. It was something terrible; another nightmare about Max, one of the many common dreams that kept me awake in the darkest hours of the night.

Another knock came, not much louder than the first.

"Yes?" I asked, clearing my throat, wiping my forehead. Avaline wasn't in the room, but that was not unusual. She wandered the castle grounds as she pleased.

The door opened and my mother, queen of Valta, walked in. Her dark hair was bundled loosely on her head, held by a jade pin. Long strands had escaped and now rested on her square shoulders. Her

A Kingdom's Possession   85

face was worn, aged more than I would have expected in the time I'd been gone from the palace. I hated to think that the worry lines had come from me.

"You're not dressed?" she said in a rush. "You are to make a speech for the festival soon. Have you done anything to get ready?" Before I could speak she placed a hand on my head, roughing up my hair. "Still warm from your bed, I see. Come, you mustn't be late."

All through the process of my getting dressed, my mother chattered on about street politics. Though she was queen, my mother was a gossip at heart. She was a keen woman with fresh ideas and a tight relationship with her husband's people. They loved her for it, and her social nature was always satisfied.

After dressing, I yawned, and followed her out the door. I was led down the hall to the balcony, a large platform overlooking nearly Valta's entire seaside city. Within the palace wall, a thick crowd of people gathered, ready to hear the heir to the Third Kingdom speak about her history and bless the Valtan Canal, Cavail's main source of fish and the place after which the festival was named.

The nobles and cousins related to the royal family gathered for dinner after my speech. My eyes were at half-mast while the hall echoed with voices, each speaking over another's. At the head of the main table sat the king. I was to his right, nearly sleeping when my brother jostled me back into reality.

Those brown eyes stared at me from across the table. He blew a strand of brown-gold hair out of his face and grinned. "I see that Avaline did not do well in coaxing you to sleep last night?" he said, his voice musical.

I smiled at him. My father often did not approve of Perido's humor and light nature, but the king always failed to notice that he was also very intelligent and caring. He would have been well suited to be king, had he come out of the womb before I. I wished that he had every day.

"I slept," I said.

"Not enough: you're dozing. Are you still dreaming about Max?" he asked.

"Nightmares."

"Father has arranged for you to meet your future wife soon."

I looked at my plate full of food, thinking about the arrangement. I had been avoiding it since the second I arrived on Valtan soil six months before. It was costmary for the heir to take a wife and the throne all in the same day. She was some distant noblewoman in Delosan, a cousin of the nobles there, intended to help tie Valta to its neighbor across the canal. It was a smart match, politically, solidifying connections all the way down to Oslo. But it was yet another reason why I had wanted to decline. When I had returned though, my father had not given me the choice. He would not have Perido as king. It was my duty; I had to bare it.

"Please, that is a sore subject," I said. "Don't burden me with the thought tonight."

"You are already burdened, my brother," Perido said. "Your nightmares have taken your spirit away."

"No. That's not it," I said.

"Max is safe, is she not? It was smart of her to flee from the rebellion, the fighting, the drama." Perido knew the story well. Of how I met Max, took her to Bortal, Dela. How she had decided to ignore the goddess instead of face her. Avaline and I had not told him about our searching for the Vault, though. We didn't want him to get caught up in our stress, worry, and rule breaking.

"I don't know if she's safe," I spat.

Perido leaned back dramatically, straightened his collar, leaned forward. "No need to shout, brother," he whispered. He leaned back again. "Avaline says that the dreams foretell a message from Max. But I say, why worry about her? You'll never see her again. You're getting married. Forget her, why don't you?"

"I could never forget," I said slowly, anger rising.

Perido knew me well. Raising his hands, he surrendered the topic. And as he did so, he also became a minor prophet, for a man in tight green pants flung the double doors wide and ran into the dining hall, waving a scroll. He stopped at my father, unrolled the paper, read to the king in a forceful whisper.

"This better be important," the king said. The messenger went on, his mouth moving faster. "Paraphrase my good man! I am in a meal," he ordered. A few people looked around, noticing his outburst. My father patted his beard, leaned in closer.

"Dela has spotted Alician spies searching the island for the goddess. Six months ago, her whereabouts became unknown, but now, her mark has been spotted. The young woman works in the port." The messenger's hands, holding tightly to the scroll, were shaking. "My king, if Alice finds Adahlia, she will win. The other kingdoms will be helpless against her rebellious spirit. Alice will become *the* Kingdom, the only kingdom."

My father merely nodded, swallowed the meat he had been chewing. "We will meet later," he said finally. With a wave of his hand, the messenger was gone.

I leaned toward the king. "Father...."

"Do not let this ruin tonight, my son." He put his hand on my shoulder, and I frowned. "There is something on your mind, I can see it in your eyes." His face searched mine.

"Yes," I said.

The king's eyebrows fell, wrinkling in thought. "We will speak in your room tonight. Perido has mentioned three times now that something was on your mind. I could never get the reason out of him."

"Good. They are not his thoughts to be sharing," I said.

The king went back to his meal.

After all the toasts had been said and the desserts were finished, Father ushered me to my room. The palace's high ceilings and wide walls always amazed me; the intricate lines of green and white on the tiles below us, as well as the roof above. There was a reason why Valta's symbol was four spirals, a maze. The palace was the most difficult to navigate in all of Cavail. And I knew it by heart.

In my room, Father closed the blinds, locked the door. Avaline lit candles with her fingers and was watched by my father the entire time.

"Will she leave?" he asked me, sitting in a chair, still watching the woman. He had not liked her from the beginning because she was strange. When he had found out about her powers, he was even more uneasy.

"Avaline, would you leave us?" I asked.

She nodded, created fire in her tattooed hand, let it disappear. My father shivered.

"Father, she's harmless," I said. "No need to worry."

Avaline grinned. "I am not harmless. But I do not harm for pleasure, only purpose." She slipped out the door and the king locked it for the second time.

"She is dangerous," the king began.

I held up a hand. "She is my friend, Perido's friend."

"I would expect this from Perido, but not from you..."

"Did you expect me to leave six years ago? Perido is loyal..."

"You are heir, Prince Jonathan. Not Perido," the king said forcefully.

I sank into the chair across the small table from him, nodded.

"Now tell me, my son, what is on your mind?"

"Max," I said.

Father's expression softened, but only a moment. "The Adahlia girl? I thought you had forgotten about her."

"I have not. She is in my nightmares. I don't sleep." I fell silent a moment, spoke quietly, "I can't stop thinking about her."

"You know your duties as prince, my son," he said, disappointment lacing his voice. It was the voice he often used with Perido.

"Yes, about them..." I went on.

"You wish to decline." It was not a question. "There is no choice, Jonathan."

"Perido."

"Do not bring your brother into this," my father yelled.

"Father, I am not right for the job," I said, my voice calm.

He sighed. "That is your concern? Every new king worries about his worthiness of the kingdom. You will be fine, my son."

"Father, I have thought long and hard. Please respect that." It had surprised me when I returned that my father still wanted me to be king. I had deserted the kingdom, and yet tradition was more important to him.

"It is not the job. It is Max, isn't it?" the king asked quietly. I could see his knuckles whitening as he gripped the arm of his chair.

"I cannot marry someone I do not love for the sake of a palace I feel stuck in," I said.

The king was quiet for a long time. "Do you love Adahlia?"

"No," I said. "But I may love Max."

Father slammed his fist on the table. The fresh candle flickered, toppled. He slammed his fist on it repeatedly until it was extinguished. "This common girl, what good would she serve when you become king? You need a woman who can rule, a woman arranged by people who know better! Valta is already hated for her alliance with Bortal, she would be overthrown come news of the new king taking a slave as a wife. That's why we have you marrying that fair noble from Delosan, to tighten our bond with the Fourth Kingdom."

I glanced at the chest at the foot of my bed remembering Max's keys hidden somewhere in the bottom. The tag was surely right beside them, under clothing and books.

"Father, there are four kingdoms, Valta and Bortal being two of them. We are not outnumbered," I reminded.

"It is the rest of the nation you forget, my son. And Alice, with her rebellion..."

"Valta is still loved, Father," I said quietly. He had struggled with keeping Valta respected since before I was born. Her good relations with the hated Kingdom Bortal did not help his struggle, but they were loyal friends that he could not bear to lose.

"But the idea of an heir, with her?" he said.

"Father, I can't forget her, not now," I said calmly. "And anyway, I doubt she'd marry me."

The king put on a delicately formed smile. "I was fourteen when my father died, as you know. I expected my older brother to take the kingdom, as is custom, but he ran off, much like you did. But unlike you, he did not come back.

"I did not want the crown, all I wanted was a woman. She ended up marrying another before I could decide my path. I was crowned at the age of sixteen and married to your mother by arrangement. I was lucky with her, son. I learned to love not only my queen, but my people. But there was always a part of me that wanted more than the palace life." Father met my eyes. "I guess you get that from me."

"I do not wish to let you down, Father," I said.

The king straightened. "I do not wish that either, Jonathan."

I looked at the drapes covering the window. They were turning from green to gray with the darkness of night.

"Please, my son, try to love my kingdom. Try to love your arranged queen. And try to forget Perido's wish of becoming king. He is a second son, and he must learn to love his life the way it is." The king put on a mask of sorrow.

We sat a moment in the near-dark, silent, pondering. "There is one more thing," I finally said. "The messenger spoke of Alice finally finding Adahlia. Max. I must go to Dela and warn her."

"That news was not intended for your ears. And first, I must meet with the messenger, I am yet…"

"I heard all there is for me to know. Please, Father, let me bring her here. If Alice wishes to use her in the rebellion, surely we can use her to stop it," I said.

"A good thought," Father said, gazing to his left. He looked back at me. "I will call for a ship in the morning, with guards and a crew. Sail to Dela, then bring her here. We will decide what to do when she is safe in the castle."

I stood simultaneously with the king, hugged him, stepped back. "Thank you, Father."

"You will make a fine king. Do not let me down," he said. "And get some sleep tonight, Jonathan."

He stepped toward the door, turned back once more and said, "I appreciate your honesty, son," before leaving me alone in the room.

I was readying for bed when Avaline slipped into the room. "So, how is your father?" she asked.

I laughed. "How would you like to visit the Fertile Hills?"

Avaline stroked her hair as if to think about it. "I'd love to. When do we leave?"

"My guess is two days," I said, slipping into bed. "Two days and Max will be on her way to Valta."

Avaline sat at the table, opened one of the other books resting on it. She thumbed through, her body glowing as it often did. "We will relieve Max of her burden."

"And relieve the nation of hers," I added, lying down. "If we can find the Vault." I closed my eyes and fell asleep before Avaline could add another word.

The next few days went by fast, and I woke early on the third, ready to sail. I fled my room, rode my horse down to the port, and tied him to a post close to the docks. I rubbed his legs and knocked on his hooves to calm his feet. It was a trick I had learned from Perido. I pushed the thick black forelock out of his eyes before walking along the shore. His tall figure was soon lost to the fog, merely a black shadow in the distance, though Jet was much like a shadow up close as well.

I breathed in the salty morning air, could smell the calmness of the ocean without even seeing the water. The spring sun cast beams through the streaks of fog, both hovering silently over the sea. It was crisp outside, but the chill of the wind wasn't what cast bumps over my skin.

My heart raced as I stood motionless looking out into the fog on the seaside road. I could feel my heart thumping with my thoughts in an impossible synchronicity. The walls of haze floated along the Valta Canal with such ease that I felt misplaced in their laziness. I was anxious, and I knew that the people in that castle would be wondering where I was. I had only told one guard where I was headed when I left the haven of the castle walls. I wanted to watch the sunrise.

I shuttered, but this time from the chill. A hand touched my shoulder and I looked back.

"Aren't you cold?" Perido asked, stopping beside me, shoulder to shoulder. Though he was my twin, he was fairer. It was as if I were looking into a mirror that gave back an image of my lighter self. Everything from personality to skin tone was brighter on his side of the reflection.

I shook my head. "It will be a nice day."

"Why are you out here so early?"

"I woke early."

"You're an insomniac," Perido said, giving me a sidelong glance.

"I am troubled," I corrected.

My brother sighed, looked back toward the east where the sun was rising over the fog and the blue canal. "There's nothing like a sunrise over the Valta Canal, especially in the spring. The sun seems to burn off the fog so kindly this time of year." He met my eyes once again. "You are anxious for today."

My fingers twitched. "Yes," I said.

"What does she look like Johnny? You've never said."

I looked at my feet and breathed out slowly, letting the warm air cloud around my face before I looked back out over the ocean. "She has long brown hair," I said. "And green eyes that I could travel in forever, and still feel lost."

Perido did not break his gaze from the horizon, but he smiled. "She sounds beautiful."

"Father does not understand," I said.

Perido laughed. "Father never understands."

I laughed a moment, then quieted. "He fears for Valta, if I were to take her as a wife..."

"Would you? Instead of an arrangement?"

"She'd never marry me," I said.

"She has Adahlia as well. If she were to die due to Alice or any other kingdom, it'd look bad," Perido added.

"On Valta or on my heart?" I said, meeting his eyes.

"Both," Perido said.

"Why doesn't Father demand I tell him where she is and kill her outright?" I asked. "It would make things less complicated."

"Is that what you want?"

"No, not by any means," I said. "But I still wonder."

Perido looked at me. "I think this is something the king will leave up to his heir."

"I can't make that decision," I said, breaking the stare.

Beside me, Perido looked away in thought.

Moments later, footsteps approached. "My prince, the captain of your ship has arrived, along with the crew." I turned to see Harold, the head of the Valtan guardsmen, and Avaline. "Princess Sarah is in the carriage. She asked that she say goodbye to her brother. Perido,"

Harold said, turning to face the younger man, "you may ride back to the castle with your sister."

"Shae is tethered down the road, I may ride him back, and lead my brother's horse beside me," Perido said. His horse was a medium sized grulla: a deep gray with dark legs, muzzle, and tail. Shae would follow Perido anywhere and, standing only to the shoulder of my horse, could fit almost anywhere as well.

Harold placed a hand on my shoulder and handed me a sword, sheathed in a gold-tooled scabbard. "I had this polished and sharpened upon your return to Valta. You may need it. Alice is getting anxious in her fight."

Harold had trained me when I was young to wield a sword, as all princes should learn. This had been the sword given to me.

I adjusted the sword's strap over my shoulder and pulled it out, letting the blade steal away the quietness of the port. The vibration rang through my right hand as I inspected the blade, running my fingers over the polished metal. I looked at Harold again and sheathed the weapon.

"It's an honor to hold this hilt again," I told the guardsman. It was true, though I felt reluctance with it now. I had killed my first man on Dela six months before, and now the sword seemed a little cold under my grasp.

"I know the feel," Harold said, and stepped aside for my sister to rush past.

She had exited the carriage only moments before, but ran fast and did not stop until she was in my arms. When she pulled away, she said, "Tell Max I said hello."

Perido gave her a flat smile. "You haven't met her."

"I know," she said, crossing her arms. "But she's a friend of Jonathan's and that makes her a friend of mine." Sarah turned to me again. "Come home soon. Perido is a pest."

"What ever did you do when he was gone for six years?" Perido asked.

Sarah tipped her head dramatically. "I spent many days in my room, do you not remember?"

"Alright Sarah," I said and kissed her forehead. Her face lit up and she brushed a strand of hair from her face.

The three of them, along with three guards and Avaline, accompanied me down the long dock to the boat. The captain stepped forward when we all arrived, his sailors only pausing a few seconds before they continued with their preparations.

"Captain Morth, this is the heir to the Valtan Throne," Harold said.

Avaline and I stepped up the ramp to the deck and greeted him.

He shook my hand, his gray eyes not leaving mine. The wrinkles on his face deepened as he spoke. "It's an honor, truly, my prince," he said, "though I believe we have met once before?"

My face reddened. This was the man who had sailed me away from Valta six years before.

He shook Avaline's hand next. "And who is this fine creature?" She smiled warmly, her dress fluttering in the breeze.

"Avaline," Perido said before she could speak. She turned to the younger prince and nodded her head. He grinned.

"Captain Morth is the best Valtan sailor around," Harold went on.

"Oh, I wouldn't brag," Morth said with an even bigger smile. He turned his attention away from me. "Harold, it's good to see you."

"All the same, my good man," the guardsman said.

Perido came and clasped my hand. "See you soon, Brother."

I nodded and waved from the deck of the boat as Harold and Sarah stepped away from the ramp. The dock jostled as our ship left port and began gliding over the Valta Canal. Avaline went to the bow, her hair waving behind her, but I stayed still.

Morth placed a hand on my shoulder. "I do hope you will come back sooner this time."

I met his eyes. "I am not looking for an escape this time, Captain."

He nodded. "Ah, it's best for the kingdom that you stay."

"It is not best for me, but a prince cannot choose," I said.

Morth nodded again, this time with his eyes cast down. After a pause, he clapped my back and strode along the deck, speaking to his crew.

My hands clenched. What would I say to her, after this long?

* Max *

I wiped the sweat from my forehead and squinted my eyes against the afternoon sun glaring off the water. Cleaning ships for a living in Dela did not bother me in the least when compared to the complications of slavery or what I might have encountered had I stayed on the quest to release the goddess. This was the life I had wanted that night when I had escaped. But something felt a little off.

Spring had come to Dela. After a quiet winter, the fields were coming to life again, the port was becoming busier, my anxiety stronger. Something about the winter had made me feel safe, whether it be the cloak of dark storm clouds or the silence it brought to the land. On the cusp of spring, pale sunlight brought on a naked feeling that went deep inside my body, like breaking from the cover of the forest into a clearing. Exposed.

Adahlia began speaking more as the days became longer and the nights less dreary. I had not seen Charlotte or any of the spies for a while. Where I would once spot them among the people in the port, the farmers in the fields, traveling along overgrown paths beside streets and through the little town of Dela, I noticed emptiness. I knew they had been watching over me just as they watched over the island, but lately it seemed less and less. I had not seen any spies from Alice come to find me, but still noticed a tingling in my shoulders when I walked to and from my work in the port. I had no need to see Johnny or Avaline either, but felt particularly lonely come spring.

Over the course of my time living on Dela, I had been careful to stay hidden. Being cautious about my mark and remaining mysterious about myself with others was easy compared to the live I would have had if I'd gone to Valta that evening six months ago. I did not regret my decision to stay.

But still, as spring progressed, I felt more and more uneasy. It was as if I were being watched, still pursued by a rebellious kingdom, despite my efforts to live a normal life.

Chapter 7

* Johnny *

The morning sun glistened along the waves as we made our journey. Sailing to Dela had only taken a day with the winds behind us. The flap and ripple of the sails filled my ears, giving harmony to the sound of the ocean beneath.

The sun was high when we got to the modest island. Dela's port bustled with activity, the hills behind it green with spring. People waved and whispered as we docked, knowing well that the four joined spirals on the side of the ship were the Valtan Seal. I smiled as I walked down to the cobbled road.

Captain Morth spread his hands. "It's just a visit, my friends. A few Valtan citizens have requested a trip to their favorite island." Delan people chattered and went on with their work. They would not recognize anyone but my father, the king. I was unknown as long as my mark did not show.

"I do not wish accompaniment, Captain," I whispered, motioning to the three guards behind him. "They will make a scene."

"You cannot do this alone..."

"I won't," I said. "Avaline?"

The woman appeared on the deck of the boat and walked to where I was standing. People gasped when they saw her, but no more. Avaline smiled brightly at the men and woman who passed us by.

I directed my attention back to Morth. "How long will you be, my Prince?" he said.

"Not long, possibly the night, I do not know. Wait for me in the port or in town. I'll find you when I wish to leave," I said.

Avaline and I turned right down the road, old buildings on one side, bobbing ships and docks on the other. People were all around, basking in the new spring sun.

The last boat in the port tipped from side to side; the medium messenger ship was being cleaned. Men my age, tossing rags and insults, laughed when someone slipped on the deck being swabbed. Avaline had turned to go to the other side of the port, but there, one of the workers polishing the railing on the ship was no man.

A woman. Her thick brown hair was pulled back but still fell around her face as she worked.

I touched Avaline to get her attention. "Av, can you excuse me? I will meet you at the top of the hill," I said, pointing with a jerk of my head.

"That is her. Yes?" Avaline asked, smiling. "I will leave for now, but be swift." On the last word she swiped a hand through the air.

My smile widened but faded quickly. "Stay out of trouble," I told my friend.

She examined her tattoos and wiggled her shoulders and head. If she were still a bird, she would have ruffled her feathers. I watched her slender figure disappear into the crowd of people. The afternoon clouds made shapes above her golden head.

I turned to the boat once again, hid behind a few barrels on the dock and studied Max. Even from so far away, I could see her pendant catch light and bend it back to the waves. Her green eyes flickered and my heart raced.

She wore tall black boots that hugged her calves tightly, slim leather pants, a loose white shirt, a band around her head. A leather vest was laced up the front so that her waist was small, her breasts held perfectly in place. Her forehead glistened with sweat in the sun.

The other men spat words at her, but her attention rarely wavered from her work, however much they seemed to try for it. A blond man leaned against the side of the boat, his head tipped, giving off an air that he often tried extra hard for her attention. He crossed his legs in front of himself and stretched, flexing his arms. Max bent to a water bucket, dipped the rag she had been cleaning with, and the blond reached forward and hit her backside with a rag.

The four others snickered, one especially, who had been looking her up and down from his perch among the sails.

"Why don't you give me some sugar when the day ends?" the blond asked her lazily.

"I don't think so," Max said, not looking up from her work.

"If not him, then me," another man said. "I'd treat you right." He pressed his lips together, squeaked, and grabbed at the air before breaking into laughter.

Their laughter turned into cheers as the shortest man went up to Max and clutched her upper thigh. But in an instant, all the bravery had drained from his eyes and the men on the ship fell silent. The short man straightened under the pressure of Max's dagger, laid flat and careful against his neck.

She had kept the daggers I had given her, sheathed and concealed perfectly by her boots. She looked the man square in the eyes before she threw him down on the deck. The others went back to work.

Behind the barrels, my legs were beginning to cramp.

I stood.

"Max," I said, possibly not loud enough for her to hear. But she turned, along with the five men, and her face tightened as she seemed to realize who I was.

* Max *

I looked down at the man standing on the dock. His clothes were clean and expensive, a fancy sword was fastened at his hip. His eyes were almost black but flecked with that unmistakable gold.

Johnny stood before me with stubble on his face and sleep in his features. It wouldn't be right to embrace him on the dock, but I yearned for it. I could feel my face go flush. "Why are you here?" I asked. My mouth was dry, searching for words to say to the Valtan prince.

"You know him?" Chara whispered, brushing his blond hair from his face. He leaned close and I could feel his breath on my neck. I pushed him away, eyes focused on the man I had not seen for so long. I could see his muscles bunch under his shirt. He stepped forward, stepped back.

"I need to speak with you, Max," he said.

I held back a wave of emotions when I heard his voice again, rough and deep, a sound musical and haunted.

The men around me called out, teasing and whistling and shoving.

I repeated my question. "Why are you here?"

"We need to talk," he said.

"Talk," I said, gathering myself, calming down.

"Not here," Johnny said.

"Adahlia?" I called. The men around me did not know of her, and the cloth tied around my head, behind my ears, pulling my hair back, always concealed my mark.

Johnny flinched with the word. "Yes."

I jumped from the boat to the dock, feeling it waver beneath me.

"You're not done," Chara yelled down. "You won't be paid for today if you go now."

I looked at Johnny again. He was watchful as I struggled with my own emotions. I'd been safe on Dela up until this point; why would he come? I thought of him often, but hadn't expected to see him again.

"It's about your life, too," Johnny said.

"My life?" I whispered.

He nodded, searching my eyes.

"Come with me," I said. I took an apple out of my pack and bit in. Johnny shook his head when I offered him one.

We walked through the port past the crowds of busy people and I occasionally waved at the few familiar faces. The crowd made walking slow and hot, but the day was cooling, the sun falling. I threw my apple core into the water.

"It's good to see you, Max," Johnny said.

I smiled and nodded, looking at his arms and how they swayed with his walk. My eyes slipped up to his lips, his eyes, dark as ever. The little flecks in them caught sunlight, made them sparkle.

"Where's Avaline? Is she well?" I asked. We had started up the hill; the highest point on Dela besides where the castle sat, just to our right. The Fertile Hills crested out in front of us, and I couldn't help but remember the first time I had seen them.

"She's here, but exactly where...I don't know," Johnny said.

"How did you know where to find me?" I said.

His eyes broke from mine and scanned the view. "I have my ways," he said. A smile twisted its way onto his face.

"I'm surprised you could leave your palace to look for me."

The smile disappeared. "I am not king yet, Max," he said. Pain laced over his words.

"So tell me then, why are you here, exactly?"

"Adahlia has been found. The Alician spies have been dormant for a while. But someone spotted your mark a few days ago. Alice is plotting again," Johnny said.

"That can't be," I said, touching my pendant. I checked the cloth band over my head as well, making sure it was in place, over my mark. "Charlotte and Kye have been watching over me. I'm not in any danger. That can't be," I repeated.

"Well it's true, Max. Valta heard it only three days ago. Someone knows you're here, and the chase is on again," he said gravely.

I looked out over the hills again. Spring had come late, and early vegetables had not yet bloomed.

I glanced back at Johnny, curious at his expression. His jaw was tight and his eyes were focused on the fields. He was watching something in the distance.

"What's that?" I whispered. A chill wrapped around my shoulders.

"We're being followed," Johnny said.

"It's probably one of the Delan spies. Maybe it's Charlotte," I said.

"They wouldn't be dressed in Alician clothing." He started down the hill, his pace quick, directed toward the town. The figure followed and Johnny broke into a run. I ran too, glancing behind me as two figures appeared. I sped up, leading Johnny through the maze of houses near the town of Dela. He almost slipped as I darted down a small path, its head shadowed by an oak tree. I veered away from the houses and into a thin wood, weaved through the familiar trails, took the long way to where I had decided to go.

Johnny closed the door of the old barn as soon as we were inside. He placed a bar across it. "Just to be sure," he said.

My heart beat inside my ears. "They won't find us here," I said.

The barn was dark, overall. Streams of light fell onto the straw floor from open places in the structure. Dust was magnified in its floating, the beams catching the particles and watching them drift, like lantern light fixated on shadows.

"Where are we?" Johnny asked.

"I come here to think sometimes," I said. Birds lined the rafters like peasants watching an execution from their perches. They chattered.

"You're here because of the goddess," I said.

He nodded. "Partly."

"And the other reason?"

His face turned. "To get away, just for a few days."

"You're bored while they wait on you hand and foot there? Oh, I pity you," I said. I took a deep breath to quiet myself.

"I have no freedom, you must understand that," he retorted. "I am to marry soon, as well. It is custom for the heir to take a wife and the throne on the same day. Start the new line of royal sons that night." His voice was low.

"What?" I asked, trying to conceal the shiver in my voice. Sorrow filled my veins as if it were a disease. He was going to marry. The thought had not crossed my mind before this. "You're going to take the throne? What about your brother, Perido?" I asked.

Someone pounded on the door, and the tension between us snapped.

"We've found you, goddess, you cannot hide."

I turned to Johnny. He looked tired. "I can't believe Charlotte and her spies aren't here, they should be here." I took another deep breath.

He pulled his sword. I yanked my daggers free from their sheathes. They glittered in the beams of light, cutting through the streams of floating dust. Birds fluttered through the cracks in the barn, leaving the scene.

The building shook as the men outside threw their bodies against the rotting wood. But another sound came too, swift and surprising. A cackle of flame, the whoosh of displaced air.

The screams rose and then subsided quickly and ended with Johnny's sword, scabbard against blade, as he shoved the weapon home, into its gold encasement.

I kept my blades out.

Johnny lifted the bar from across the door and opened it slowly. A ray of outside light flooded the barn, widening as the hinges screamed. He made a sound with his one last cautious step, and then rushed out. I followed reluctantly.

Outside, two bodies were face down, their clothing and skin charred with the mark of fire. I shoved my blades back into their scabbards. Between the men was a woman, dressed in an orange fluttering dress, her pale skin barely showing behind the fabric, as if it were a screen.

"Avaline," I said, my smile widening. She stroked her hair.

"Max," she said, embracing me. I was surrounded by warmth in a moment, and when she pulled away, I shivered.

But then I thought of Johnny's words right before the men had come, and the smile left my face.

"We had better go into town. We aren't safe here," Johnny said.

"We can stay the night at my house, leave early," I said.

The old barn was east and south of the town of Dela, but a short walk nonetheless. I led Johnny and Avaline into town, past the popular taverns and stores. The street was nearly deserted; everyone was inside having his or her first ale of the evening with the fading sun. Light was still in the sky, illuminating the nearby clouds in pink and purple while the darker clouds slowly rolled in. I pushed past Johnny again and turned down another path, then the final one that snaked toward my house.

It was a modest path, barely wide enough for two. We began to pass houses, huddled and small. When we arrived at mine—it was lonesome, so far from the others—I went through the crooked gate and pushed against the heavy door. Inside, it smelled of spices, familiar and appetizing. I closed the door behind Johnny and

Avaline, slid the key into the lock, and listened until the last of the tumblers had fallen into place.

* Johnny *

Avaline and I followed Max deeper into the sweet smelling house. She motioned to Avaline and, without a sound from the tips of Av's fingers, the room was brightened; candles flickered on a shelf near the door and on a small table in the center of the room. Three chairs were at the table, two of which were tucked neatly under the lip of it while the third was angled to one side. The windows were deserted of any curtains and a pot hung over a dead fire. Surely when it was ablaze, the pot would be full with soup or stew.

"Sit down," Max said while she slipped her boots off and let the daggers clatter on the floor. She proceeded by letting her pack slip from her shoulders. I took my boots off as well, as Max unlaced her vest and hung it on a hook by the door. Her shirt was wrinkled. I fingered my expensive wool, silk, and stained leather, decided to leave it all on as I sat down. Avaline leaned forward on the table from her seat, pale hands together in front of her, white fingernails resting on her lips.

"How did you afford..." I spread my hands.

"I work hard," Max said. "And it's required of me by the man I work for. I used to sleep in that old barn." She started the fire beneath the cooking pot as Av and I watched. It grew quickly and I could feel the heat warming the cool house as the outside became darker.

"I'll start some dinner," Max said, and began adding spices and vegetables. The room was quiet as she worked, so I began a conversation with Avaline to break the silence. As I spoke, I could hear the pot starting to bubble and Max's feet still shuffling across the floor.

When she was done, Max wiped her hands on a rag and sat down. "It will be done soon," she said quietly. She placed her head in her hands. "How did they find me?"

"It was inevitable, Max, you know that," I said.

"You're saying I was wrong in staying here, ignoring the goddess?" she said, looking up. Her eyes were red, but not wet.

"I'm saying you knew this would happen. Regardless of whether you wanted to face her. Adahlia is still in you, and Alice will not stop looking until she is out."

Max frowned. "I thought I could live here in hiding and be fine," she said. "I knew something felt strange lately, like I've been watched. But what about Charlotte? The Delan spies didn't come, I can only think the worst…" she cut herself off. "You came here why? To warn me? You said you wanted to escape the palace for a day or two as well, yes?" she said.

"Yes," I said.

"You're not king yet though?"

I was relieved to shake my head.

"But you will take the crown," she said quietly.

I glanced over at the pot of soup that continued to cook over the fire. She waited for my answer, but I didn't want to talk about it anymore.

"Is that finished yet?" I said instead. She shot a look over at the pot and then looked at me once again. Her eyes pierced me as she stood up and ladled some soup into a bowl. She plopped it down on the table in front of me.

I looked up at her, but she didn't return the glance.

Avaline remained silent.

Max dropped down into her chair with a bowl of soup in hand. She started eating, but then hesitated at her third bite and looked up at me.

"Is the soup ok?" she asked.

"Yes," I said.

We sat in silence for a moment, then Max looked up again. "What is she like?" she asked.

"Who?"

"The one you are to marry," she said, taking another bite of soup.

"I haven't met her. It's an arranged marriage," I said.

"I see," Max said. She set down her spoon. She sounded bitter, perhaps just as bitter as I felt toward the subject. "A noblewoman? Untainted, unlike me."

I swallowed the lump in my throat. "What are you saying?"

She shook her head. "You look tired," she said. "Go through that room and to your left is a hall with a bedroom on your right. Go sleep," she said, and I stood, left the kitchen.

Once I was in the bedroom, I laid back on the bed. Had the distance treated Max as it had me? Had she missed me? Did she care as much as I did?

It took forever for me to fall asleep.

* Max *

I went about cleaning once Johnny left the room. I worked around Avaline, who brooded in the middle of my activity. What had come over me? The thought of a man I barely knew living far away with another in his bed? It did not matter to me.

I stayed in the kitchen the rest of the night, staring, cleaning. Avaline did not speak; she only helped with the work, sat quietly when there was nothing left to do.

It was early when I leaned against the window, looked at the stars blinking out from behind the leaves of the trees outside. I paused my thoughts to hear Avaline stirring.

"He has not decided, Max," she said.

I stepped away from the window, sat at the table with her. The candles were wilting and the fire was nearly dead. I did not intend to tend to either of them. "Hasn't decided about what?" I said.

"The kingdom. He wants to leave the palace, but his father urges him to stay. He has not decided what he will do just yet."

"He sounds pretty sure," I said.

Avaline shook her head. "That's his intention. He has to be sure, it's his duty. But he is unsure of the very ground he walks on. He does not sleep, does not wish to sleep most of the time. He sits in his room, thinking. I can't urge him to bed and I know the thought of another there beside him makes him sick."

"He looks tired," I said.

Avaline played with a small fire on her fingertips, extinguished it. "He is troubled. By the kingdom, by his father, his brother, his nightmares. You," she said. "Adahlia, the politics of it all."

"I trouble him?" I said. "How?"

"He thinks of you, cares for you. When he does sleep, he has nightmares, moans your name until someone wakes him, and when I ask, he does not answer. You haunt him, and I must only guess why, for he does not say," she said.

A new dark figure entered the room. Johnny's eyes were sagging, downcast. He sat down, yawned. "Couldn't sleep," he said.

He looked at me waiting, and I realized it had been a question. "No," I said in a small voice.

"I slept only a little," he said. His face was speckled with stubble and his hair was messy. "And I'm sorry," he added.

I shook my head, began to speak.

He raised his hand. "My decision remains unmade about the kingdom, Max. My father's wishes are clear, but mine are not. You must try to understand. Please don't be angry with me, it's been too long that you've wondered at my intentions."

"What do you mean?" I asked.

Johnny briefly looked at Avaline. "You didn't trust me six months ago, nor do you trust me now, but there are reasons why you must, the first being your life. My intentions are clean, I promise you."

I did not understand completely, but I nodded. "Alright," was all I said.

"Tell her why you're here, Johnny," Avaline said, her solemn, echoic voice ringing with impatience.

"We must take you to Valta," Johnny said. "Dela is not safe for you anymore, and the only place for you to go where you will be safe is Valta. We can decide our next move from there."

"I am not a pawn in a game, Johnny," I said, alarmed.

"Please Max, you know I didn't mean it like that. You will be safe in Valta; we may visit the Vault, free Adahlia. Please come with us," he said. "It's time that we finish the politics."

"The king, he knows your plan to enter the nonexistent Vault?" I asked. I could hear Avaline snort with my comment.

"No, and he would not allow it anyway," Johnny said.

"So we're to sneak in?" I said.

"Yes."

"You think it can be done?" I said, intrigued. "You think we can even find it?"

"Yes, Max," Johnny said, standing, smiling.

"And why, in my right mind, would I ever do this? I am happy here," I said.

"Because you will die here, Max," Johnny said. "And you have no right mind, just one with a goddess that speaks and enough stubbornness to outdo an ass."

I laughed. "Calling me an ass will not convince me to leave with you to Valta."

Johnny laughed a little as well. "I'm trying here," he said.

"And what about Charlotte?"

"Something must have happened, but it is safer to have Valta send messengers than for the three of us to investigate the situation ourselves," Johnny said.

I didn't speak for a long time, but when I did, I could see Johnny's face brighten. "I want a room with a view. I hear Valta is beautiful this time of year," I said.

Johnny cocked his head. "That can be arranged."

"Well then, when do we leave?" I asked, standing. I stroked my mussed hair so that it fell in place over the mark.

Johnny looked at Avaline. "Now."

Avaline nodded in agreement, her red hair rippling.

"I will start packing then," I said.

* Johnny *

Max grabbed her pack and headed down the hall into her room. The candle on the table was melting into a puddle of wax and the cooking fire had already gone out. The room started to feel cool from the morning chill.

I shifted in my chair and looked at Avaline. "What is it like to rebirth?" I asked.

Avaline became still. "It has been a long time since I've done that without interruption. You must understand Johnny, the last time I rebirthed I woke under the veil of wizard's cloth. I was turned into a woman."

I nodded solemnly, knowingly.

"But," Avaline said, "I do not remember how it all happens. I remember letting my fire loose, completely. I remember feeling young and fresh again, but never what happens in between. The fire must cool at some point for the new phoenix to be born. Then the old soul must harness her power again, resume her ways."

"You mentioned a man once. Who was he?" I asked.

Avaline closed her eyes again, her body glowing slightly. "There are some things I wish to let die. His memory will stay alive in my mind but please do not ask that I relive it."

I nodded, stood, put an arm around Avaline.

She stood too, to meet my embrace fully. When I had met her in the forest, I had not expected her to become such a close friend.

"Are you always so warm?" I whispered, smelling the forest that was her hair.

Avaline laughed a little, pulled away. "I guess it is a bit chilly in this room. And yes, I am. An internal fire will do that." She smoothed her dress. "Would you go check on Max? Possibly change your shirt, to blend with the Delans for our journey back. Alician spies will be looking for your wealthy attire," she said. I still had many questions for her, but all would have to wait.

I stepped away from Avaline, leaving her aura of warmth. When I arrived at Max's room, I stopped in the doorway. She was bent over her bed, shoving what little clothing would go into her pack. Her hair hung around her face, but her mark was concealed.

She straightened, turned around. Her eyes widened to reveal she wasn't expecting my figure in the doorway, but she gathered herself quickly.

"I was," I started, "I, ah, may I borrow a shirt?" I said.

Max's brow creased and her lips scrunched. "Yes," she said, relaxing. She bent over a large chest, empty, save for just a few garments in the bottom. When she turned around, she was holding a dark red shirt. "Will this do?" she asked.

I took the shirt and held it to my chest. "Yes, thank you," I said.

"I sleep in this, mostly. I like the loose feel when I sleep," she explained, as if I had wondered why she had a man's shirt in her room.

I hadn't wondered, until she brought it up.

I breathed in more of the pleasant smell. It made me enjoyably anxious. "Thank you," I said.

The smile she gave me then was broad and warm, tight-lipped as if she were keeping a secret from me. I could have searched her dark green eyes forever and still not have found the meaning behind that smile. I walked past her and tossed the shirt on her bed. I loosened my own, pealing away my vest and various other gray and green layers. Max stood to the side, looking at her feet, then back up at me as I took my shirt off. I tensed at the piercing cold in the room and saw her coyly look away again. I put the red shirt on quickly and laced my vest, everything back in place. "Perfect," I said. "What do you think?"

"It fits well," was all she said as she buckled her pack and swung it over her shoulder.

We went back into the kitchen; Avaline was sitting at the table again, but stood when we came in. "We should go," she said.

I slipped on my boots as Max dressed, first her vest, then her boots and daggers. She laced them all roughly, jerking with her fast moving hands. She slipped on the cloak I had bought her so many months ago. I was surprised she still had it, wondered if it reminded her of me.

When she was finished, we left the house, walked briskly down the road.

I asked Max if she needed anything else from her home. "This is all I need," she replied. Apples and bags of spices bulged out of her pack, making the whole air around her tangy.

Everything was quiet in the frosty morning; even the trees remained still. The sky was clear; a haze of clouds clung to the earth in some places, but not in others. It would be a warm day and the Delans would be out for all of it. Yet something seemed too quiet about this morning.

Max quickly rounded a bend and led us along a skinny path that soon cut out of the oak trees and bushes and revealed the town of Dela. The early coolness of the morning wafted along the main road. People dappled the cobblestone street, some stumbling out of the bars groggily, and others yawning with a big exhale of warm air. We kept walking, hearing whispers that didn't seem to belong.

"What's going on?" Max asked, pulling the hood of her cloak over her head.

I shook my head. I did not know. Max and Avaline stayed by my side as I made my way down the street, approaching a group of people, all gathered, all alert. They watched us as we neared, every stare silently shouting out its own warning. When we reached the little crowd, I pushed past a few onlookers to see. A little gasp came from Max, but that was all.

A big man, bigger than just an ordinary soldier, lay face down on the cobblestones surrounded by a lake of blood. The blood ran thick through the dust on the quiet road. His muscles were bunched and bulky and the leather shirt on his back was torn open with one long gash. Flesh was ripped like fabric on his back and I stood, just as wide-eyed as all the other viewers, taking in the sight. I could hear people whimpering and muttering questions, but there was no useful information tossed into the words.

"What happened here?" I finally asked. Just as the blood was leaking from the body, people shuttered and left the mess in a trickle. They eyed Avaline as they fled, but other than that, there was no comment. "Can anyone answer me?" I insisted a little louder. More people turned and soon there was only one person left. He was a heavy man with a dirty white apron and a thick beard.

"Who did this?" Max asked forcefully. The man walked around the body to finally confront us, stopping only close enough for us to smell the ale on his breath and the sweat on his brow.

The man eyed Avaline suspiciously before speaking. "Three men came into my bar last night," he said. "They seemed different, obviously travelers. I didn't bother to ask them their business in Dela; I served them their ale. They sat in the back, left after only a few drinks and began talking to this fellow outside." The tender nudged the man with his foot. Nodded at him and said, "He was with the royals, I suppose. He was wearing the common garb of the castle people. It seems to me they stripped him of his fancy attire.

And his life." The bar tender trailed off, his casual demeanor changing.

"Why did they kill a royal worker?" I asked.

"Can't really say, other than for information. They weren't from Dela, I can tell you that," the man said. He wiped his hands on his apron and shifted awkwardly.

Max kept her eyes low, her body stiff. I returned my attention to the tender.

"The three men who came into your bar, could they have been from Alice?" I asked. Avaline shifted and rested her eyes on me.

The tender shrugged again. "Sure, but why they'd kill a higher up from the palace, I'm not sure. Must have been an inside job, meant to leave a mark for sure. It's why they left him here in the street, no doubt." He kicked at the dirt on the road, covering a little stream of blood that had almost reached his foot.

"So they were working for someone else?" Max asked.

"Promises are cheap," said the tender.

"But keeping them is not," I reminded.

"Ah, but when it's a fat royal like this you're after, it's an easy purse to gain," the man said.

I stepped a little closer to Max and looked around at the people still huddling in groups down the length of the main road. The trees, bending slightly in the distance, were the only movement now.

"Av, Max, let's go," I said, moving away from the scene. "Thanks for the help, sir," I added to the bartender. He waved casually, left the scene quicker than his demeanor suited.

I looked straight ahead, keeping my eyes set on where the hill to the port reached the pink-kissed sky.

"Johnny, what happened to the Delan spies? They would have kept this from happening," Max asked quietly. She swallowed. "What does it mean?"

"It means we need to leave Dela. Now," I said.

Chapter 8

* Max *

It wasn't the mid morning breeze that made my skin crawl. It was apparent that I couldn't run any faster, anymore. The spies would find me regardless of my efforts to flee or hide from them.

We hurried into the port, down the hill, and past dock after dock until we arrived at the Valtan boat. Not many were in the port this morning; it was clear, but too cold by the water.

"Here it is," Johnny said. He took a moment to study my face. "Are you okay?"

"Where's your crew?" I said.

Johnny climbed onto the boat, called for the captain. A moment later, an older man with a red nose and matching ears arrived in front of Johnny.

"My Prince, is your purpose here fulfilled?" he said.

"Morth, we must set sail. It is urgent we get to Valta. Now," Johnny said. His sturdy voice made my heart lose track of its rhythm. But laced underneath were the tones of a troubled man, more troubled than when he had spoken with the tender about the body on the road.

This is how Johnny is when he is with Valtan people, I thought, this is what Avaline meant when she said "troubled."

"Did you find her?" Morth asked Johnny, leaning in.

Avaline swung up onto the ship gracefully. I followed, and as soon as I was on board, the captain came forward and shook my hand.

"Max, ah," Morth said. "I am pleased to meet you."

"Captain Morth, our departure?" Johnny said.

The man nodded, "Now, I presume?"

"It is urgent," Johnny said, nodding. "Sailors?"

The captain clapped his hands and one trotted up, saluted the captain, us. The sun beamed down warmer, but the sailor still had bumps on his uncovered arms.

"The others are in the hull, still sleeping, my Prince," the captain said.

Johnny's face wrinkled into a handsome frown, "Sleeping?"

"They'll be up with a bottle and bell song," the sailor said. He was young, no older than Johnny or me. His blue eyes glistened in the pale sunlight and he scratched his closely shaven chin.

The captain shrugged, "They are men, my Prince."

"We will be free of port in an hour," Johnny said.

The sailor smiled at him, "We can start our preparations now, my Prince."

"Good, thank you," Johnny said, smiling briefly. "I will take Max and Avaline to my room to get settled." Johnny turned to walk away.

"My Prince, my ladies," the captain and sailor muttered as we passed them.

Johnny led us into a room laced with green velvet and dotted with white candles. He closed the double doors when the three of us were inside.

"This is where we can stay for our journey," he said. Sunlight peered in through a small window and fell warmly onto a table littered with books. Avaline seated herself on the bed in the corner, stroking the sheets with her tattooed hand.

"They were nice," I said.

"It will be worse at the palace. More formal."

"How so?" I asked.

Avaline laughed. "It's worse for *me*. His father is afraid of me, for one."

Johnny shot her a glance and she grinned even more. "You have it good. I'd love him to avoid me, shoot me quick glances," he said.

"I suppose."

"How so?" I asked again, touching Johnny's arm. He was warm, his muscles big and relaxed.

He faced me again. "You will have to curtsy to the king and queen. And remember to nod acknowledgement to my siblings."

"Perido?" I said.

"Sarah too," Johnny said. "My sister, she is very sweet, she'll want to talk to you all day." He smiled distantly.

"What do I call them?"

"Prince Perido, Princess Sarah, King, and Queen."

"Your parents don't have names?"

"You *never* call Father by his name, nor my mother," Johnny said.

"Why's that?"

Johnny shrugged. "They have their preferences."

"Do I have to do anything else?" I asked.

"Will you?"

"You know me, Johnny," I said.

"I doubt the strength of that knowing," he said, "but I will require nothing more from you in Valta."

"I'm going to get some fresh air, would you like to join me?"

Johnny shook his head. "I may come out later."

With his last comment, I stood and left the room.

The coastlines of three islands surrounded us on our journey. The sun had finally warmed the air and its reflection bounded off the waves of the sea. We tore through it, a seam splitting with our wake. I swayed against the railing and gulped the wind, tears streaming down my face from the salty ocean spray in my eyes.

The heat of a body came up beside me and I turned my head away from it, still enjoying the cold. "We'll be there by nightfall," Johnny said in a quiet, gentle voice. His arm brushed against mine and rested on the rail.

I turned to look at Johnny next to me. "Have I been standing here long?"

His hands rubbed together. "Since the sun was high."

The water was pink and gray, changing fast with sun as it slipped farther down the face of the sky. I looked into Johnny's eyes, admiring the way the water reflected on the darkness in them.

"Come with me," he said, and placed a hand on my back. I wondered, briefly, how it would feel if he were to run his fingers through my hair, if the hand on my back was meant to pull me closer instead of guide me to the front of the boat.

"There it is," he said faintly. A smile swept across his lips as fast as the wind across his face. "The palace is beautiful, despite my loathing for the duty it comes with."

With the sun behind us, the castle was turning more purple than the clouds. Behind it, the sky was nearly black, letting in only the light of the moon as the sun fell lower. The castle, silhouetted by the evening, stood proud. It was the fortress of the prince beside me, and yet he seemed unhappy to be home. He walked away, leaving me at the bow.

Captain Morth bustled about the deck, yelling orders as the coastline came closer. The sailors turned blue or gray in the dusk-light, blindly pulling ropes and bounding here and there.

Johnny returned dressed as a prince, in silk and velvet and wool and leather all magnificent in their blacks and hues of green. He acquired a look of lost purpose on his face as he stared at the palace, now only peeping up over the trees. He straightened as the boat bumped against the dock and a sailor jumped off to fasten it in place.

Avaline strode up and handed me my bag; Johnny already had his, and was adjusting the sword at his hip.

Water lapped up against the dock lazily. It was getting dark fast. We waited in silence until a four-horse carriage rolled out of the mask of the night. Johnny swung onto the dock, and helped Avaline down from the boat. I got down on my own, and followed the two of them to the carriage along with Captain Morth.

Johnny simply saluted the driver, as the captain greeted him. I was ushered into the carriage by Johnny, and Avaline joined the driver on his seat.

"You're not riding inside?" Morth asked the pale woman.

She shook her head, glowing faintly. "I enjoy the fresh air," she said simply.

Johnny closed the doors of the carriage and waved to the captain through a window before we rolled away.

He sat across from me inside, and though he was close, I could barely see him. The carriage lurched forward as the horses broke into a trot.

"How long to the palace?" I asked.

I could see Johnny's dark figure shrug and settle. "I assume we'll take the long way there, considering there are often bandits at night on the main road to the port, so it will be over an hour," he said. "My family will have finished dinner when we get there, I presume," he added in a hollow voice.

He was tense, quiet. But it had been too long of a day for me to ask why.

I tried to sleep on the way—I had been up for nearly two straight days—but I couldn't with our jostling over the road. The goddess pushed at my dreary mind; I tried not to let her through. Her tormenting was not welcome, and she knew it, yet she still pleaded to be heard. And I continued to fight back, tired of her presence.

"Are you ever tempted to kill me, Johnny?" I asked. I could hear his breath catch, but I went on. "Your kingdom would benefit from releasing her, Alice would fall in her own rebellion, and you'd be free of me."

In the grainy light, I could see his face become grave. "I don't understand how you could think that. Are you really that afraid of me?" he said. His voice was shaky.

"I'm not afraid of you. I just do not understand you," I said.

He leaned forward so there was only an inch or two between our faces. I could feel his warm breath on my face, light with the smell of apples. I breathed in the breath he offered willingly, wondering if he'd move closer, hoping he would not. "I am here to guard you, not betray you. It is not just you and Adahlia in this, Max. I am here too, and so is Avaline. We will not leave your side until you are safe, do you not understand?"

"I don't understand, Johnny. Why you would do this for me. And last time I asked you, you had no answer. Is that still the case?"

His expression changed in the darkness of the carriage. With his face so close to mine, I could see the emotion swirling in his eyes.

"Yes," he said. "Am I required to know?"

"You are not," I said quietly. "I'm sorry I asked."

In a rush he placed his hands on the sides of my face. His eyes were cold and filled with longing before they closed and his lips pushed into mine. Rough hands moved through my hair and cupped my neck as he kissed softer, deeper. And when I leaned for more he pulled away, shook his head as if a mistake had been made. And possibly that was the case.

"I am sorry too," he whispered. One hand lingered on my cheek before he placed it back in his lap.

I placed my hand where his had been, trying to remember the feeling and finding it difficult, even so soon after. My lips tingled and my body felt a little numb, flushed with excitement. The goddess was silent, and for a moment I felt uncomfortable hearing only my own thoughts. Looming inside me was a shutter of regret, a fluttering of fear. This would complicate things. This would make it harder for me to endure the pressures of death already crouching behind me.

Outside the carriage I could hear whinnies and voices piercing the dark, taking me out of my shock. The driver pulled our horses to a stop with a gentle "ho." The sound of their feet prancing on the crisp, hard ground subsided and then stopped. Their harnesses clinked and creaked as they shifted uneasily, quivering the wheels of the carriage. The sound of hooves approached us and I could hear firm voices questioning others.

"What is the meaning of this?" Avaline said in the confusion of horses and men.

With her voice, Johnny stood up and swung the door open. He stepped out into the cold and walked toward the chaos. I followed him out, stopping at the edge of the carriage, peering over the horsebacks at the scene unfolding. I shivered; my breath hovered in clouds around my face.

Johnny walked toward the men, completely in the open, and stood straight as if to ensure all the men could see him clearly. Whispers waved over the group of riders. From what I could see, they were each dressed nobly, with a green sash and many hilts to various weapons. The leader of the group, riding a tall white horse, swung from his mount and landed squarely in front of Johnny. He saluted the prince, gave him a slight bow, and then stood with his shoulders proudly back. "Prince Jonathan, it is my deep apology to have stopped you," he said, waving his hands through the air in a series of lowering circles.

"By whose orders are you following, sir?" Johnny said.

"Of your father, the king. I am to carry the news of war," the man said.

"War? With whom?" the driver asked. Avaline put a hand on his shoulder and he quieted. Under Johnny's harsh eyes, he began checking the horses' feet and harnesses.

The man in front of Johnny gave him a questioning look.

"Well go on, answer his question. I admit it is mine as well," Johnny finally said.

"War with Alice, my prince. She is beginning to take action in recruiting men for her cause."

There was a frown in Johnny's voice. "Who will this message meet?"

"Bortal, Oslo, Dela," the leader said.

"Mala in hopes she will get on our side, Delosan in the idea that the young town is willing to fight," a man in the crowd of horses said.

Their leader shot a glance back and then addressed Johnny again. "They are anxious for their journey. Please do not take their speaking out of place as disrespect," he said.

They both stood in silence for a moment. The call of an owl echoed in the distance.

"I would not dare question my father's men," Johnny finally said. "Move out," he called to the rest of the mounted men. They waited for their leader to mount his horse and then all were off down the black road, back into the darkness.

I shivered and rushed back into the carriage, ready for Johnny to enter. "No more delays," he said to the driver, then boarded the carriage. The horses lurched forward eagerly and Johnny shut the door.

"Sorry for that," Johnny said, settling, only to be jostled by a sharp turn.

"War?" I asked.

Johnny glanced at his feet. "You can see why Alice is eager to find you."

"I'm sorry." It was all I could think to say.

Johnny adjusted his clothes. "I worry that when I take the crown the war will become my burden," he said quietly. "You must understand that. I do not wish this on my father, or Valta, or anyone."

"When you take the crown?" I asked, feeling the tension rising.

"If," Johnny corrected instantly.

"I..." I looked at him a moment, the tiredness on his face, the intelligence in his eyes. "I didn't mean to..."

He shook his head. "No. You're right."

I coughed. "You mentioned on Dela that you marry and take the crown all in the same day?"

"Yes, that is the customary way in Valta. The king is always the one to perform that ceremony, which is why he is preparing for it now, rather than on his death bed." His lips twisted away from a frown as the carriage slowed to a halt. People spoke outside, but this time Johnny made no move toward the door. I settled into the seat, fell into a light sleep.

When I woke, the cart had come to a stop and the door had been opened to let the coolness of the night seep in. Johnny placed a hand on my shoulder and squeezed gently, saying my name like it were silk slipping from skin.

Rain pattered on the roof of the carriage and the ground outside.

I followed Johnny out into the night, shifted the pack on my back and drew my hood, glanced up at the stone walls and up again at the towers of Valta until I could see the sky. Candles lit the little windows of the fortress.

Johnny and Avaline walked as one toward the gate, only to be met by three large men. I stood behind them as the guards shifted in their places.

After squinting down at Johnny a moment, the tallest guard's eyes widened and he cleared his throat. "My prince," he said. The three guards moved swiftly to unlatch the gate and let us pass and we hurried through the weakly lit yard toward the palace. The hinges on the gate screeched back into place and the guards settled in their posts.

Inside the palace was just as dark as outside, with very few torches lighting the way through the maze of wide, spacious halls. Johnny knew exactly where he was going over the white tiles, though. Besides the occasional torches, there was nothing else in the hallways; just plain white walls or a blanket of green fabric hung from somewhere high. It was an eerie and formal place, so far.

We came to two huge doors guarded by more men, but Johnny barely acknowledged them, besides the quick order that they were to take our packs to his room. Together he and Avaline led the way inside.

A magnificent chandelier hung high over three long tables filled with people. The room was bright, only colored in green and white. The people were dressed in bolder colors, filling the room with vibrancy and making my clothing look plain.

The man at the head of the middle table stood and spread his hands, gathering the attention of the diners. The bustle of the room quieted as he adjusted his robes and the scarcely but beautifully jeweled crown on his head. My knees shook. I followed Avaline and Johnny between the tables.

"My son," the crowned man said, grasping Johnny's hand.

Johnny smiled, bowed slightly. "Father," he said.

The king peered at Avaline only for a moment before addressing his son further. "I thought you would plan your arrival from Dela in a more timely manner than this," he said, sitting.

"I found it urgent to return. Dela is..." he spread his hands, "unstable at the moment. I apologize for the unexpected entrance tonight."

The king nodded briefly. "And this is Max," he said. It was not a question.

Johnny looked at the floor.

I took of my hood and bowed deeply, still shaky.

"She's pretty," a small voice said.

I looked in her direction and found that it had been a young girl in a purple dress speaking. I assumed it was Johnny's sister. Across from her at the table was a lighter version of Johnny. I tried not to stare, but it was startling how similar they looked, and yet, at the same time, how different. He stopped chewing a moment and raised his glass at me, a flicker in his dark eyes.

A slender woman in a green gown stood and embraced Johnny. "You're safe," she said into his hair.

"You knew I would be, Mother," Johnny said, pulling away.

"Avaline," she said smiling at the woman. "Max," she said, resting her gaze on me.

"My queen," I said, falling into another deep bow.

She smiled widely and went back to her seat. "Come sit, my son. I'm sure it has been a long day," she said.

"Long, yes," Johnny said absently, sitting in the empty chair beside his father. I lowered myself into the seat next to Sarah. Avaline left the room, at only the brief acknowledgement of Johnny and the watchful eyes of his brother.

The other diners in the room began to chatter again and I felt a little more at ease.

"So tell me," the king said between bites, "what information did Dela offer to my heir?" Waiters arrived to the table, offering plates and bowls of rich smelling food.

"The island is saturated with Alicians that common folk best not be messing with," Johnny said. He went on to tell his father more, but I did not pay attention. I fingered the silk napkin in front of me.

"So tell us Max, what was your obligation to Dela?" the queen asked.

I looked at the napkin again. "I worked in the port," I said.

"Oh," she said, "and how long have you known our son?"

I brushed a strand of wet hair out of my face and looked at Johnny. Before I could answer the queen had moved on to more questions for her son, her enthusiasm for his return evident on her face.

I directed my attention to Perido. There were great similarities, but also great differences between the two brothers. Perido's hair was lighter, his eyes more gold, his skin fairer, his body more bulky. He looked sharp, intelligent, and humorous, obvious by his attention to the room, the laugh lines by his eyes. I could not break my eyes from him, but felt nervous at how comfortable he seemed. Looking harder, under all the laughter on his face, I could see a hint of an anxious man, always under the shadow of the heir of Valta.

I forced my attention off Perido and looked to Sarah.

She returned my glances right away. Her eyes glittered with excitement as she finished a bite of food and leaned toward me. "Jonathan never said how pretty you were," she said.

I smiled at the frail face looking up at me. Perido looked up, gave me a furtive grin, took another bite of food.

"Well he mentioned you, princess," I said.

She giggled and pointed her attention back down to her soup.

I still hadn't lost Perido's stare; I turned to him. "You must be Prince Perido," I said, remembering to use his title when I addressed him.

He bowed his head, cast his eyes away from me to where Avaline had exited the room.

"Johnny didn't say much more than your name," I said.

Another giggle escaped Sarah. "You mean Prince Jonathan?" she asked.

I could feel my face color. "Yes."

Perido paid no attention to the informality. He grunted. "My brother has mentioned you countless times," he said dryly.

"Oh," I said, and returned my attention to Johnny.

He was saying: "Father, we came across your messengers on the road home. Is it true you're sending word of war?"

"It is precautionary," the kind replied.

"Precautionary? My travels proved that more than just precautionary actions are taking place," Johnny said. "Are we not expecting war?"

The king shook his head and spread his hands. "The tides are rough now, son. It will be hard to predict what will wash up next."

Johnny was heated in the conversation, but his father seemed to have other matters on his mind.

"What about Max?" Johnny whispered. I looked in another direction as the king rested his eyes on me.

"We must not speak of this now, Jonathan," he said slowly.

"Later, then," Johnny said forcefully.

The king nodded. "Later."

I slouched into my chair and played with my napkin until the dinner was over. Perido continued to make me feel uncomfortable by openly staring at me. But I was relieved when Johnny finished and decided to retire to his room. I followed him readily, along with his escort.

"You are to stay just down the hall, your bag's already there, he will show you," Johnny said. "I am going to meet briefly with my brother, have a bath, and then I will come to your room. Hot water is ready in the room adjoined to yours, so get clean and fresh, it's expected. I'll see you later tonight."

I was led to a room not far from Johnny's. Once the guard had opened the door, I walked in, and I could hear his footsteps disappearing down the hallway. I closed the door and turned around.

The room was huge, with only a few furniture pieces. Every linen in the room was either green, or had four green spirals stitched into one of its corners, it seemed. Artwork dotted the walls, and a fire was nearly exploding out of the hearth. Avaline walked out of the adjoined.

"I started your fire. It was deathly cold in here," she said.

"Thank you," I said. I went to my pack resting on the large bed and rifled through, searching for clean, dry clothes.

"Did Johnny seem alright during dinner?" she asked.

I shrugged. "He seemed tense."

Avaline laughed for a moment. "You will find that he will remain tense until he is out of the palace once more," she said. "And Perido, was he kind to you?"

"He was," I searched for the correct word, "strange," I decided, still a little unsatisfied. "I cannot describe how I feel about him. He was kind though."

Avaline laughed openly. "Ah, yes you have met Perido indeed."

"He watched you leave," I said.

Avaline gestured as though that was not unexpected. "Perido and I have grown to be good friends in all this. He is sharp and kind, a man destined to be a great king, if given the chance. He is at a difficult place under his brother." She paused, "Anyway, we have spoken many late nights together. He is strange, but give him a chance to warm. He will keep you on your toes," she said.

"Well," I said, "I should bathe. Slip into some new clothes. Johnny said he would come to see me later tonight."

Avaline nodded. "Very well."

I stopped in the doorway between the rooms. "Thank you Avaline," I said.

"For what?" she asked.

"For burning down the door for me in Bortal," I said.

"I'd do it again." The corners of her mouth turned slightly upward as she turned away and I closed the door.

When I was finished grooming, I went back into my room to find myself alone. The room was still warm, though the fire had dwindled in the hearth. A few candles had been lit, but that was the only light to see by. I sat on the bed and stroked the tangles from my wet hair. My fingers brushed the chain of my pendant briefly, felt the place where the mark would be. I closed my eyes.

Light footfalls came from outside my door, and it screeched only a little as someone entered. The hallway was bright when I opened my eyes.

"Feel better?" Johnny said as the darkness of the room closed in on us. The door made one last click as it fell into place.

"Yes," I said. "You?"

The dark figure shrugged and came to sit on the bed beside me. I could hear him breathing, a shallow, tired sound.

"What time is it?" I asked.

His wonderfully deep voice echoed through the room. "Midnight," he said calmly.

He placed a hand on my leg, lifted it awkwardly when Avaline came into the room.

"We need to go to the Vault," she said.

Johnny stood up and moved the chair at a small desk in front of the bed so that Avaline could sit and face us. I scooted back on the bed and sat with my legs crossed and when Johnny came back he did the same.

"Right now?" Johnny asked. "Avaline, we've been looking for months. What makes you think we will find it now?"

Avaline cocked her head, sat down. "Because Perido knows where it is."

Johnny shook his head. "Has he seen it, Av?"

"Close enough," she said.

"How can you be sure?"

"He would not lie to me."

Johnny grumbled. "Why must he tell us now? After we've been looking for so long?"

"We never asked him, never told him about it," Avaline said. "Is he busy tonight?"

"He's asleep. You know how Perido is," Johnny said. "We can meet with him in the morning."

Avaline nodded. "Why don't we all get some sleep?"

"Why don't we talk tomorrow, Max?" Johnny said. He stood and went to the door. "Good night."

Avaline followed him out. Without the goddess speaking, alone in the darkness of the room, I laid back on the bed and fell asleep almost instantly.

* Johnny *

Perido was not free that morning. Avaline found him riding his horse in the orchard where she normally took her morning walk and later she had come to my room to inform me that we would meet with Perido that evening. I told her to tell Max to relax the day away, as I would. I wasn't ready to see Max alone, not after kissing her as I did. I wasn't sure what I'd say if she brought it up.

I was lying on my bed after a solitary dinner when someone knocked on the door. Before I could speak or open it, Perido burst in.

"What is this talk of the Vault, Johnny?" he said. "Avaline said we would discuss it later, well I'm here now."

I smiled. He had always been more enthusiastic than I, and now it was no different. "We should go to Max's room."

Perido led the way out the door and down the hall. Inside, Avaline was on a stool. Perido dragged another chair next to hers and Max was on her bed, just as she was the night before.

"The Vault," Perido said, getting right to the point. He looked at me. "This is not a joke. It is real, and you three expect me to just show it to you?"

I touched his shoulder. "You've seen it?"

"You were gone for many years, Johnny. And I had many days to wander around the kingdom, without the care of my father nor anyone else," he said, quieting. "I have not seen it though. All I know is where it is."

"It's a legend," I said.

Perido shook his head, serious. "It is real, my brother. But why do you wish to see it? Is there a reason besides curiosity?"

Avaline nodded. "You know that Max has the mark of Adahlia," she said.

Max looked a little nervous at the goddess's name.

Avaline went on. "You know my history," she said. Perido nodded, his eyes intent on Avaline. "I have seen the Vault," she said. "I have been inside. I have looked for potions, spells, ways to…" she broke off, resumed. "I believe that there is another way to release Adahlia, besides death. And the answer lies in the Vault."

"Do you remember how to get there?" Perido asked.

Avaline shook her head. "I do not. I remember the passage, but I could not lead the way."

Perido nodded again. "Johnny could lead the way, though he does not believe so. But I can guide you. Do you know how to get inside?"

"I have the key," Avaline said.

Perido smiled, wide and mischievous. "Then we will enter the Vault tomorrow night. Late, when even the servants are sleeping. Is that an idea? Is that our plan?"

I smiled too, looked at Max briefly before I said, "That is our plan."

With that, Perido stood and left the room. "I'd ask that you don't tell Father, but I know you wouldn't. Even if you did, he wouldn't believe it," Perido said, his voice disintegrating behind the closed door as he walked down the hall.

He was right. Our father wouldn't believe there was a Vault, and he certainly would not believe that Perido was the one who found it.

"I'm going to take a walk," Avaline said.

I went to tend the fire as she left the room.

Max's emerald eyes followed me as I moved a wooden chair to face her. My hands were restless in my lap. "Thanks for coming here, Max," I said. "And I'm sorry about the other night, in the carriage."

Her breath caught, but she regained herself quickly. She sighed. "I saw your sister in the hall today. She spoke of your sleep problems. Avaline has mentioned that you are restless, tossing and turning in your sleep, calling out my name. Is that true?"

I swallowed my emotions, urging my face to show nothing of how I felt. "Why would Avaline tell you that?"

"She worries." Max shook her head. "Is it true?"

I looked around the room. At the ceiling, the floor, the windows and walls. Finally I told her, "I'm not sure what to say."

Max took a deep breath. "Neither do I," she said calmly. She stood, ushering me to the door. I opened it, stood in the doorway and looked into the dark room at her. Kissing her had been a mistake. Not in the way I felt, but in the nature of the situation. It had caused my feelings to grow, and I feared that by loving her more, I'd be more afraid to take the chances necessary to release Adahlia. I'd perhaps refuse to make decisions in the kingdom's best interest, and if I were to be king as my father hoped, I could not push Valta aside for Max.

I stepped back into the room to meet her in the dark. Tracing her cheek, I leaned in, slowly, and she met me the rest of the way. Her lips were cold, supple. I drew her closer but as I did so, the hand on my neck that had been pulling me in slid down over my heart. She pushed me away, gentle but firm, into the hallway.

My heart sunk into my stomach, my mind raced, as she smiled innocently, the light catching the silvers and blues amongst the green of her eyes. She cast her eyelashes downward.

"I'm sorry," I said as she closed the door.

She shook her head. "Maybe it was not right that I came."

The sound of the door's final click into place was enough to make my mouth dry. I had a feeling my sleeplessness would come back this night.

Chapter 9

* Johnny *

I had always liked Perido's room better than my own. His was perched high over the Valtan countryside, where he could see the orchards, the farmland, and the large, whitened peaks of the Lomic Mountains. I was right above the town and courtyards, forced to gaze upon the kingdom I would once rule.

I was seated in my favorite chair, in my favorite room in the palace. My brother was happy and brooding next to me, sipping hot water with mint. Dinner had been bland with just the family. Av and Max had stayed in Max's room. Max had been brought food, without the inconvenience of royals breathing down her back as she ate.

"So," my brother said, "how is Max doing in Valta? She is a strange girl I must say. Do I scare her?"

I snorted. "You scare and surprise many, Perido. And I'm not sure what she thinks of Valta."

"Does she know that you love her?" he asked.

I sucked in a breath. "What?"

"Honestly Johnny, for a man so sensitive, so typically open with your feelings, you do have trouble admitting this, don't you?"

"No. I...ah, don't love her."

Perido threw his arms up in the air and laughed. When he calmed, he settled deep into his chair and wiped the smile from his face. "You amuse me, Brother," he said.

"Perido, do not make this matter your own," I said.

He took a mindless, hasty sip of his tea. "This matter," he said calmly, "may not be my own, but it affects me entirely. It is the least you can do to keep me informed."

"What are you talking about, Perido?" I asked.

He pointed a finger at me. "You know very well what I'm talking about. If you love her, you won't take the crown. You don't want to anyway, but the love of yourself and what you want won't deter you from the kingdom. The love of someone else will." Perido frowned, looked into his cup. "Do not play with me, Johnny."

"I'm not playing with you," I said. I put a hand on his shoulder, and he grasped it. "I know you want the kingdom, but Father…"

"Father will do whatever he can to keep me from it," Perido finished. "I am not sent with guards when I travel, though danger may follow. I am not invited to dinners. I am not recognized by any other kingdom, and barely my own. I have been made invisible and you a celebrity. You were born first, and the winner of that battle is not satisfied with the prize. Do not think that your matters are not my own as well. My life has been dictated by yours since you fell from Mother's womb into Father's hands. I have always come in second, my brother. But my heart deserves happiness too."

I took my hand back. Drank the last of my tea. "I know all this, Perido. And I'm sorry for your troubles."

"And I for yours," he added.

"I will make my choice swiftly, and tell you first," I said. "What more can I do?"

He shook his head. "You have certainly done enough, just as my brother."

"I am honored." I paused. "And you certainly maintain your reputation of being different."

"I flaunt it!" Perido said, suddenly enthused. "With you more than others, though."

"You are hated for it," I said. "Everyone thinks you're strange, if not just a little mad."

Perido jumped out of his seat and the lick of tea left in his cup sprung into the air and landed on the carpet. He looked down at it as if it were some kind of tiny demon. Then he looked to me. "I know," he said. "And I'm glad, too. Let them hate me, despise me, but also let them know that I'd be a better king than *you*."

"I believe they already know," I said quietly.

Perido sunk back into his chair. "And that is what I could never begin to understand."

A small rap on the door drew both of our attention away from the subject. We waited and heard it again before Perido said, "Come in."

Max and Avaline formed in the doorway, walked over to replace and sit on the empty stools in the room. We were all in a little circle, settled for the most part, before Avaline spoke. "Tonight," she said, glancing out the window, "will be the first time I've seen the Vault in hundreds of years."

"We must do this in haste," Perido said.

Max nodded. "Where is it exactly?"

"Well," Perido said, "let me show you." He stood and went to the door, opened it. "Let's show Max the Vault."

I blew out the candles and the room went black. We followed his hasty steps down the halls in the palace of Valta. I knew all of them, including all the artwork hung above the marble tiles. I knew the tapestry we came to. It was the story of Valta's long ago king. The one who had ended Bortal's civil war.

Avaline's breath caught. She touched the soldiers, the men fighting below a wall. The Great Barrier. She touched the man standing upon it, the woman by his side, dressed in red. The familiarity with which she stroked the scene was eerie.

Perido paid no attention. He brushed the tapestry aside, revealing a hole in the wall. I gasped and Max took a step back. Avaline drew her hand away from the cloth. Her glazed look became fresh again. She glowed slightly in the dark halls.

I grabbed a torch off the wall beside the tapestry, thrust it forward into the hole. I took a step inside.

It was another hallway, one that had been covered, shut out by the broken wall I stepped through. Dust had taken over the green and white floor, the art cluttered on the walls, the unlit torches.

I took one from its holster, lit it, and handed it to Perido. He led the way around the turns in this old part of the castle, only to stop abruptly at a seam in the floor, a small metal hook. Perido handed his torch to Max and bent to lift the marble slab. Avaline took my torch while I helped my brother move the slab aside. It clattered, but the echo was dampened. A waft of cold, damp air drifted up from the darkness with a howl. My eyes focused on the steep stairs leading into the blackness.

Perido briskly fastened his wool jacket tighter around his chest, took his torch back, and started down the stairs. I let Avaline and Max go ahead of me, then fell in step down the stairs into the passage that would lead us to the legendary Vault of Valta.

* Max *

Perido began to sing. This strange, shut-out prince walked slower as the paths narrowed. Soon the walls were on either shoulder, wet and cool, and Avaline stopped glowing. We passed dark, thin hallways, Johnny keeping close behind me the entire way. The goddess pushed at my mind, manipulating, speaking, but I shut her out. I focused on Perido's voice.

"*Banilgar/He comes to a crossing in the road,*" Perido sang. "Go left," Perido stepped to the left, down a hallway, "*and there will be no more warmth here/He'll be all alone.*" A wave of bumps pocked my arms. I shivered. In the pause I could hear a rat scratching at the walls.

Johnny hummed the tune behind us as Perido went on. I recalled that the queen of Bortal had given Johnny a book, his favorite story; that of Banilgar. This must be a children's rhyme.

"*Banilgar/He passes right along/He passes all that's left/He passes three civilians comforting their children/Go right away/Banilgar.*" Perido, meanwhile, went past one right hall, one left, and three thinly carved passages until he got to the next right turn, and took it. Johnny all of a sudden seemed to understand his brother's madness. He began to sing as well, with more enthusiasm.

Together, they went on, singing louder. "*Banilgar/The journey's almost over/Don't slow because you're covered,*" on that the brothers bent at the waist. Avaline nearly ran into a low tapered ceiling, but bent too. We crawled under it, walls closing in to our bodies. Panic was about to take me when Perido's voice cut the air.

"*Banilgar,*" he sang slowly, holding his note, "*the hero of the Valtan Land/Guide us to the hidden pass/Where Valta's love of magic has,*" Perido paused and then entered a cavity where he stepped aside to let us in. I sighed, relieved at the space. "*No end.*" And there, at the end of the song, Perido revealed a large wooden door.

Johnny dropped his torch and fumbled along the floor to pick it up. Avaline gasped, her face tight with a smile. Perido watched her, his attention genuine, his expression filled with excitement. He directed his gaze at me, waited a moment, then turned back to Avaline.

"Brilliant," Johnny said, but Perido paid no attention aside from a small, unwavering smile.

"I believe you have the key, my lady," Perido said to Avaline. He bowed slightly and she laughed.

Avaline searched in the folds of her tattered dress and finally drew out a slender vial. Johnny muttered something as she uncorked it. She bent to hear him a second time. "What did you say?"

"Dragon's blood and lily nectar," Johnny said.

"Not only is it good for my nails," Avaline said. She pulled out a brush and began painting over the keyhole in the door. "It is the most precious thing I could have: The key to the Vault."

The hole began to glow white and Avaline stood back. "Storret Airet, I wish you could be here to see this," she said to herself, shaking her head. The door clicked, sending a huge echo into the winding halls under the castle.

And then it swung open.

Avaline rushed past Perido inside, but he followed close behind her. She breathed deep and the huge hall ignited with her light. The chandeliers went on forever, hung from a ceiling that seemed to reach the sky—I reminded myself that we were *under* a palace. Avaline's power lit each and every candle it seemed, and they all worked together to reveal the legend of Valta, the room after which the Second Kingdom was named. When we were all in, Johnny closed the door behind us and smothered his torchlight on the floor. Perido only dropped his, but when Avaline's dress passed over it, it extinguished.

Avaline grinned as we all gazed upon the magnificent hall. On either side were bookshelves and cases. Scrolls and books burst off the shelves while others were plainly stacked on the ground in large disordered heaps. The cases held vials and jars of all shapes, filled with every color imaginable, every texture, some liquid, some solid. Some glowed and others were almost empty, save for a single drop or speck in the bottom of the container.

Down the middle of the hall were paintings, sculptures, large cooking pots, an array of surgical utensils and knives, clothing, shoes, bags, pouches, hats, a case full of sticks, staffs, jewelry, armor, swords, shields, potted plants, strange animals that were stuffed and in cages, huge books on stands, furniture, instruments, and above it all, on a high wooden block, was a very thin, deep red dress.

Avaline stopped below it, did not dare touch the fabric. It seemed as if she would cry, but she did not. Beneath the dress was a small piece of paper that Avaline did pick up. She read it slowly, traced the letters, and then tucked it into her dress, somewhere amongst the vial of dragon's blood, I assumed.

"Now," Avaline said quietly. She cleared her throat, went on in her magical, fluid voice. "We are looking for a scroll, much along the lines of a recipe. Once it is found, we will be looking for ingredients, clear?"

Perido and Johnny nodded. I bowed my head and took the leather band out of my hair, revealing my mark, to ensure Adahlia knew what we were doing. The goddess began to mutter, her voice soft and rhythmic in the back of my mind.

"Let us search, then," she said, and began to pace the Vault.

We were down there for a long time, rifling through scrolls and books. When Johnny finally found the case of recipe scrolls, down on the right side of the Vault, nearly opposite the place we came in, we began to open them.

We found recipes for sickness, some for sleep, some for even love. One could heal a broken leg while another could make the body more fragile. Poisons, medicines, potions that could control the mind, heart, body; in the Vault we were finding everything imaginable, and some unimaginable.

Perido was the one who found the recipe that would release the goddess. Avaline would not let us see it; it was recognized plainly by the seal that bound it and the small lettering in the corner: Adahlia.

"Here," Avaline said, "this is what will save you, Max." She embraced me, smiling wide. "This will bring you to freedom, as long as it is done right."

"And if it is done wrong?" I asked, pulling away. I looked into her purple eyes, searching.

"If it is done wrong, you will live between the gods and Man forever. You will have no choice but to be a slave to both, and your soul will be lost," Avaline said gravely, matter-of-factly.

All of a sudden the Vault didn't seem so big. It felt impeding, tense under the pressure of the castle and the gods and goddesses looking down at us inside it.

"Very well," Perido said, clapping his hands. "We have ingredients to find, no?"

Avaline directed her attention to him and grinned. "We do. Let us see what those are." Avaline broke the seal and unrolled the scroll. Dust sloughed off the paper as she read it to herself. "Look for a slender case, with gold lettering. It will have the seal of Oslo on it, as the contents were gathered in her desert."

We all began to look. I went to a large cabinet, unlatched the doors, and pushed trinkets aside to see the items hiding behind them, ensuring that I searched everywhere. I did not find the case, though. When the case was found, not too far away from where Avaline stood, Perido handed it to Avaline. The box was nearly the length of my arm. A golden sun had been carved into the lid.

"Good," said Avaline. "Johnny, find me a pouch with gold dust in it. I also need a brush, a small one that could be used for painting. Perido, I need you to find me a jar. It will be filled with orange, shimmering liquid. The consistency will be that of honey." When the men left on their tasks, Avaline turned to me. "Max, find me a dagger. Its handle will be silver and gold wire, and it will be sheathed in red leather." I nodded and began to look.

I searched down the center of the Vault in the mess of weapons and tools but I could not find it. I began to look elsewhere and finally found the dagger with Avaline's description. It was on the edge of a bookstand. A large book was splayed open to a map, and the dagger was unsheathed, sticking straight out of the wood where it had been plunged. I wondered how long it had been there, why it was there, if it was magic, because it was placed in the Vault.

I grabbed the handle and pulled it out of the wood. I sheathed it and found Avaline. She took the dagger, made it disappear in the folds of her dress.

When the other objects had been found, Avaline directed us to the door. It would be morning in the castle soon.

When we had left the Vault, Avaline stopped just outside the door. "Oh," she said, turning back, "I will only be a moment. I have one more thing to retrieve." She disappeared in the Vault and we waited patiently outside it, in the small dark cavity beneath the castle.

Avaline arrived a few minutes later, holding a full vial of dragon's blood and lily nectar. "We may need passage inside this Vault again," was all she said as the chandeliers extinguished and she closed the door. The contents of the Vault were once again sealed away in darkness.

Perido led us out of the tunnels and back into the hidden hallway of the palace. It was early morning, and we snuck quietly out from behind the tapestry and went into Perido's room. There, Avaline spoke to us only once before leaving for privacy, to study the recipe and think about how it would be preformed. "I am not sure if our find today is good or bad," she said. "Without this, Max would die in peace. But if we do this wrong, Max will be subject to something much worse than death." She turned to me. "I fear for you, sweet woman. I do not wish a harsh future upon you. All we can do is try, and pray and sing plea that the gods will grant you success in your releasing of Adahlia. Without you, she will perish, but with her, you may suffer an afterlife not worth anything in this world. Let us all hope for the best."

My heart sunk into my stomach, and my throat closed. A fear powerful and sudden took me, and I fled to my room.

* Johnny *

The next morning, after we had all rested, I could not find Max anywhere. Perido advised that she would be walking somewhere inside the palace, but I doubted that. Something had gone wrong.

I rushed from my brother's room and began to ask the servants if they had seen her. Most had not. I began to worry that she had gone back down into the Vault, thinking she could remember the way. I imagined her lost down there, calling out, eventually perishing in the dark. I shook my head to clear it.

I ran down the hall and slipped behind the tapestry when no one was near. But when I found the slab of marble leading to the passage, it was covering the hole completely, just where we had left it. Max would not have been strong enough to move it out of the way.

I checked the kitchens, the courtyards, and finally I strode out in the bright spring sunlight and decided to check the last place she could possibly be.

The stables were nestled back against the palace walls and as I walked to them, I doubted myself over and over that she'd be there. She had no reason to be there. When I went inside, a groom was seated on a stool, polishing leather. I could smell the wax and manure, hear a few horses whinny in greeting or curiosity. Perido strode out of a stall with reins in his hands. He would often take up the groom's job by dressing his own horse.

"Care for a ride, my brother?" he said, leading Shae out into the walkway. The little horse was well groomed and tacked, the bridle without a bit, as usual. Perido stroked his horse's legs, knocked on his hooves. "Stay grounded, feel those," Perido said to the beast. "There," he cooed, stroking his neck.

I shook my head. "Perido, Max is still lost somewhere," I turned to the groom, "Have you seen a young woman, brown hair, my age?"

The groom stood up and the bridle he had been polishing fell to the floor in a clatter. His eyes were wide. "My prince," said the groom, bowing low, "I fear I am at fault." I could see Perido roll his eyes, but the groom went on, "She asked for a horse to be tacked, that she was to meet you in the orchards behind the palace for a ride."

My heart sunk as my anger rose. She had escaped. I looked at the man. "She could be dead," I said harshly.

The man shook.

"Value your life, for in any other palace you'd be hung for letting a guest flee under no supervision." I took a deep breath. "Ready my horse."

The man shuffled down the hall to where Jet was and began saddling him.

"Perido," I said, "help me find her."

"Does this mean we are to escape the palace as well?" he asked, smiling.

I nodded at the irony. "How much food can you fit in your saddle bag? We should bring blankets too. It is late in the day and I will not stop until she is back," I said, and added in a whisper, "Alician spies have infested this land, it is only a matter of time before she is caught."

"I will get food from the kitchens and call for Avaline," Perido said.

I shook my head. "Avaline can stay here."

But Perido protested. "She may be of help, my brother. Just ready a horse for her." Perido tied Shae to a hook and burst out of the stables, running for the castle.

I turned to the stalls and came upon not only my horse and the nervous groom, but another horse, perfect for Av. I opened his stall and tacked him swiftly, noticing that his neighbor, Moon, was gone. My mother's mare must have been who Max rode out on. I hoped that Moon had taken care of Max so far.

Perido arrived in the stables only a few minutes later, his arms full of food. He packed it all into his saddle bags, strapped blankets to my saddle behind the seat, and put a wad of cloth in a pouch hung from his belt.

"What's that for?" I asked.

Perido only smiled. "You readied Aurafax for Avaline?"

"I figured he would suit her well," I said, motioning to the well muscled, sleek white horse. He pawed impatiently at the ground, and I was quickly reminded that Aurafax was quite large. He was one to test the hugeness of my own horse. And dwarf Perido's.

Avaline entered the stable, her arms full of weapons. "Perido, take these," she said in frustration. He took the swords, handed one to me, along with a dagger. I fastened the straps over my shoulders, so the larger blade lay at my hip. Perido did the same, and Avaline was left with a small dagger to have at her waist.

She nodded at the large white horse taking up the walkway of the stable, Perido's little gruilla standing quietly behind him. "Whose horse is this?" she asked.

"Yours, now," Perido said. "His name is Aurafax. He's very light in the mouth so you must only guide him. Be gentle."

Avaline nodded as the groom took Jet into the walkway as well. I took his reins and led him out the far door. "Let's ride," I said, mounting once we cleared from the stable doors.

Perido swung onto Shae and patted his neck, smoothing the soft fur. Avaline mounted Aurafax with the same grace. He responded to her every command as soon as she had settled in the saddle.

I maneuvered Jet toward the stable and called for the groom. The black beast shifted eagerly underneath me and I could feel his energy swirling from where my calves met his body all the way up to the top of my head.

The groom stumbled out. "Open the gates," I said to him. He looked reluctant, but did so in a hurry.

"Is this where she was headed?" I asked him before he returned to the stable. I pointed to the orchard in question.

The groom shook his head. "She left only a few hours ago, heading toward Drew."

"The deserted city," I said to no one in particular. My palms began to sweat. "When he asks, tell my father that you did not help us in our escape." I laid my heels against Jet. His hind legs dug deep into the soil as we took off northeast toward Drew.

The groom closed the palace gate behind us.

* Max *

Old feelings had crept up on me. They were the same as they had been on Dela, a sort of defiance for the goddess and the quest to release her. When Avaline had spoken about releasing the goddess and the consequences if it went wrong, I had began to panic. This time though, I knew I could not run or hide. I would not be so selfish. The spies from Alice would find me just as they had before, and so I had figured that killing myself would be easier.

Without me, Johnny would have no need to worry over Adahlia again. I would not suffer at the hands of Alicians nor would I be trapped in a state worse than death if the releasing with Avaline went wrong. I had no need to feel nervous or cry. I was beyond that. Disappearing and killing myself was easiest for everyone. I was doing good by the individuals I had come to love. Releasing them of their pain, as I would release myself of mine, and Adahlia of hers.

The wind blew across the barren land as I rode onward, away from Valta to find a place to die. I ignored the cold, refused to close the front of my cloak against the weather because I liked the feeling of numbness it gave me. The goddess screamed in my ears, perhaps more intense than the night she had entered me. I could imagine what she was saying, her pleas for me to refrain, that this was not how she was intended to be released, that a kingdom was supposed to do it. Or possibly she was screaming in anticipation, yearning for freedom.

I stroked the neck of the horse I rode, fingers intertwined in the thick hairs of its mane. Yes, I thought, this would be best for everyone.

* Johnny *

There were no tracks from Max, but there was only one path to the city. While the sun lowered, the wind picked up, whipping the changing land. On the hill behind the palace, I looked down over the kingdom, the canal, the town, farms, orchards. The tip of Lake Nomp curled into the very right of my view. Jet was uneasy, his gait choppy and big. I reined him in, just to see the view for a few more seconds. Perido and Avaline waited part way down the other side of the rise.

This was the kingdom that I'd inherit. My heart sank, knowing very well that it was too much; it was something I did not want.

A Kingdom's Possession

As we made our way, the path became flatter, muddier. We could now see fresh tracks on the road and it felt good to know we were heading the right way.

Storm clouds began to hover over the wavering sun, rising from the ground like mountains, darkening the grey scene. Everything looked like it was made of stone in the twilight and the horses became flighty.

We rode hard with the sun and the castle behind us, searching for a girl who could very possibly be dead. When the day was as dark as my mount, we decided to pull away from the road and make a small camp. Intertwined in the trees, it was easy to stay concealed. Though we were on a path to the deserted city, there was still a very high risk of encountering bandits. Shepherds and other common folk would often wander down this road too far, in search of a lost animal, and a bandit could take away everything the farmer had. The outside civilians of Valta were not poor; they fed many inside the walls and were well rewarded for their hard, honest work.

Avaline had quickly made a small fire while Perido tended the horses. I touched Shae's neck as Perido bustled around me, checking legs, hooves, eyes, noses. He took the cloth he had packed and wiped the dirt from their nostrils, to lower the chance of them snorting. It was better to remain concealed.

"Shh," Perido cooed to his horse. He rubbed him between the eyes then went to the fire. I went with him to enjoy its heat, prayed that the clouds would not burst with rain. Avaline's aura was warm and was cast deep into the shadows.

Perido and I had laid down to rest—though I doubted I could sleep—when we heard a horse whinny in the distance. Perido rushed to our horses before an answer could be made. If it was bandits, we were best undetected. But the whinny came again, one that was familiar. It was not a blind call into the dark. Our horses became restless, though they did not call.

Perido crouched on the edge of the path, waiting for the stranger. I got up and joined him in the brush, hoping it was Max.

A single rider fell into view under the dark clouds of the night. The silhouette of the rider was thin, head hung down, long hair tangled.

"Max?" I said. Perido shot me a scolding look and the figure shot her eyes our way.

"Yes?" Came the reply. It was her.

I rushed from the underbrush and seized Moon's bridle. The horse flipped her head, but calmed. I led the two of them into the underbrush and tied Moon with the other horses. I helped Max down, and she cried out sharply when her feet hit the ground.

"What happened?" I asked.

"I fell from her, I think my ankle is broken," she said, hobbling to the fire to sit next to Avaline.

I slipped off Max's boot, felt her ankle. Above her foot were many scars, most flat, pale, and smooth. Only a few were pink and raised.

"Just a sprain," I said, ignoring them. "But we should have you rest a day before we go back. We're only a third of a day's ride from the palace, but riding will be hard on your ankle."

Max shivered, nodded.

Perido returned from tending to the horses and sat beside Max, spoke to her about nothing in particular.

Avaline nudged me. "Do not question her tonight, Johnny. She looks tired."

I nodded, moved my attention to the night sounds. The fire cackled at the sky, little birds and mammals scuttled in the bushes. The clouds overhead began to sprinkle, but that was all. Perido covered the tack next to the horses, and settled down to sleep under the blanket he had brought. Max had one too, in her saddlebag, so she laid down to sleep as well. She gave me one final glance before she put her head down. It was a look of thanks, I hoped. Her eyes were soft and the small smile in the corners of her mouth gave away her feeling of being secure.

I touched Avaline's shoulder. "Will you be alright if it rains, Av?"

She ran her fingers through her hair. "I will be alright. I can keep watch for you three and tend the fire so it stays warm."

I tipped my head. "I thought all the warmth was coming from you," I said.

A Kingdom's Possession

Her eyes flickered. "I can't keep all of us warm all night just off my own powers," she said. "Now go to sleep, Johnny. Your Max is safe again."

Chapter 10

* Johnny *

"We need some fresh water. I'll be back before dark," Max said, standing up.

It was past noon, the sun was lowering from the peak of its arc in the sky, and we were just finishing a very late lunch.

"Don't stress your sprain. We rested today to let it strengthen for our ride home tomorrow. I don't think carrying water will be best for you," I said.

"I'll be fine." She brushed some breadcrumbs off her pants.

"I'll come and help," Perido offered.

She placed a hand on his shoulder so he wouldn't stand up. "I will be fine alone. It is only a short walk away. Where are the water skins?"

Perido nodded over to the packs by the horses. "There, somewhere," Perido said.

Max secured the daggers hidden by her boots and took the water skins out of sight. I sighed, promising myself that if she was not back in an hour I'd go to her.

"Well then," Perido said coming to his feet, "shall we practice some swordplay? It'll be like old times." He picked up two slender sticks off the ground.

I grinned. "We haven't done this in a long while, my brother." I snatched one of the sticks from his grip. "Are you prepared to die?"

The cold air burned my lungs as Perido and I jousted. It felt good to play as if I were a young prince again, without a care or worry. When we were tired, Perido retreated to the fire to speak with Avaline. I decided to find Max. After all the things that had happened to her, I did not find myself comfortable with having her out of my sight for too long.

I followed the sound of trickling water through a slight wood, out into another clearing. There, Max was sitting on the very edge of a slow stream. Her knees were bent up to her chest and her arms were hugged around them. The water skins rested in the grass around her, empty and unorganized. Her hair hung around her face; the leather strap was beside her. Her arms were bare, and she was holding her pendant, the chain dangling through her fingers.

I sat down beside her, but she did not move her stare away from the stream.

"I look tired," she said. The figure in the reflection had red eyes, dirt on her face.

"I don't really blame you," I whispered. Then she did look up.

"I don't either," she said. Neither of us spoke for a while. Then, "Why are you here, Johnny?"

I shrugged. "You deserve to live, Max," I said. "I had to come and find you."

She shook her head, "No. That's not the reason." The setting sun cast her face in a golden glow, made her hair catch fire with the light and glisten with tints of red and orange.

I looked at the water, and her reflection stared back at me. I closed my eyes. "No," I said, opening my eyes. "It is the reason."

Max shifted, met my eyes with hers. "Only part of it," she said.

I breathed deep. "Max, I think I'm starting to..."

But she interrupted. "Stop, nevermind," she said, placing her hands on the ground to stand. I reached for her arm, but she was already up.

"Max, wait," I said, scrambling to my feet. "What are you so afraid of with me?" I asked. I looked down into her eyes; they were harsh and impeding.

"I'm not afraid of you," she said, meeting my gaze. "Why would I be?"

"Because you've never felt this before," I said. "Everyone wants to be loved, Max."

"Yes, we all want to be loved. But so far I've gotten by without..." She paused, tightened her lips. "Johnny, I couldn't do it to you. In trying to release the goddess, what if a mistake is made, what if I..." she trailed off.

"You came here to kill yourself," I said quietly. "You escaped to die in peace."

She nodded, her eyes getting wet. "I couldn't do that to you, Johnny. I would never forgive myself, even after death, if I left this earth, if a mistake was made. I had to go and do it alone, where it would be peaceful. Where you wouldn't worry about me."

I shook my head. "Max," I said, touching her face, "it is better to try."

"No, Johnny," she said, pulling away.

"Do not take the easy way out this time," I blurted. I grabbed her shoulders. "Face what it is that scares you."

"I am," she said quietly, as my fingers slid from my hold on her. "He is staring me right in the face, waiting for me to make a decision that I do not want to make."

"You said that I did not scare you…"

"I lied," she said. "You are the scariest thing I have ever come across, and yet you're the one thing I think it would be hard to live without."

"Don't kill yourself," I said.

She shook her head. "It will only cause more trouble if I am alive."

"I don't care," I said. "We are so close to freeing you completely, but you must try. Think of the freedom you could have."

Max looked at her feet, picked up her leather band and secured it in her hair. "Fine, Johnny. It will only get more difficult for us now," she said, and then she disappeared into the shadows of the spread trees, leaving me with all the water skins and her pendant, resting in the grass.

"I know," I said aloud, once she was gone. "It's worth it."

I gathered everything and walked back to camp. The day was at the tail end of a faint twilight that meandered through the trees, creating a fog of shadows. I dropped the full sacks of water down on the ground and sat next to Avaline by the fire. Max was on the other side of her, facing Perido.

"And where are you from?" he was saying. He took a bite of dried meat, staring at her intently.

"Alice, I guess," she said.

Perido grunted, picked up a roll of bread. "Did you like it there?"

Max shrugged. "The land was nice."

"Yes, yes a very good location." Perido waved his empty hand through the air, shoved the last of his meat into his mouth. "Who are your parents? I know you were a slave, but is there something that came before that?"

"I don't know," she said. "All I can remember is serving other people. I do not remember a time when I had a mother or a father or siblings. I like to think that if I did, they loved me very much, and that I was taken when I was too young to remember. Or something like that."

The younger prince smiled. "That is a nice thought."

At that the conversation was over. Perido began speaking with Avaline, and Max sat quietly. I watched her through the flames, noticing her perfect nose, her tight lips, the way her eyebrows arched above her eyes like a mountain would arch above the sea.

She placed a hand on her chest, her face creased, and she glanced at the ground. I leaned back and reached around Avaline to touch Max's shoulder. I pulled her pendant out of my pocket, handed it to her. Her expression softened and she returned her attention to what was happening around the fire.

Perido and Avaline only talked another few minutes before we all lay down to sleep. Avaline stayed seated, playing with the fire, supposed to keep watch.

It wasn't the crack in the nearby woods that made me stand and draw my sword, nor was it the fact that one of the horses startled and blew out a breath of fear. It was Avaline's expression as I looked up at her from the ground, the expression that changed so instantly upon the recognition that men approached.

I shoved Max and she silently came to her feet, daggers out. Perido unsheathed his custom Valtan sword. Like mine, the hilt and scabbard were cast in a gold and silver netting of wire and leather and had the Valtan Crest etched into the blade. Both swords rang in harmony as we brought them into the silky light and gathered a stance of readiness.

When the men came into sight—there were six of them altogether, but no horses—they all simultaneously grinned. The biggest one, over a foot taller than me at least, spoke like he had downed a little too much ale. "So what have the thief's heavens granted us tonight? Valtan royals, with those swords. But, ah, could it be? The princes? They do look alike, don't they? This is splendid: the chance to rob the most promising royals in these parts! But surely I would suspect they would be a little smarter than to be wandering around in unmarked territory without a guard," he shrugged. "But I am not the one to question or complain."

"You'll complain when we're done with you," Perido said. "But if you leave now, you'll avoid all the trouble."

"I do not fear the *other* prince."

The men laughed, Perido looked only irritated.

"Who are the fine ladies behind them? One for each prince I presume?" one man said.

"Bitches for their doing," another offered.

"Noble whores," a third said.

On that I rushed, clattered on the impact of one sword meeting another. Avaline went into the crowd after me, ignited a man. He fell to the ground charred, face down. I couldn't see Perido or Max, but I could hear their fighting, blades hitting other blades. All was encompassed by the sound of phoenix fire. I focused back on my own fighting, one more step left, two more right, a jab...

Everything went still as I ran my blade through the bulky man in front of me. His face went lax as I yanked my blade from his chest. It was too late. A cry had escaped Max and now her silhouette was sinking to the earth. The blackness of her figure merged with the blackness of the ground and her attacker stood above her with a blade raised to make the final kill. There was not enough time for me to get to her, to stop the man above her. But I ran anyway, frantic, trying to close the space between us and save her life. Perido made it there before me though, and thrust his blade cleanly through the man's chest. I dropped to my knees beside Max and cradled her head as Perido yanked his blade free.

* Max *

"Johnny?" I whispered. But the man behind my attacker was not Johnny. It was Perido.

From behind my tangled hair and teary eyes, I could see Johnny. His eyes broke from his opponent and fixated on me. His eyebrows creased and his muscles bunched under his shirt. In a surge of anger, it seemed, he ran his blade into the man in front of him.

In the same series of moments, Perido must have done the same, because the man above me had lowered his sword and tumbled to the ground. I closed my eyes, felt the blood pooling around me, hot and sticky. Perido uttered a curse and I could feel hands lifting me, voices calling my name over and over.

I must have passed out, because I woke by a fire, hands moving fast around me in the darkness of night. Someone unlaced my vest roughly, other hands brushed the hair out of my face. Avaline was brighter than the others; her glow bounded into the night, pushed back the shadows.

I could feel more blood around me, see it on the hands that were fumbling with my clothing. The goddess spoke to me, her voice loud and tonal. She lulled my mind, but I pushed her out.

"Here," Avaline was saying. "Here, Max, this will help. It will hurt, but it will soothe you too, here."

Something new came to my wound, and it was something I could not stand. I sucked in air so that my body would not deflate with agony. Little, intolerable sounds escaped my mouth, but screaming arose in my head. Liquid was poured down my side, cool and grueling. And there, I slipped back into the dark night of pain and wandering. Unconsciousness took me.

When I came back, I was hot. Beads of sweat had broken on my forehead, and my stale mouth tasted of sickness. But my eyes were open and everything was in focus now.

There were small trees that grabbed onto a fuzzy blanket of grass, and a slanted horizon that left the spring-blue sky tilted on its side like frozen water. There was a little fire flickering lazily in a blackened pit, and there were bags and pots that littered the immediate area. I could hear horses snorting between hasty bites of grass and heavy breathing in my ear. I was wrapped in someone's arms, warm and relaxed. A chest expanded into my back and suddenly my whole side ached. My arms felt like they were weighted with all the water of the ocean. It was pumping through my veins and sloshing as I tried to grab at my wound, just to see what it would be like. Soon I was struggling to sit up, but the water sloshed me down and anchored me to the bottom of the clear, cloudless sky.

Someone walked up. I let my eyes travel up the contours of the body until my eyes strained to see his face. Fair, attractive, yet not as captivating as Johnny, Perido knelt down in front of me.

"Finally," he said lightly. "You are so lazy."

I tried to speak, but my voice was drowned out by the heaviness pounding in my head. I could feel it coming on stronger. "You," I managed, a smile forming on my dry lips. "What," I mumbled.

His smile broadened and he squatted, rested his hand on my forehead. "You have been out a whole day, a night, and now it's the afternoon of your second day," he explained. "As for who is sleeping next to you, well, you can probably guess that for yourself. You were cold beyond any reason for the past few days and so Johnny, Av, and I have been taking shifts keeping you warm so you don't get sicker. He was up all night keeping watch and worrying; I would let him sleep now."

"Sicker?" I mumbled.

Perido nodded, his tussled hair blew in the breeze. "You had the chills, now a fever is peaking. If we don't get you back to the palace, you'll get a risky fever for sure. You're already starting to heat up a little too much, I have to say." He stood. "You're lucky Avaline had the dragon's blood. If she hadn't used it, you'd probably be dead right now. But you're healing nicely." He poked at the fire and I wondered where Avaline was.

Finally I could lift an arm. I expected to feel a proud wound, dry blood caked on a dirty shirt. But when I reached down I felt fabric. I was wrapped in bandages, and my shirt was different. My side ached even under the light touch of my own fingers. I took a deep, shaky breath. A thought came to my mind. "Who changed me?" I said.

Perido put his hands on his hips. "We had to, or else an infection would have spread. The scar from this will be bigger than the ones on your back." I lifted my head to speak but Perido went on. "I did not study them. We were more worried about your wound. You look concerned. Does it bother you that we saw them?"

I licked my lips. "They're just something that I'd like to forget. Something I want to keep to myself."

Perido tipped his head. "Max, they are a part of you. Do not forget them, accept them. There are things that I..." He broke off.

Johnny lifted his head. I could feel his breath on my neck.

"She's awake," Perido told his brother.

Johnny got up, jostling me. I turned onto my back so I could see him. Both Johnny and Perido squatted next to me, darker features on one side, lighter on the other."Hello," I said.

"You're awake," Johnny said, grinning.

"Finally," Perido muttered. The brothers exchanged looks and then rested their eyes back on me.

"You," I said, repeating my first words to Perido. "I am not lazy," I added. He laughed and Johnny looked confused. "Can I sit up?"

Johnny shook his head but Perido said, "Yes."

Together they lifted me. My wound pulled and stretched and I winced at the feeling, but soon I was sitting up with Johnny behind me so I could lean against his chest. His legs were on either side of me, and I rested my elbows on them.

"Are you hungry?" Perido asked. He handed me a small piece of bread and I ate it with haste. It tumbled down my throat.

"Water?" I said hoarsely.

Perido handed me a water skin. I was still sweating, but it was good to have nourishment.

"Avaline?" I asked the men.

Perido shrugged. "Out walking. She's watching for bandits too, making sure no one disturbs us while you are like you are."

My head began to spin, and my stomach churned. I became hotter.

"She should be back before dinner," Johnny said, but his voice was a hum in the back of my mind.

Adahlia began to speak and this time it was hard to push her away. My head rolled back and I strained to retain strength. I couldn't this time. My stomach seized and my wound pulsed. I fell over to one side and vomited, felt Johnny's hands trying to lift me. Perido's voice swirled away from me.

And then everything went black.

Voices buzzed in my head like bees, only louder, and they were drowning out everything else. Someone was moving me somewhere, hoisting me up clumsily. I could feel it in my side more than anything; the tear of unhealed skin ripping apart in strings of dried blood. I moaned and then the voices started to make sense.

"Careful."

"We have to get her back to the palace or she'll be a lot worse off."

And then I was on a horse wedged in front of someone in the saddle. His breath was heavy and a cold wind blew my hair all around my face, sweat chilling my skin.

Pounding of hooves were the next thing I could hear. My wound hurt like nothing else. It was a blunt and constant pain. The horse's body swung side to side, making me feel even more nauseated, but I didn't have the right mind to think about vomiting again. I couldn't function that complexly, it seemed.

A soft, deep voice was saying comforting words. I let them float on the horizon as I felt myself dip back into a dark pool of sleep and serenity, and the next time I woke up, I heard unfamiliar voices shouting and felt unfamiliar hands grabbing at me and lifting me down from the horse.

Through squinted eyes, grey walls closed in, carriages waited, and green flags fluttered. I closed my eyes and when I opened them once more, I was in a room, completely alone. Grey light entered from a break in the curtains and rain pounded on the walls outside. The hot air of a sickroom filled my nose and the door leading out had just closed.

* Johnny *

Father hadn't bothered to speak to Perido or me and even with us standing in his doorway, he didn't turn around. The study was small and cluttered with richly colored furniture, rugs and drapes. It was in the second highest tower in Valta, and had a view of nearly the entire kingdom. Papers were crammed on shelves, although it seemed like most were just thrown on the floor. The deep blues and greens that filled the room were enhanced by the warm glow of three torches strategically placed so they wouldn't catch anything on fire. Father had heard us come in, but was still looking out the window at the grey rain pounding on the castle walls. Water speckled and streaked down the window with rage, and with the same emotion, Father clenched his fists and pivoted to face us.

His aged features were stern and his eyes were fixed. We had entered with no word from him, and now I knew it would be best that we go. But this scolding was unavoidable and Perido and I would not wait any longer. We did not regret leaving the palace unattended. The only thing we regretted was that Max had gotten hurt.

"We demand a word," Perido said. I had not expected him to speak first, although, Perido often did things that were not expected of him.

"Granted," Father said. His crown was tipped to one side and he was wearing the robe he commonly wore in his study.

"Place all the blame on me, Father," I said in a rush. "I became frantic and did not think before I acted. And then I dragged my brother into my quest. Max had escaped the palace and I feared for her. She is important to not only me but also the kingdom. All the kingdoms. She is useless dead, so I went in search of her," I said.

Perido grabbed my wrist and squeezed until his grip was uncomfortable. "But I was the one to follow. I should have thought rationally, suggested that we request a guard to search for her, instead of putting ourselves in danger," he said.

Father looked at us, scratched the beard forming on his chin, and straightened his crown. "Do you regret this mistake?" Father asked.

Perido released my arm and stepped forward. "I do not, Father," he said. "I do not regret a thing."

The king adjusted his robes. "I was speaking to my other son, Perido. You are of no importance to the kingdom, and you often forget that your brother cannot be risked. Remember your place." Perido cast his eyes on the floor and stepped back. "First, Jonathan, you fell for a woman who is not your betrothed…"

"I have not met my betrothed," I said.

Father took a breath, resumed. "Second, you deliberately left the safety of the palace to run off and find this woman. You did not put just you and your brother…"

"And Avaline," I added.

Father took another breath. "In danger, you put the future of Valta in jeopardy," he said. Now he turned to Perido. "You," he said. "You are a disgrace. You followed your brother deliberately, something a king would never do. You had the chance to stop him in his flee, to keep him safe, and you let him down. You have continually let everyone down. A leader should never follow, and you proved to be the follower that you are. You are lucky that I do not cast you off into the streets."

Perido's eyes were still on the ground. "A king must know how to follow, so that he may be a better leader," he said quietly. He did not move, though I could see that his hands were shaking.

My body was boiling with anger. "Do not insult my brother," I said. "You will have no choice but to bow down to him; I decline the crown. You cannot disown your only heir. You will have to accept him for the king he will be, for the king he is. This is a man who cares for Valta much more than I ever will, and this is a man who will treat his kingdom with nothing but the highest respect and priority. Father, I have made my decision. I officially decline the crown. I nobly hand it to the deserving prince, and I will gladly serve under my brother's power. I believe in him completely. Regardless of what you will say, he is your son and he is your prince. Regardless of what you want, he will be king." They both looked stunned. Onto Perido's face crept a very small, private smile. He lifted his head and looked me in the eye.

Father's jaw tightened. "The girl, she did this," he yelled. "She convinced you to leave our kingdom."

I shook my head calmly. "My decision was my own," I said.

Father shook his head and slammed his fist down on his desk. Papers fluttered around, shuffled back onto the table. He leaned back in his chair, his demeanor suddenly quiet. "I should have known," he said. "I should have known from the day you left that you would not sway. You're a lot like I was, Johnny. A lot like my brother too. Neither of us wanted the crown either. I know how you're feeling, how horrible it will be for you to be married off and take the thrown. I was lucky, came to love it. But I should have more sympathy for you. I should be grateful that I *have* a son who wants to be king. My father did not."

"Grant me this, father. Have sympathy. Perido sits here eager, ready. It's time that you stop underestimating him," I said. I placed my hands on his desk and leaned forward, looked him in the eye. "If you have been through the same thing, felt as trapped as I feel now, how can you deny me?

The king took a deep breath "I can't." His voice was low. "I have no choice but to accept your decision. Perido, I congratulate you. We will declare this publicly in a month."

Perido bowed reverently. "I will treat this duty with nothing less than pride, dedication, and nobility. I thank you, my king."

Now I bowed. "I respect your acknowledgement and understanding of my choice, and I thank you for your kindness. I will serve Valta with energy and enthusiasm, but in distance to the seat of high power. Have a nice afternoon." And then I turned for the door. Father pivoted to face the rain outside again and Perido fell in step with me as we made our way down the stairs.

"That went well," Perido said.

I laughed. "He was calmer than I expected, but I suppose that's how Father is. He had no choice," I said.

"Thank you," Perido breathed. I knew he would be headed now to tell Avaline.

I shook my head. "I am the one who should give thanks. You have lifted the awful job off my shoulders," I said. "Congratulations."

He smiled. "Thank you."

I didn't speak. I merely nodded and headed down the hall for Max's room.

It had been ten days since Max had gotten hurt, nearly a week since she spoke, and five days since we arrived back at the palace. She hadn't woken up yet, and although she still breathed, it wasn't enough just to stand by her bedside.

A maid was wiping Max's forehead with a cool rag when I closed the door behind me. Immediately the woman bowed and scurried out, leaving me alone in the room. Max was not awake. I strode across the room and opened her curtains, went to her bedside.

Her skin wasn't as pale, but it had the same feverish tint as it did the day before. Her wound was healing slowly.

The hotness of the infection had fled throughout her veins the night we were still on the road, and she had been shivering with hot flashes the next morning. And she was still unconscious, even now.

I had been the one to let her leave. I had not kept a close enough eye on her.

I went to the window and watched the streaks of rain darting to the gardens outside.

The room began to blur as I remembered that dreaded night: Max was in my arms and I was shaking. Perido and Avaline had both insisted on changing her clothes and I finally agreed. We did it quickly and efficiently, only getting glimpses of the scars on her back. The vague image of the ones I did see haunted me. With every scar, there had been pain. It was hard to wrap my mind around that.

The wary light coming in from the window laid a hand on the smooth contours of her body. I stepped out of the line of grey radiance and treaded lightly over to her bedside. Looking down at her face, I told myself that no matter what happened, she would always be the one I cared for the most.

I bent over and gently kissed her forehead, smoothing her hair with my hand as I came up. Her eyelids fluttered this time and she shifted in her bed. She took three shaky breaths and I went to find the maid.

Chapter 11

* Max *

I kept my eyes closed as I heard the door gently slide and latch. Footsteps disappeared down a hallway. "Johnny?" I mouthed. I wasn't sure of the chances that it had been him, but I knew I was in the Valtan castle.

I opened my eyes and a damp grey light met them. Rain knocked on the walls and the windows like an unwanted guest. The curtains had been opened, and a draft was leaking in. It thinned out the hot, sick air. I lay in a bed of green silk sheets, and three other beds were placed in the big room, each empty. There was a table with jars of herbs and cups of water on top, and blankets and furs were piled up in a corner.

I sat up in my bed and threw the blankets off of my body. The stale air was smothering. I twisted my legs off the edge of the bed and felt my side prickle in pain, stretch and pull as I adjusted until my feet were solid on the ground. I ached in every muscle, but this pain wasn't nearly as extreme as before.

I wondered how long I had been there.

I braced my hands against the headboard of the bed and stood. I let go, wobbled, and fell to the ground. My muscles seized in pain, but I rolled to my side and used the bed to crawl back to my feet. This time I stood still, gained some balance, and then walked. I managed it all the way to the window before I had to tumble the rest of the way into the wall. Sliding to the ground, I put my back against the cold surface and sighed.

Looking down, I saw that I was dressed in a green and white nightgown. There was a thick, white bandage wrapped around my torso underneath. I stood back up and wobbled toward the door.

As I crossed the threshold I was embraced by the ghost of winter. A wave of chills cascaded down my back as I slid one hand along the wall and continued down the hallway. I didn't know where I was going, but I did not stop.

And then I thought of Johnny. I wished for a familiar face. Johnny or Avaline, or even Perido. What had happened to them?

Keeping my eyes on the floor and a hand on the wall for balance, I stumbled down a wide hallway. The green and white tile, the artwork and heavy doors, it all looked familiar, like in a dream. But something stopped me in my tracks. Someone caught my arm and gently turned me around so I could face him. Slowly I let my eyes wander from the feet, up the immense torso, and to the face of the person in front of me. He was a memorable face, but not one I was hoping for. Not anyone I could name, either.

The sun-dark skin, brown hair, those piercing blue eyes, welcoming and icy, every feature looked familiar. But I still couldn't remember who he was. He scratched his clean-shaven jaw and a smile was painted over his tight lips. His hand was still clutching my wrist, but I didn't try to pull away. I didn't have enough strength.

"From my gathered knowledge, you should still be in your sickroom, safe in bed," he said kindly, although his deep, stern voice was all but light. "But I have also found that you are not the one expected to be in a safe place for long, Max."

Frustrated that my own mind could not call forth this man's name I asked, "Who are you?" My voice was hoarse.

His fingers let my wrist slip and fall to my side. "Let's see if you can guess," he said, raising his hands in a challenging invitation. He continued in a boyish voice, "How did a girl like you get a jewel like that?" He broke off and kept his gaze on me. I lifted the hand that was free of the wall and felt my pendant against my chest. I was surprised, thankful that it was there.

"I watched over you for some time, Max," he said.

Thinking a moment, I realized who he was. I could almost feel the warm air wafting over the Fertile Hills. Taste the mint tea and the fresh apples that came with his memory. "Kye?" I asked. He waved a hand through the air in little circles that led him into a dramatic bow.

When he straightened he said, "Yes? Would I be wrong to guess you're surprised to see me?"

I shook my head and forced out a laugh.

"My, you're certainly more beautiful than I remembered you," he continued. "Though for many months it was only from afar. And don't tell Johnny I said that or he'd have me beheaded, I'm sure."

I didn't know if it was right for me to blush right then, but I couldn't help it. "He knows you're here?"

Kye nodded. "Of course! This is his home, his palace, I would expect him to know a lot about who comes and goes."

It is his kingdom, I thought, suddenly saddened. "So then why are you here? What happened? I knew you and your mother and the spies watched over me on Dela, but you disappeared so suddenly."

He glanced around. "That is a story that I will have to save for later," he said, sounding a little shaken. "Right now, I will walk you back to your room so you can rest." He placed a hand on the small of my back and walked.

"But I've been resting for days now," I said. "How long has it been?"

He started to walk again and I pivoted against the wall to walk beside him.

"I'm not really sure," he said. "Johnny told me that he arrived at the palace five days ago with you, Perido, and Avaline. He didn't say how long it has been since you acquired that ghastly wound."

I frowned. "Five days," I repeated.

He nodded.

I must have been unconscious that entire time.

After a few more steps we got back to my room and he stopped in the doorway as I started in.

"Here is where I must leave you for now, I was headed for a meeting with the king and I'm afraid I'm already late," he said.

I forced a smile.

"Very rude of me, I know, but I'm not used to being in the presence of such a beautiful woman. I'm sure the king will understand." He grinned.

"I expect you to tell me why you're here the next time I see you."

"At dinner, I presume. Or maybe after would be better. That is, if you're well enough," he said. He touched my cheek briefly.

"I could eat a horse and the rider," I said.

He gave me a single nod and started down the hall.

It had only been a few minutes when someone knocked on the door. I was seated in a chair by the window, watching the rain still coming down with purpose.

"Come in," I said quietly, but the door was already screeching open.

"You look very ugly in that dress," were the first words.

The door re-latched and I turned around and laughed, though it hurt my side. "Perido, why am I not surprised that it is you?"

"Because I'm the only one who would dare such a rude comment," he said, "but you must know I am kidding of course. You look very pretty." He strode over and sat in the chair next to mine.

"I liked the first comment better," I replied. "That way I have an excuse to stay in clothes that I'm used to. As for the sarcasm, it wouldn't be you without it," I said. "It is good to see you."

He grinned. "Good to see you, Max. Alive and well it seems. I wasn't expecting you to be awake just yet, but I had been hoping today would be the day."

"Well I am," I said. "Alive and awake."

He laughed.

"Where are Avaline and Johnny?"

"Avaline, I have no idea. I was looking for my brother, actually. He has been visiting your room often; I'm surprised he wasn't here," Perido said, he stood and poured two cups of water from a pitcher and handed one to me, sipped out of his own.

I shook my head. "I feel like I haven't seen him forever."

Perido let out a little laugh. "Hardly. He has barely left your side this whole time. But I can send him up when I find him myself, if you'd like." I nodded as he continued, "Anyway, I'm sure he hasn't told you the news, since you just woke up."

"That Kye is here?"

Perido shook his head.

"So what is it?"

"Oh, he'll have to tell you. But how did you know Kye was here?" Perido asked. "I only met him when he arrived, but Johnny said that you two had met him on Dela in your travels."

"I snuck out of my room for a test walk and I ran into him."

Perido crossed his hands over his chest and tipped his head to one side. "A test walk? And how did that go? I'm surprised you were standing at all with that fiend carved into your skin."

"I didn't get far and Kye quickly ushered me back to my room," I said.

"Well good. And who were you looking for? I assume you were looking for someone," he went on.

I shook my head. "No one."

He snorted in disbelief and then stood up, turning for the door. "Well, I'm off to find my brother, expect him to be up very soon. He'll want to see you after I've told him you are awake," he said.

"Thank you, Perido," I said.

He paused for a moment. "For what?"

"For helping me after my escape. I barely know you and you helped save my life," I said.

"It was my brother who went after you. I just followed. I trust him with my life," he said. "Anyone he loves, I have to love as well."

I didn't voice my wonder out loud. "Well thank you," I said instead.

"Don't give it a second thought."

Contrary to Perido's promises, Johnny didn't visit me. And the chance of seeing him, or even Kye, was lost when my fever spiked again that night and I became too sick to be at dinner. For the next two days the maid, Laura, kept me in bed with all sorts of herb juices in my stomach. She let me get up and walk around in the afternoons and helped me bathe, but I was still restless.

Avaline was the only one to visit me in those two days, although from time to time I could hear Perido's voice outside the door. I assumed Johnny was busy doing royal things. I doubted he wanted to talk to me.

But on the third morning, Laura came in and asked me if I felt well enough to take a walk through the gardens. "Why do you ask?" I said.

The maid curtsied again. "Prince Jonathan wishes to speak with you in the gardens if you are well enough."

"Really?"

"Yes, my lady. He wanted me to ask you, and I tell his words: 'I assume she would appreciate an excuse to leave her room, but if she is not well, tell her I will come to her.'" Laura said, imitating his deep voice. She returned to her high tones. "So would you like me to dress you?"

I laughed at her imitation. "Only if I can wear pants," I said. Her round, weathered face creased in question. "Yes," I said plainly. She curtsied and then scurried over to an old wooden dresser and pulled out a set of clothing.

The maid dressed me quickly and efficiently and soon I was wearing my old clothing from Dela. She handed me a thick cloak and slowly led me through the wide and impressive halls of the castle, down to the main floor, and stopped in front of a door.

"You're sure you are well enough to walk outside, my lady?" she asked before letting me leave. "You are still recovering and I wouldn't wish for you to undergo more stress than necessary."

I nodded. "I'll be fine. It's only raining a little?"

"Yes, my lady. You will tell us if your clothing is too thin for the cold?"

I nodded again, this time more impatiently. "I will."

She curtsied and then spoke to one of the guards standing at the door. He opened it and let me step outside into a small courtyard smothered in a damp grey glow. There was a light rain drizzling down, making the leaves on the spring-ready plants snap with the prickly droplets.

I hobbled down the wet path, looked around at the ponds and statues and flowerbeds, all shaped and pristine as a peasant would expect a palace garden to appear.

"I'm glad to see you're well enough to walk out in the rain," Johnny said, coming from a side path and falling in step with me.

I startled slightly. "Anything to escape that prison," I breathed.

He smiled and stopped me by a touch on the arm, faced me. Suddenly he pulled me toward him and wrapped his arms around me.

I grunted in pain and he gentled his hug, but didn't let go. "I'm so sorry for everything Max," he whispered in my ear. He felt warm and perfect against me and I almost forgot to speak.

"You didn't do anything wrong, Johnny," I said, pulling away. "You saved my life."

He shook his head. "I shouldn't have let you go. I was not watchful."

I placed a hand on his arm for balance, but he seemed to take it as an act for comfort. "I wanted to relieve you of my problems," I said. "But you were right. I cannot run away any more. It is time I face this. Please do not burden yourself. You have many things to worry about. Your kingdom, your arranged marriage."

Johnny shook his head. "This is my journey too. You and I both know that I have made this my concern from day one. From that first encounter. I'm not leaving now."

We walked another few steps into the fog. Johnny ushered me down to a stone bench and I drew my hood over my head so the rain didn't give me a chill. He scooted closer, sharing his warmth.

Next to me, I could hear Johnny swallow, take a deep breath, and speak in a very low voice like he was telling me a secret. I let my eyes travel over to his as he spoke. The grey sky made them a deep velvety brown with blue flecks instead of gold. All the steel in Cavail couldn't measure up to their inflexibility.

"About the kingdom," he started, breaking the impossible stare. "Perido and I spoke with my father days ago, before you had woken up. He was furious, especially with Perido. He threatened to disown him, but I think it is I who he wants to disown now." His eyes met mine again and I felt the fever freeze in my veins. "In case you haven't already realized, I hate it here," he said. "I find it a close partner with physical torture, being watched everywhere I go. The very thought of having to live like this for the rest of my life makes me sick and the only thing that sounds worse to me is an arranged marriage. So Max, I'm telling you right now: there was nothing I wanted more than to decline the crown and leave this place with you at my side." He stopped and brushed the hair out of my face, tipped my chin up so the shadows of my hood disappeared. "So you want to know what I told my father?"

I shrugged mutely and he took his hand from my chin, placed it back in his lap. "I told him that I officially declined the crown. That he could not disown Perido if he was the only heir. I haven't spoken to my father since."

I couldn't move. "You can't do this," I said, though relief flooded through my body so rapidly I felt like I would drown. "You're not leaving your home because of me, are you?"

"No, I'm doing this for myself. And I will not leave completely, though I will surely not be in the line of focus. I never wanted the kingdom. It was always Perido's dream, ever since we were little."

"And you're telling the truth?" I whispered.

Johnny did not speak for a moment. Something passed over his face and he said quietly, "I'd never lie to you."

I nodded. "Okay, so then tell me this: Do you pity me, or is there another reason why you're still here? I have asked you time and time again, but you have never told me why you have helped me over and over. Do you love me, Johnny? Is that what this is?"

He held my eyes so perfectly that I started to doubt if I had spoken out loud. But then he whispered, with a surrendering note in his voice, "You know every single answer."

I shook my head. "I want you to tell me."

He paused. "Do I love you?" He shrugged, shifting his weight. "It's something like that. I could never leave your side without a weight in my heart pulling me back." He touched my hand briefly. "But I do not know how you feel about me, and I wonder."

"Are you expecting an answer?" I asked flatly.

"Only if you're willing to tell me the truth."

I cast my eyes away, thinking for a moment. "Then I guess this conversation is over," I said.

Johnny breathed deeply and stood up. "Good, because I am starving and cold. Will you be joining us for dinner?"

"Only if I can make it there," I said.

He laughed and helped me up. "I think we can manage." He put his arm around me and aided me back to the palace without another word.

* Johnny *

A small knock came on the door and moments later Perido burst in, followed by Max. "It's my room," he said to her. "No need for quiet knocking." He surveyed the room, sat down.

I was sitting in the chair opposite his, speaking with Avaline who was standing behind Perido's chair, gazing out the window. She had been reviewing the recipe and objects obtained in the Vault for days. Perido ushered her to a place next to Max on the bed, and reseated himself. "I wonder how Valta will handle a madman at her helm."

"Well," I said to him. "Her royals are all madmen. I couldn't break the cycle." We laughed, settled when we heard another knock on the door.

"Who's there?" Perido asked.

"It's Kye, may I enter?"

Perido surveyed the room again, then said, "Yes."

Kye walked in and closed the door. "I see that this is where everyone went," he said lightly. "I just came from a meeting with the king. There is some news you need to hear."

I glanced at Perido.

"Shouldn't the king himself be informing us of the latest politics in Valta?" Perido asked.

"He wished for me to tell you because it involves information that I myself gathered. He is a busy man, as you should know," Kye said. He dragged a stool over to join us.

"I believe I can speak for both my brother and I that we know very well how busy a king can be," I said rudely.

"Johnny," Avaline warned.

"Oh, I apologize if I seemed haughty. I merely wanted to lighten the mood," he said.

"We still don't know why you're here," Max said. "Or at least I don't."

Kye flickered his serene blue eyes over at her and smiled perfectly. "I believe Perido knows, but Johnny hasn't taken the time to ask either," he said.

"Well tell us," I said coolly.

"It's really not the story for tonight, I don't think," he said quietly. "We could talk about something else."

"They should know, Kye," Perido said. "After all, they met you before..." he trailed off.

Kye looked from one face to another, clasped his hands in his lap. "A few months after we helped you escape the Alician spies, more came," he said. "Mother was head of the Delan spies, and though she was small and did not fight well, she was witty, and very much a part of their family, as you know. They wished for her to be safe but the Alicians came continually, looking for you," Kye directed his speaking to Max, smiled at her. She smiled back. "I assume you also know that we watched over Max for many months, but as more Alicians came, the situation turned dire. The Delan spies made a deal with the royals of Dela, hoping that they could protect Mother as well as continue to watch over Max. It was arranged that Mother would be interviewed and given the security of the palace at no cost. The Delan spies would still be about their business and speak with her often about their plans because she was, after all, their leader. She would be safe from the harm of the Alicians' interrogation, and live happily amongst the king, queen, and princess of Dela. As you know, the Delans are a welcoming people. I believe that if they could, the royals would house every one of their citizens within the safety of their palace." He paused and looked past Perido and me out the window at the dwindling light outside. "Mother, upon much convincing, agreed to the plan under the condition that she was not confined to the palace at all times." Kye met my eyes a moment, then continued. "My mother met a man inside the palace, though I do not know who he was. Quite recently, he invited her to a drink in town, and she accepted. My father was long gone and this man was kind, I won't elaborate.

"As I heard it, some strange men entered the bar where this man and my mother were drinking and left near the time the man and my mother left," Kye continued. "From what was seen on the streets, my mother had been hit until she was unconscious and her companion had been murdered and left in the street for all to see."

The image of the man we had seen in Dela flooded back to me, and I could hear Max take a quick breath. I cursed silently.

"Mother spoke of the night to the royals an eve later. That next morning, she ventured out of the palace to visit the port. She always loved the water. It was the last I saw of her." He stopped there, choking back the tears in his voice.

"I'm sorry," Max said. She reached from the bed and placed a hand on his leg for a moment.

Kye went on. "They found her body but I never looked. The spies of Alice must have been humiliated by their slip in revealing information, so they disposed of the problem." He choked off again and we all sat in silence for a moment.

"And I decided to come here. The royals of Dela gave me their seal and informed me that the Valtan Guard would let me in if I showed it to them, so that's what I did. In all the chaos, the spies lost track of Max, so I hoped that she'd be here with Johnny and I could tell you both my story."

I exchanged glances with her and she flicked me a crooked, ironic smile. It warmed me a little.

"You were the only ones I thought to go to, after my mother was suddenly gone," Kye added.

"But the Delan spies?" Max asked.

Kye shrugged. "I spoke with them, but I was never close to them like my mother was. They were there when I left Dela, wishing me the best, but though they were family to us, I could not stay with them. I was not a spy."

"So what is the news with my father?" Perido asked.

Kye didn't seem to notice the sudden change in subject. "Your father has officially decided to send out the question of alliance to the Four Kingdoms and, of course, Dela as well. This war is very real and it is expected to happen."

"When are they being sent out?" Perido asked, a note of urgency in his voice.

"Next week," Kye said.

I shared a look with Perido.

"And?" Max asked.

Kye sat back a little. "I offered to be one of the messengers, so he decided to send me back to Dela as a familiar face."

Perido said, "It seems you would fit the standard for a messenger quite well."

Kye smiled, if not a bit distantly. "I thank you," he said. "I think I should get going now, it's getting late." He stood and left the room with little more conversation.

After Kye's footsteps could no longer be heard, Avaline stood and went to the far side of the room, where the items from the Vault and the nearly-empty vial of dragon's blood were scattered on a table. She fingered the vial, rocked the last drops of white blood and lily nectar back and forth in the bottom. After a moment she said, "We need to go back to the Vault."

I sat up straight, turned to Avaline. "Why must we venture there again?"

Her eyes glittered. "Because I ran out of blood," she said, tossing me the vial. "And I have a note to return."

Chapter 12

* Johnny *

Upon Avaline's words, we ran down the halls toward the Vault. It was dark in the palace, and though the last servants were still awake, we could not waste time: war was coming. We would gather the white blood and nectar as medicine for Max during the releasing. Av said that Max would feel much agony, but that the liquid would dampen it.

"Here," Avaline whispered. She lifted the tapestry from the hole, all the while keeping her eyes wide for a servant walking down the hall. Perido grabbed a torch and went into the secret passage, Avaline close on his heels. I followed, leading Max down the abandoned hall. When we came around the bend, we found Perido already hunched over the marble with Avaline standing above him holding the torch. It flickered abnormally and she watched it, moved her hand over and through it, making it dance.

I bent to help Perido move she slab of marble aside, revealing the stairway into the depths of the palace. Avaline glowed slightly, handed the torch to Perido once again.

I ushered everyone inside, placing a hand on Max's back as she passed me. She met my eyes briefly, but her expression was cold. "Hurry now," I said as I began down the stairs.

"Not so fast," said a voice from above, "I am coming as well."

Perido rushed past everyone on the stairs to see who had spoken, though I'm sure he knew before he could see the speaker's face. Perido looked angry, frightened, and shocked all in one as he gazed out of the hole. I felt very much the same, though I tried not to show it. Father was crouched above us, not questioning our venture, but asking to come along.

"Do you know where we are going?" Perido asked him.

"I've heard the legends," was all Father said.

I looked down at Avaline, who had begun to glow. With her rising brightness, Father's eyes widened. "Oh," he said, "I hope I will not be adding one too many."

I shook my head and Perido said, "Not at all, the Vault is big enough for armies."

"You really know where it is?"

Perido grinned. "Trust your new heir," he said.

"Have you been there before?" Father said, a hint of anger lacing his tone.

I nodded. "Yes. I will explain as we walk," I said.

It took the king a long moment, but he straightened on his legs, stepped into the hole in the palace, and began to follow us deeper into the passage without another word.

At the bottom of the stairs, Perido began to sing and lead the way. I ushered Father behind Avaline, but he did not mention his fear for her. He was intent on our path, on our adventure.

Along our passage, Perido sang, "*Banilgar/He comes to a crossing in the road/Go left/And there will be no more warmth here/He'll be all alone.*" Father looked surprised, but when I began to sing along with my brother, he sang too. "*Banilgar/ He passes right along/He passes all that's left/He passes three civilians comforting their children/Go right away/Banilgar.*" We made our turns and soon Father was nearly dancing through the passage. Perido's voice carried us through the darkness with enthusiasm. "*Banilgar/The journey's almost over/Don't slow because you're covered,*" The king came close to knocking his head, but did not. Avaline bent lower than was needed, and I recalled that she had bumped her head the last time.

"*Banilgar/The hero of the Valtan Land/Guide us to the hidden pass/Where Valta's love of magic has,*" Perido paused in the cavity, then sang, "*No end.*"

Father simply gasped at the large wooden door. He patted my hand and smiled at Perido. "Perhaps he will grow into a fine king," he whispered to me.

"Perhaps," I said, knowing well that there was no question about Perido's abilities as king. He would rule with confidence and grace.

Avaline pulled the vial of dragon's blood and lily nectar and painted the last drop over the keyhole. We waited a moment, but nothing happened. Avaline stood there, staring at the keyhole, and took a breath of relief as it began to glow and the door clicked, swung open.

On the sight, Father swayed on his feet. "Magnificent," he muttered. Perido led the king inside, presented the Vault to his father.

Avaline smiled at me, then Max, and walked into the brightly lit hall.

We stayed down in the Vault well into the night. I told Father about our plan with the items we gathered; we could release Adahlia without permanently harming Max. He did not speak as I explained what we had done. I thought he would be angry, but he simply nodded, scratched his chin, adjusted his robes, or touched the gray hair that usually had a crown nested among it.

When I was finished, he seemed to ponder something. "I think I have an idea about how that would work, my son, and it would solve our problem with Alice as well," Father said finally.

"Perido and I were thinking the same thing. May we all meet tomorrow night to discuss?" I asked.

"Yes," Father said.

"Father, this war…" I trailed off and spread my hands.

"It is not a war yet, my son, only severe doubt of safety for the kingdoms. Alice knows that she is weak in support and that is why she searches for the goddess, so she may gain control. Do not think of it as a war, think of it as a perspective, a hunger for power. It is nothing less than a hunger for love, or a hunger for freedom." He looked me square in the face, looked at Max, back to me, continued. "It is dangerous, senseless, but it is planted deep in the hearts of the Alicians. All we must do is take away Alice's chances to succeed. She must come to rationality and I believe Valta is the only kingdom with the means and the bravery to face Alice and take away her greed. We will simply let her fall back into her place among the other towns and kingdoms in Cavail. But," Father said, waving his hand through the air, "let us speak of this later."

"Tomorrow," I said quietly.

"Yes," Father said. "When we are fresh."

We walked under the bright chandeliers for a long time after that, waiting for Avaline to fill her needs in the Vault. I found her reading a passage from a book, smiling at the wrinkled pages. Father kept walking, and I went to read Av's book as well, but she closed it, raised her eyes to meet mine.

"What is it?" I asked.

"An old story," she said. "One that brings me great joy."

"Will you keep the book?" I said.

Avaline shook her head. "I should not. It brings me great sorrow and great anger as well."

"It is a true story," I said quietly.

Av nodded, placed a hand over my heart. "Do not let another dictate how this grows, Johnny," she said as she patted my chest. "As soon as you lose control of your own heart, there is nothing left, do trust me. Never lose sight or feeling, it is your own, and only you may direct it," she said. Max came from behind some shelves, moved toward us. Perido led the king in our direction as well. But Avaline leaned in close. "Do you remember when we met, Johnny?" she asked swiftly.

"Yes," I said.

"You had asked about my being magic," she said.

"You told me that you had no magic, only skill," I recalled.

Av nodded, grabbed my arm. "I am no more magic than you, Prince," she said.

I could smell her breath, sweet and clear.

"We both have hearts, and that is where it all lies. Mine simply has a larger capacity for fire and healing than yours, but we are the same. Remember this, Johnny: You do not find magic here in this room, though it seems to be filled with it. The magic is here," she rubbed her hand over my heart. The others disappeared behind an isle of objects and Avaline leaned in closer. "Remember that, Johnny." She leaned into me and kissed my brow very briefly. It was not out of love or desire. It was as if she had stamped her words onto me, imprinted them into my mind. And I had felt nothing but that intention.

"Do not think loosely of this," she said. A warm hand came to touch where she had kissed. "It is so you may remember."

"I know," I said. "Thank you Avaline, your friendship is more than I could have asked for."

She bowed her head. "And yours, Johnny, means more to me that you will ever know. You have taught me to love Valta again."

I did not know what she meant by that, but I took it to be personal. Everyone arrived where she and I were standing, then. They had not heard our conversation, not seen the kiss. No one looked surprised or angry or hurt, only curious. Max came to stand by me and placed her hand on mine for a short moment. My chest warmed.

Avaline disappeared, came back, and slipped six vials of dragon's blood and lily nectar into the folds of her dress. "I may not be back for a long time," she said quietly. "Now, let us return to the light. There is less air here and my fire feels as though it is dwindling."

"Indeed," Father said. "My wife will be wondering why I have not yet returned to our bed."

It took us no time to leave the Vault, though we all paused as the doors closed and the keyhole ceased to glow. Perido led the way back out, though Father or I could have done it too, knowing the song in full, forward and back. When we arrived in the palace again, it was completely dark, all except for Perido's torch and Avaline's slight glow. The Kingdom of Valta was slumbering.

We returned to our rooms with little talk. The king left first, turning down the hallway that led him to the royal wing, where the king, queen, and any young royal children stayed. Down that hall were also the stairs to his study and the rooms of many high ranking royal guardsmen.

Silently, Max headed down the hallway to her room.

"Perido, Avaline, goodnight," I said. Perido walked Avaline to his room. She often stayed there, looking out the window and reading his books while he slept peacefully. Their closeness was sweet and the thought that Perido could be close to another in the way he was close to me reminded me of his capacity of acceptance and love. He would make a fine king.

I entered my room, closed the door, and collapsed on my bed. As I drifted into sleep, my mind rushed around Avaline's words from the Vault. It had made Perido, Max, and me more magical. And I fell asleep at the thought.

In the morning, we all climbed the long spiral stairway and met in the king's study. Perido and I sat in our usual chairs and the women were given stools.

"What did you find that first time in the Vault, Avaline?" Father asked. All the small talk in the room fell silent upon his voice and Avaline rested her eyes plainly on him. I expected him to flinch under her stare, but he did not. His fear for her seemed to have diminished.

"We found a recipe," she said. "A series of events to be preformed to release Adahlia from Max. A way other than death."

"Magic," the king said.

I expected Avaline to disagree, but she looked at me, smiled, and turned back to the king. "If that is what you would prefer to call it, then yes."

"What does the recipe call for?"

"We gathered items in the Vault listed on the scroll, Avaline has them at the moment," I said.

Max made a small, brief sound, shifted in her seat.

"And how do you wish to perform this final event of the goddess?" the king asked.

I leaned forward. "We must do it so that Alice can watch."

"Indeed," the king said, scratching his chin. He adjusted his crown. "We can use Max as leverage, show Alice that we have found Adahlia. Show Alice that she has lost."

"So not only will we be releasing the goddess from Max, we will also be ruining Alice's rebellion," I said.

Avaline nodded. "Yes."

"But that could backfire," I said. "Bortal would be offended if we ignored her. Oslo is a kingdom, she'll want to be a part of this."

"How can we do that?" Max asked. "Even if all the kingdoms were present, Valta still would be the only one releasing the goddess, the only one getting rewarded."

"That could cause problems for us," Father said. "We'd be opening ourselves for a larger rebellion, with all the kingdoms against us, if we aren't careful."

"But what if," Perido paused, thinking. He'd been quiet until now. "What if all the kingdoms performed the recipe, the releasing? That way, each kingdom rests on an even playing field again. They would all be equal."

The king nodded. "Yes, that is a good point. We should make all the kingdoms neutral again. Avaline, is it possible to organize the event in that way?"

Avaline bowed her head. "Yes, as long as I am not interrupted. This must be done properly."

"Then may we meet this afternoon to organize this in more depth?" The king asked Avaline. "I want to see the, ah, ingredients to this recipe as well."

"Yes," Avaline said, "that is a good idea."

I spent the rest of the day in my bedchambers, bathing, reading, eating, and resting. It was dark and rainy outside when I heard a small knock on my door. I stood, opened it to see Max standing in the hall. She had no shoes on, no vest, only a pair of loose trousers and a wrinkled shirt. Her hair cascaded around her face and the only thing that appeared to be in place was her pendant, which hung perfectly in the center of her chest.

"Come in," I said quietly.

"Alright," she said. She sat on the bed with an evident strain and crossed her legs. I sat next to her, noticing the way the candlelight and the outside grayness mingled to illuminate her face.

"How is your wound?" I said, trying to break the silence. Her expression was solemn.

"It's sore," she said.

"Why are you here?" I asked.

Her face tightened. "I wanted company. Should I go?"

"No, you're welcome here." I placed a hand on her leg.

She glanced at the window and sighed. "I never thought I'd be somewhere like this."

"Valta?"

Her eyes were soft when they met mine. "Somewhere where I have no control over what happens."

"I don't understand. Your whole life has been dictated by others, dictated by chance."

She shook her head. "When I was a slave, it was solidly in my control whether I was treated poorly or well. I could behave, or I could not, but my actions drove what happened," she said.

I brushed a strand of hair from her face.

"The goddess was not my choice, but I was the one who chose what to do next. I always knew what was happening, or enough of it to feel safe among people I didn't trust."

"You don't trust me?" I asked, interrupting.

She blinked. "I trust you more than anyone else, and I fear that." The chill in the room intensified. "But now my fate rests in the hands of Avaline, the others releasing Adahlia. I can't control what happens, if I die or if I live. And frankly I do not know what to fear more, because if I live I have nowhere to go. You and Avaline and Perido are not bound to me."

"But we are," I said, standing. A smile brushed her lips while confusion creased her brow. "You're part of our lives now, Max. We help because we can, because you mean a lot to us, goddess or not. When you survive the releasing, you will still have us here for you." She touched my leg very lightly, met my eyes. I went on. "And you've never had control besides the decisions you've made. You did not choose to be a slave, or have the goddess enter you. You did not choose to meet me. You have made the best out of what you got, and that is not control, that is living, Max. But remember this: you do not need to rely only on yourself. Avaline, Perido," I paused, "We are all here for you."

She smiled again and this time it stayed on her lips, lit up into her eyes. "Thank you," she said.

I shook my head. "Thank you."

She stood up and rushed into me. I held her while she shook, whimpering. Her breath was heavy on my neck, her hands spread wide on my back. I ushered her to the bed, told her to sleep. It took her a while to calm herself, but when she did sleep, it was as if she floated on the surface of the green sheets, a flower on a lake. I stayed there for hours while she slept, on my back listening to the rain still coming down in solid walls outside the castle, her hand in mine.

* Max *

I opened my eyes and ran my fingers across the silk sheets. In the dim, gray light I could see Johnny's outline next to me, his stare content on the ceiling. I propped myself up with one elbow and looked around the room. The candles were extinguished, most of them forming pale gray lumps of wax on their trays. There was no light to see by except what leaked in from outside, shards of moonlight.

I sat up a little more and glanced toward the window. Rain was still falling, only now in light boughs of mist rather than the earlier downpour. The clouds were thin; the moon was shining through brightly.

"It's calm on mornings like these," Johnny said softly.

I nodded, but he still lay on his back, eyes on the ceiling. "Quiet," I agreed.

He sat up and looked down at me with a changed expression on his face. "You look fresh," he said.

I sat up slowly, feeling every dreadful tug and pull of my wound. "I'm not as tired as I have been."

He shook his head. "No, not from sleep. You look different somehow."

"Well thank you, then."

He looked away. "Are you happy there is hope for you? With Adahlia?" He clasped his hands together.

I frowned. "Are you okay?"

He looked at me so instantly, my breath caught in my throat. "I'm fine."

"Something's bothering you," I insisted.

He sighed. "I've just been thinking too long I guess. I haven't slept."

"Tell me."

His expression softened. "I can't stand the idea of this recipe failing. I know what will happen to you if it does. And the dangers of the other kingdoms being there, participating, are huge. Where will we do this? It has to be neutral, but Bortal hasn't crossed the wall in hundreds, possibly thousands of years. How will she handle it? How many guards will Alice bring? She is uprising and there will be attempts to ruin this compromise."

I grinned at him.

"What?"

"These are matters for the king, for the heir. You are neither, why worry? You do not have a kingdom to protect."

A smile touched his lips, then was gone. "But it all comes down to you. That's my concern. I have you to protect, and you are more than a kingdom, in my eyes."

I felt a touch of redness come to my cheeks. "Well..." I trailed off, consumed by thought.

"What?"

"Have you been to Shor? It is just south of the Great Barrier isn't it? Open fields, and the travel is short," I suggested.

"Smart idea," but that wasn't Johnny's voice.

Perido closed the door behind him and silently went across the room, sat on the bed with Johnny and me.

"What are you doing here?" I said.

Perido's grin was ironic. "I could ask the same of you."

"I fell asleep here. By accident," I added hurriedly, a bit embarrassed. "Now, why are you here? It's not a usual hour to be visiting Johnny."

The brothers exchanged a humored look.

"Actually it is," Perido said. "Now, I wanted to discuss the very topic I walked in on, and frankly, I'm glad I walked in on conversation, rather than something else." Perido only paused a moment for emphasis. "We need to speak with Avaline to hear about her conversation with the king. There are details in this plan that need to be revised."

"Like what?" Johnny asked.

"Shor sounds good, actually. It is open, fairly central as far as the kingdoms go, and away from civilization in the chance that war breaks out. Very clever thinking, Max. Have you been there?"

I shrugged. "Once, maybe. I do not remember it well, but I know it is mostly fields, from the talk I've heard. South of the wall, so Bortal will not go far," I said.

Perido seemed to think for a moment. "Johnny, Shor is open. If Alice decides to rebel, she will have three other kingdoms, and Dela, possibly, on her back in an instant."

"Alice is not stupid, brother. She will not act if she has no advantage. Only a madman would rush his kingdom into failure. She has no choice but to agree to this compromise. If she refuses, she has no leverage, and less power than the kingdoms who reaped the goddess's rewards. If she comes and rebels, she will be pummeled into the ground by her sister kingdoms," Johnny said. His deep voice carried through the darkened room, sounded stark against the night.

There was a light rap on the door and the three of us looked toward it. Without waiting for permission to enter, the door opened and Avaline stepped across the threshold. She cocked her head and small sparks emanated off of her hair. She was glowing more than usual. The dead fire in the hearth caught on the blackened logs and came to life. Her body light ceased.

Avaline's purple eyes fixated on us. "Good to see all of you."

"We're just speaking about the recipe, the final event for the goddess," Johnny said.

In a flurry of her tattered dress she was seated on the bed between Perido and me. "I know, I heard you from outside the door," Avaline said. "I spoke with the king earlier tonight about how this will be done, and his ideas are good. We had not decided where to go, but I heard someone here say Shor."

Perido nodded. "Max did. I think it is safest."

"I agree," Johnny said.

"As do I." Avaline paused. "Max are you settled on Shor?"

I shrugged. "It is out of my hands, isn't it?"

"No," Avaline said. "It is up to you after a certain point. The kings and queens and members of the kingdoms and I may perform what the recipe entails, but in the end, it is you. You are our focus. You must be strong. Do you understand?"

"Yes," I said.

Perido shifted on the bed. "Is everything ready, Avaline?"

She placed a hand on his knee and looked into his eyes. "I will alert the king of our adjustments to the plan. After that, he will send word to the kingdoms. We are ready," she said. "But I have a fear."

"And what is that?" Perido asked.

Avaline took her hand from him as if she had forgotten it was there. "Cooperation," she said. "Alice may sabotage this plan. Not by rebelling right then and there, but by holding onto her ingredient. I must give the kingdoms their pieces to add before the ceremony begins but the recipe is dead without all the ingredients. What if she holds back? A rogue plan in Alice could kill Max and worse. By letting Alice partake in this, we are giving her leverage."

"Exactly," Perido said, looking to Johnny, then back to Avaline.

"So then what do we do? Perform it on our own after all? Just Valta?" I asked.

Johnny shook his head. "We go along with the united releasing," he said. "She will be under the pressure of all the other kingdoms. She will have no choice but to cooperate. There is no gain if she doesn't."

"But she will have an ingredient. What about her leverage? It is small, but she may use it, regardless of if there's a gain," Perido said. "The king may not act with any sense. He may just use what he has."

"But Valta has the most leverage of all," Johnny said quietly.

"And what is that?" I asked.

He grinned. "You."

Chapter 13
Three weeks later...

* **Johnny** *

The sun sprinkled golden dust along the slivery Valta Canal and the crisp morning air filled my lungs, bathed me in light. Two ships were already on their way to the Northwest Island, full of soldiers, and ours was just setting sail with its own set of guards. Oslo and Alice would already be there, camped in their orange and golden tents on the fields of Shor. Bortal was rallying her troops for this particular meeting, striped in crimson red, and Valta had agreed to be the last to arrive, her green flags proud. Dela was to set sail as well, for in the agreement among the hardheaded rulers, it came to a common accord that the Fertile Island would receive her own blessing as a new kingdom. The reward of the goddess was held only to the original Four. Dela would be a witness.

Much had been decided already. Alice was to be almost naked of guards while in Shor, but would receive the goddess's rewards nonetheless. Bortal was expected to sail down the coast to Mala as Oslo, Valta, and Dela would, and her freedom constraints would be discussed later. There was no need for complications.

All was set for the next day, but I was taking this one slowly.

Max was in her temporary room in the hull of the boat with Avaline, going through the items required for the event as well as getting comforted by the wise woman. I was with Perido, discussing mild topics as we kept our eyes on our destination. Father was in his vessel suite, guarded by five men as we spoke and at all times until he was back safe at the castle. He was busy going over the messenger's notes and agreements he had received by the other kingdoms.

"And to think we never once thought our sword skills would be that handy, and for such a use too. Who would have guessed it?" Perido was saying.

I knew the story well. He was reminiscing on one of our childhood adventures, one of the many that seemed so trivial now.

Perido placed his hand on my shoulder and squeezed. "It'll be alright, Johnny. Everything is in place. Father has mapped this out a hundred times in his mind already, I'm sure. He has been ever since we proposed the plan. You know him. And Avaline seems confident as well."

"Thanks Perido," I said. "For everything. You've been nothing but kind to me since the beginning."

He bowed slightly. "I'd do anything for you, Brother." He patted my shoulder again and strode away without another word.

"Lovely day," came a most wonderful voice. Max strode up to my side, leaned on the wooden railing, and took a deep, shaky breath of sea air.

"Yes," I said.

Her green eyes flickered with a small wildness that I had never seen before.

"Nervous?" I asked.

Her shoulders rose and fell in one fluid motion and she spread her hands. "Secure, insecure, and everything between," she said. "You?"

"I feel similar," I said. The water was glistening with the afternoon sun. The day was slipping.

"And frankly I'm not sure what I prefer. Security or fright."

"What do you mean?" I said.

"I'm not certain. I don't really know *how* to feel. Should I be nervous? Calm? In both settings I feel vulnerable." Her forehead creased in thought. "It's all relative to the circumstance I guess."

* Max *

We stood quietly against the rail until we could see our destination. Low piers hung out from the land, tattered, lonely.

Johnny seemed to startle out of a thought when the port of Mala came into view.

He turned to me. "I have something for you," he said, touching my arm. He disappeared into the hull of the boat and came back a moment later, a hand in his pocket. "I believe we have had these among us for too long."

Johnny pulled out a ring of keys.

At their sight, I sucked in a mouthful of air, let it out not as steadily as I had hoped. "Why do you still have those?" I said. "Where is the tag?"

"The tag is in Valta, locked. It will never be opened again, not with the keys gone. I hoped that we could cast these into the water. We do not need them anymore," he said, jingling the keys a little.

"Why did you keep them for so long?"

He handed them to me; they were cold and heavy in my hands.

"When you stayed on Dela, you gave them to me. They were the only piece of you I had. I kept them so that I would not forget you," Johnny said.

"You do not wish to rid of their partner as well? The keys kept me bound but the slave cuff gave me more grief, caused more pain."

Johnny squeezed the railing, released. "I wanted to keep the tag. It reminds me of when we met."

I laughed briefly and it seemed to startle him. I lifted the keys over the water. "Then we will let these go, never to lock or unlock the cuff again. They will have no power at the bottom of the ocean."

I did not let go. I pulled them back from out over the water, looked at the prince by my side.

"What is it?" he said.

"Let's do this together," I said, lifting the keys again.

Johnny took hold of the ring. Our fingers wrapped around the metal together, we lifted the keys high above the sea, high above our heads. "Ready?" Johnny said.

"Yes."

"Alright. One, two," Johnny paused, looked into my eyes, and held them as he said, "three."

The keys made only a small splash when they hit the water. Insignificant. "Thank you," I said. Johnny bowed his head and I walked down into the hull of the boat.

We arrived at Mala soon thereafter. The traveler's town had been expecting the Valtan ships specifically; when we got there the little streets were overwhelmed with soldiers under the rich green Valtan seal. No one else was around; store windows were covered with sheets and all doors and windows were shut.

I walked with Johnny, Avaline and Perido by our sides, a line of four down the empty cobbles. Leading the way, on the edges of the street, and behind us, there were Valtan guards. The king had his own specific entourage of ten.

Though there were no town's people in sight, there was much whispered conversation. The guards seemed to be wary of Avaline, but I could not blame them. Her dress was tattered and flowing, as if it were made of satin and autumn leaves. Her tattoos were in plain sight, and certainly the epitome of strangeness on such a beautiful young woman. Her golden hair emanated no sparks, yet still glowed in the twilight. She was beautiful and intimidating all in one.

In all the chaos of my mind, thoughts racing, the goddess whispering again, I had hardly noticed Johnny reach for my hand. His was warm in contrast to mine, but he seemed to want to comfort me. I knew I looked anxious. Avaline made it a point to place her hand on the small of my back once in a while, as if to steady my feet. My pendant seemed to burn a hole in my chest, the amber trying to draw the goddess out as we walked.

"Are you okay?" Johnny asked quietly. The buildings were becoming fewer.

I nodded blankly, looked past the guards, past the last inns and taverns to the fields of Shor beyond. The tents of Oslo, Dela, and Alice glistened in the very last shards of sunlight, and looked even more magnificent with the fresh green hills and the pink clouds among and above them.

"She's ready," Avaline told Johnny.

I sighed and agreed, "Ready. Yes."

"We'll take care of you," Perido reminded.

Avaline touched the small of my back once again and smiled down at me. Her eyes glittered and sparked like a flame itself and with a simple stroke of my back I felt warmer inside.

I touched my pendant and found it cool, but the goddess's presence was getting stronger. She was just under the surface ready to breach. I felt the urge to rip open my chest, tear her out, and cast her to the sky. Her voice drummed in my ears with an eerie synchronicity to the beating of my heart and I felt a sorrowful longing for her to leave. Soon, I promised her. Soon.

* Johnny *

My pulse rang in my ears as we arrived. The Valtan tents were up and night was falling quickly. There was chaos among the other rulers as we marched in. Father immediately retired to his large tent in the center of all the others, his guards following close at hand. Max was to share one with Avaline, split down the middle with a canvas sheet to house Perido and me on the other side. We had guards of our own, encircling the tent just as Father's was guarded.

The green tents were huddled together, and as it got darker the fields of Shor became eerier. Something was not right. The king had made sure that we were inside for the night as soon as we got there. No one was to be met with until the morning. "No need to be wandering the camps," Father had told me, no doubt referring to both his sons. He knew us well.

Perido was lounging on one of the makeshift beds, Av and Max were on the other side of the tent whispering to each other, and I was pacing. Candles flickered as I strode back and forth over the ground, my sword still at my hip.

"Bortal is not here yet," Perido said calmly. That was the problem.

I turned to face him. "Bortal was directed to be here. Why isn't she?" I asked, hitting the wall of the tent.

Perido sat up. "No need to be hasty, she has the night. Remember, she's the…"

"The Third Kingdom, cut off from the rest of Cavail," I interrupted, waving my hand.

"Bortal's troops are few, and they are to load onto borrowed boats," Perido reminded me.

"But we were to be the last ones to arrive, that was the bargain."

Perido stood up, guided me down onto his bed and held my shoulders. "Brother, this is not your worry. You are here to protect Max and lend support, not anger. Bortal has limited travel experience, but she is on her way. You must remember: Bortal has not crossed the wall in thousands of years. This is big for the kingdom. Her people will be wary." He squeezed my shoulders and sat down on the ground in the middle of the tent.

"But Perido, aren't you worried too? Bortal has always been loyal to Valta, and us to her in return. She is the kingdom we trust the most, and yet she is the kingdom that is gone." I rested my elbows on my knees.

"Bortal is respectful and loyal, yes, but she is an extremely independent kingdom whose people work on a different set of rules and calendars than we do. She will arrive, don't fret about that, but if she is held up it is for a noble reason, and this will not go on until she comes," Perido said.

I sat up. "Of course it won't," I said loudly.

"Then why are you so eager? Relax, my brother," he said. "For as much time as you spend alone you do get hasty, don't you?"

My anger flared and subsided in one swift motion inside my stomach. "Do you blame me?"

"No. But I do wish you would harness yourself better."

I snorted.

Perido laughed for a moment and then quieted. "Your emotion is no good unless it is in check. Do you ever see me lose control?"

I wasn't comfortable taking his actions as examples, but he had wisdom in his words and that was nothing to be surprised about. "Not in the way that I do, but you have your own ways of making things difficult."

He laughed again. "That I do, my brother, and I have learned well from you over the years to suppress my, ah, directness, but I think it is your turn to learn from me now." Perido stood and grasped my upper arm in a strong hold. My muscle tightened. "I intend not to demean you, only to open your eyes in a new direction as you have done with me countless times. Do you not agree that I was always the rude one and you the emotional?"

"We were a tiresome pair for everyone weren't we?"

Perido dropped his hand and turned to sit next to me on the edge of the bed. "We still are, I'm sure," he said.

"Yes," I said, smiling.

* Max *

I stared at Avaline sitting across from me on the bed. Herbs and small oil bottles splayed across the sheets between us. She bent over them, naming and stating the significance of every blossom or leaf or liquid she held in her hands. The ingredients for the event were among the herbs and bottles, casually resting on the bed.

The recipe was unrolled and pinned down on a table and she studied it under the candles for a moment, went back to sorting the herbs.

"Why are there poisonous elixirs and plants among medicines and healing potions?" I asked in a whisper.

She didn't look up but kept going through the recipe step by step. "This is a complicated releasing recipe, and I may have need of these. I carry them with me everywhere." She looked up, "It is not the poison but the nature of the plant that is significant."

"Are they magic?" I asked.

"They are common, non-unique herbs," she said.

I nodded. "What of the recipe? Who wrote it?"

"It was developed by a great castle wizard of Bortal thousands and thousands of years ago, much like Storret Airet is currently. The writer was likely among the first to practice such an un-barbaric releasing such as this, but I find that there is no magical element in the recipe. There is enough magic supplied by the goddess herself. This is merely a restoration to her abilities. Think of it like broth to a weakened body: it supplies the nutrients and support for the healing process, but doesn't heal it directly. When all is placed in your hands in the right order, and once all that must enter your body has entered, then she will leave."

"Just like that?" I said.

Avaline lifted her hands and then settled them back into her lap again. "I couldn't promise you it's that simple, but we will hope it is."

* Johnny *

The sun slipped above the horizon and spread yellow across the fields like butter over bread. Bodies inside and outside the tents stirred in the crisp air. Whispers could be heard piercing the quiet morning, not as musical as the first birdsongs, but just as lively. I lifted my arms above my head toward the sky and sucked in my stomach, embracing the stretch. When I was done, I let my shoulders settle and looked around. Gold tents. Orange tents. Green tents. Dela too had her tents; pale-cherry colored. But there was no red.

My face felt flush with disappointment, but I took a deep breath and thought of Perido's words the night before. The feeling wouldn't get the best of me, but it would stay there for now. Until the last kingdom came cresting over the hills into the valley, dressed in fine silky red, just like the sunset...

Until then.

Footsteps approached and I turned to see Avaline, in all her radiance, coming toward me.

"Good morning," I said.

She bowed slightly and grasped my hands in both of hers. Her white fingernails looked gold in the fresh light and her eyes were lazy, the rich purple especially deep this early.

"Good indeed," she said. "How are you this morning?"

I took my hands from hers and spread them, as if that would explain everything. "What about you? You're supposed to lead the recipe today."

"Yes I am leading this, to the high disappointment of all the rulers, surely. They fear me, but that has never stopped me before."

"You are the only one who knows how though. It would be foolish to have someone naive do it," I said.

"And that they luckily understand," she said. "As for your question, I'm well. Meditation, as well as releasing some fire, has cleared my mind."

"I hope you kept out of sight for that," I said.

She snapped her fingers and a small flame erupted with the sound like any spark would make between two stones. The flame played across her knuckles and crawled up her arm, igniting her markings for a moment before it extinguished. I would always find that impressive.

She cast a smile over at me. "I play like a child," she said happily. She seemed intoxicated by the fire this particular morning, but became sober as my father strode toward us.

"A gifted child," I mumbled before saying, "Good morning Father."

He waved a hand through the air as if to wipe away the easiness that hung around Av and I. "What are you doing here without a guard?"

I grinned. "Avaline isn't threat enough?" He caught my sarcasm with an ungrateful air, but he knew it was true. Avaline was powerful in the least and could wipe out four times the men I could, and in half the time. "Has there been any word on Bortal?" I asked.

"None that I have heard. Valta has offered to send a group of messengers up north to straighten the question," the king said.

More footsteps came near and Perido yawned. "Wouldn't it be a little cruel to send our men into the Forest?"

"A light comment in reference to your people, Prince Perido," Max said, running a hand through her tangled hair as she approached.

"I didn't mean for it to sound that way," he said. He turned to Father, "A risky idea nonetheless isn't it?"

"Kye returned from Dela and met with me this morning. He has agreed to accompany our soldiers along with a Delan friend of his to sail from Mala to Bortal's Port and visit the castle. A much safer rout than the Forest," he said, then mumbled, "a suicide to send them into that thicket of terror."

"Not as bad as you would assume," Max said.

I laughed but Father didn't seem amused. Avaline shared a look with Perido and all fell silent for a moment.

Father clapped his hands together. "I'm off to speak with the queen of Dela. She and her little town will be welcomed into their kingdom position today, the fifth." The king of Valta turned, walked away. "Find a guard, you four," he said over his shoulder before he was out of sight.

I turned to Max but she spoke first. "Don't ask, my mood keeps changing."

"Well I'm fine, in case you were wondering," Perido said to me. "And how is Avaline?"

She smiled briefly. "Fine."

"Is everything in place?" Perido said.

She nodded, sending a ripple through her hair. "All but Bortal," she said, "and I'm afraid that the ceremony can't start without every kingdom present."

Shouts suddenly came from the Delan camp and soon people were rushing amongst the tents in a frenzy. Valtan guards, as well as a handful of Oslo's, Alice's, and Dela's, ran up a rise toward the north and moments later a boy appeared at the top to greet them. He waved his hands expressively and it wasn't until Perido and I got closer that I saw he held a scroll.

"I am here, I am here," the boy was saying. His eyes were wide and youthful and his skin pale, scratched in places. He looked to be no more than eleven years old.

"And who are you?" Perido asked as we pushed past the group of guards circled around the boy.

"The..." The boy trailed off, straightened his back and cleared his throat. "I am Hammond of Bortal," he said. His shoulders slumped forward again and he handed Perido the scroll he had been clutching. My brother took it and removed the red ribbon, let it bounce open in his hands. He read it a moment and then looked up at the boy.

"*Prince* Hammond," Perido corrected. "May I see your Royal Brand?"

Prince Hammond cast his eyes downward and revealed a small B under his right collarbone. Perido nodded and flashed him his Valtan mark as well. I did the same.

Hammond turned to me. "My mother likes you, prince Jonathan. Didn't you just recently visit the castle? I did not see you."

A Kingdom's Possession 191

"It's been a few months," I said.

He grinned up at me for a moment then looked at Perido again. "I'm sorry," he said, but didn't add anything more.

Perido extended a hand to the boy. "You may come with us. My father will wish to speak with you, I presume."

Prince Hammond of Bortal grabbed Perido's hand and walked with us to the Valtan Tents. The other guards ran back to their appropriate camps to tell their royals of the new arrival, muttering or calling out to their royals with the news.

"So," Perido said once the boy was seated in our father's tent. "What happened exactly?"

"It says here that there was a mishap in your travels. That your borrowed boats were cut from their ties and floated out of reach." The king of Valta said, glancing up from the scroll to the boy.

"That's signed in my father's hand," he said, as if the king didn't believe what he was reading.

"I see that," Father said coolly. "I presume that each of you read this scroll already?" He waved his hand. "I will summarize it. The king of Bortal is at the kingdom's castle at this point in time. He wishes his son to carry this on, as he has fallen ill and his wife intends to stay with him."

Prince Hammond nodded, his eyes intent on the king. "Father is very sick. And yes, we couldn't sail into Mala. The boats were cut and Father believes it was Alice. There is no proof, though. I was sent to stand in for Bortal's rulers." He let his eyes fall on his shoes and he rubbed his legs as if he was cold.

"Where is your guard? You didn't go through the forest did you?" the king asked.

"Oh, but I had no choice," he said.

"You mean to tell us that your parents sent you, the prince of their kingdom, into the menacing Forest of Bortal?" Perido asked slowly.

Hammond tipped his head to one side. "You forget that I am not heir, my sister is."

Father shifted in his chair. "Your sister? That is against tradition," he said.

"Not Bortal's tradition. They have had many queens in first rule," I reminded him.

Hammond nodded. "As does Oslo," he added. "My parents love me very much. They sent me with food, and horses, and a hundred guards."

"Then where are they?" Perido asked.

"Most of them are at the wall with the horses and carriages and supplies. They should be here shortly with tents. I ran ahead by Mother's wishes. She had told me to be the first Bortalan in hundreds of years to step on ground that was not ours." He smiled proudly. "My guard will be here soon," he repeated. The king nodded.

"Most of them? What of the others? And how did you cross the wall?" I asked.

Hammond looked away for a moment. "The Great Barrier is very old and crumbled now. It's not hard to find a space to walk horses and carriages through." There was a commotion outside and Hammond paused. "There they are," he said.

"Most of them?" I repeated. "The others?"

Instantly, Prince Hammond's eyes welled up with tears and he grabbed on to my sleeve.

"It's okay," I said, "No need to tell us."

"Bortal's Forest is a horrible place," he said. "We went along the coast, but I could hear cries from deep within."

I patted his hair down and glanced over at Father.

"The other guards panicked with fear from the noises and fled. Some did not make it home."

"Prince Hammond?" The king said.

The boy sniffled, wiped his eyes.

"Would you be more comfortable if you slept in a Valtan Tent? With Perido and Johnny perhaps?"

Hammond lifted his head and nodded. "Yes, I would. Thank you Prince Perido, Prince Jonathan."

I wrapped my arm around him and squeezed. Perido leaned over and ruffled his hair.

"I've never housed with other princes before," the boy said.

Prince Hammond met Max and Avaline that night by candlelight. The rulers had argued for hours over the lack of order amongst the kingdoms and the late arrival from Bortal. They postponed the releasing to the following day, so Hammond could settle.

"Those marks, are they scars?" Hammond asked Avaline when she strode into our tent. Max was right behind her.

"And who are you?" Av asked.

"Hammond of Bortal," he said quietly.

"I am Max," she said. Her hair was pulled back, exposing her mark just as boldly as Avaline always did hers.

"Adahlia," the boy whispered.

"Adahlia's chosen body, but not her soul," Max said and sat down next to me on my bed.

"Oh," Hammond said.

"You are here to represent Bortal?" Avaline asked. The boy nodded. "Dangerous to send a young royal past the Forest," she whispered to Perido. She had already heard the story.

"A royal must be here to perform, otherwise the reward spreads to three kingdoms and a villager," he said quietly, a small grin twisted his face.

She smiled at his jest, turned to acknowledge the boy. "I am Avaline," she said, bowing slightly.

"I am Prince Hammond of Bortal."

Avaline laughed. "It is nice to meet you."

Hammond turned to Max. "You are very pretty. Are you going to live when we release Adahlia?"

It was blunt, but Max didn't flinch. "We will hope so."

"That would scare me I think," Hammond said.

"It is scary," Max said, "but I try not to think about it too much. I have no choice, do I?"

Hammond looked up at her with big, innocent eyes. "You don't have a choice, is what my mother says. But I will ask the gods to keep you safe."

"Thank you," Max said.

"She will be okay if we all do the ceremony correctly," Perido said.

Hammond looked over at him. "Will you do it?"

"Our father will, the other kings will," I said.

"I will be the only prince?" Hammond asked. His face became very serious.

"You do not need to worry, you will be fine representing Bortal," Avaline said. "Just follow my instructions."

"I will do exactly that," he said.

Max smiled at me and placed a hand on my leg. Morning would arrive swift and eager.

Chapter 14

* Max *

The night brought thunder and rain and pulled it into the morning. I woke early with a chill and saw Avaline up already, a dark grainy figure studying the recipe by the small light of a single candle. I pulled the blanket up and over my shoulders and curled my legs to my chest. My body felt heavy on the mattress; all my muscles were clenched and I could not ease them, not even with sleep. I shivered. It was hard to believe this was a spring morning.

But then, there were many things that were difficult to find true.

"Are you rested?" I heard Avaline ask me. It was too dark to see her lips move, and she was not glowing now.

"I'm tired," I said. I shut my eyes and tried to swallow. My mouth was dry and sore. The wound in my side, scabbed and jagged, ached with the cold. It was a blunt pain that I had somehow gotten used to over the night.

"You shouted once in your sleep," Avaline said. I could hear her rolling the scroll, the soft paper whispering against her fingers. She tucked it into the folds of her dress. Soundlessly, she came to my bedside. I didn't notice her presence until she sat on the edge on my bed.

"Dreams?" she said softly. "Or is she simply speaking to you?"

I looked up at her shadowy outline. "Adahlia's words are never simple." I said. "And no dreams, just a tight feeling in my body, as if it doesn't want to let her go. She's speaking now, Avaline, but I try to ignore her," I said.

She sighed. "Adahlia knows why we are here." She brushed the hair out of my face. "Today will be costing."

"For the both of us," I said.

She patted my hip. "For the three of us," she said. "You, me, and the goddess. It mustn't be easy for her either, being trapped in a woman's body."

I lifted my head. "Like you," I said.

Avaline bowed her head as her body began to glow. "Like me," she whispered.

We stayed there for a long while in the dark. Nearly an hour went by before the gray haze began to lighten in shade. Rain still drizzled on the fields of Shor and the tents of the kingdoms. Thunder threatened closer.

But I knew there would be no more delays. This was a day that would come with tremendous change. For better or for worse, I was not sure. And I was terrified deep into my bones.

As day grew older, the storm pressed on. Lightning cracked, surrendered to the thunder, cracked again, and so it went on. Rain pounded the ground. The rulers gathered in the middle of it all, on top of the highest hill in Shor, their coats whipping around their bodies. Avaline was among them and she remained aglow in the haze, her hair alive in the wind, streaming around her head like an angry sea. Avaline's dress thrashed around her pale legs like a wild fire.

I could see Perido, standing at the base of the hill with the soldiers and guards, watching intently as their rulers tried to speak over the snaps and booms of the sky.

I pulled the canvas flap closed and took a deep breath. For a moment, I bathed in the green light of the tent, gathered my nerves, and readied myself to step outside. But before I could, Johnny entered from the other side, wind whistling as he laced the canvas shut.

"Wait," he said. I turned around and he was near me in two strides, close. Our faces almost touched and I could feel his warmth.

"Yes," I said.

He shrugged and took a step back. "Be careful, Max. And may the gods be good to you."

I reached up and ran my fingers through his dark hair. I smiled. "They have not been kind this far, but let us hope they will now." I touched the amber pendant at my chest and went to leave, but Johnny caught my arm and turned me toward him once more. He placed a hand on my cheek as if trying to remember my face, brushed my lips with his fingers before retreating his hand. They tingled long after his hand drew back.

"Take care," he said softly. Then he pushed past me and stepped out into the storm.

I tried to regain control of my breath, but I couldn't. He made it hard to grasp the situation. I couldn't relax, couldn't breathe. I stood there, dumb, thinking about how Johnny had become such a large part of my life.

He had become just significant enough to overwhelm me.

My feet didn't want to move but they did, slowly, as my hands lifted for the opening in the tent. My breath kept reaching the wall in my chest, built by Johnny's hands and Adahlia's instruction. I inhaled air to push past it. The goddess was ready. And I was as ready as I would ever be.

The wind clawed at my clothes like an animal, groping my hair and body and teasing the space around me as I stepped out of the Valtan tent. I couldn't hear a thing but the buzz of the wind, and even then it was a mute sound next to the captured divine screaming in my ears.

I felt as though I was walking up into the sky, and despite the thunder and lightning, I kept going with no pause up the hill. Avaline, three rulers, prince Hammond, Perido, and Johnny now waited at the top. Guards of all the kingdoms waited at the bottom, hands on their hilts, bodies tense, their feet anchors. I weaved through them as if through a forest, avoiding the snags of elbows and sheathed sword tips. As I made my way the storm sounded louder, the rain poured harder, and the wind grew wilder. Grass grabbed at my feet, clinging, cutting. The goddess's voice became more piercing.

It was at the top that all of the weight and thought of everything going on around me drove me to near insanity. My body shook.

The circle of royals stepped back so I was alone with Avaline, Perido, and Johnny. The twins instantly grabbed my wrists as if I were their prisoner. Johnny's grip was surprisingly tight, his breath heavy in my ear; Perido's hold was gentler, but his demeanor eerier. Avaline stood in front of me with the recipe flapping in one hand and her pouch of herbs and vials in the other.

And then she began. "Adahlia, we call you to the surface. We wish to release you from this earthly body and bid you immortal once again."

Johnny squeezed my arm for a moment and then relaxed. He was making me nervous. Avaline's purple eyes fixated on me and I felt myself pulling against the Valtan princes' hands.

"Queen Foe Josalind of Oslo, please step forward with your gift of releasing," Avaline said coolly.

The little queen stepped forward, her golden hair twisting around in the wind as much as her thick red dress. She didn't look like a queen, but more a peasant wrapped in a soaked noble's gown. When she got closer her eyes were wide with a sagacity that made up for her slight appearance.

"Please present the gift, Josalind," Avaline said. Her voice was calm but I could see her hands shaking with tension.

The woman drew a small, slender case from her robes and held it out before her. "I, the queen of the Fourth Kingdom Oslo, give this gift to the goddess," she said.

Perido released my arm and, using both hands, grasped the container from the woman so that she could step back.

I thought for a moment about when we had retrieved the case, deep in the Vault. I had thought lightly of it then.

"Prince Hammond of the Third Kingdom Bortal," Avaline said. The queen stepped away from the circle altogether and the prince stepped forward. He looked rough and weathered from the storm, but uttered his words perfectly, as if they had been rehearsed. Once he handed Perido the small-sheathed dagger, he looked at me, worry and curiosity on his face. He paused for only a moment, then walked over to where the queen of Oslo stood.

Avaline held up her hand as if to silence the thunder and stop the rain, but the pair continued on. "I will now perform the first part of the recipe," she said, "the Dagger and the Golden Spines. This will draw Adahlia to the surface." She shoved the scroll into a fold in her dress and looked around. "This will sting," she said to me quietly, as if she were telling me a secret. I could see the royals strain to see and hear.

She opened her small bag for some herbs and unlatched queen Foe's case. Avaline grasped my free hand in hers, uncurled my fingers and held my hand tightly. Her eyes gained and lost contact with mine in a swift, sorry glance and then she pulled a long golden spine from the case.

Johnny's hands slid from my arm, up to my neck, softly, as he had when we kissed. But this time, his fingers pulled my hair back, away from my mark, and he held my head down. I could see nothing of what was going on, only my feet, and those of Avaline's, coming closer.

The goddess screamed in my ears as Avaline drove the spine into my neck, through the mark. I froze a moment in shock and then twisted my head as the pain arrived. It was unimaginable, agonizing. A small noise escaped my mouth. She pushed in another spine. Tears streamed down my face as she added three more, into the skin along the swirls of my mark. They barely pocked the surface and yet it felt like Avaline had pushed them inches deep.

My temperature spiked and chills taunted my body, crawled like bugs over my flesh. The goddess howled and shook my ribs like they were the steel bars of a dungeon door. I gasped and wreathed in Johnny's hold, but Avaline wasn't done. She pushed herbs into my mouth and told me to chew. I did, but I couldn't swallow. My throat had closed. If I tried, I knew my churning stomach would press them back out.

"For your consciousness," I heard Avaline whisper in my ear, "and the pain."

Johnny pulled my head up, his hands cold and wet on my face. Blood was on Avaline's hands as she reached for the dagger. Perido pulled a small vile from her pouch. I couldn't guess what it was, and I didn't want to know. Avaline unsheathed the dagger and put the point on my neck near the spikes. I looked deep into her sorry eyes as she pressed it into my flesh, carved lines along the spikes on the very surface of my skin. It hurt more than it should have. The goddess shrieked. It felt as though she moved inside me, up toward the pain, rushing, like blood.

Perhaps Avaline was creating the opening for her to leave, right through the mark she had given me.

I cried out and Perido uncorked the tiny bottle, poured the liquid on my neck.

I could feel remnants of it sliding down my front, no doubt mixing with the little trails of my blood. I became hot, like I had been shoved into fire. Soon my flesh felt so hot it was cold. I shivered and shook and thrashed in Johnny's hold and I could hear him yelling too. Maybe he was trying to calm me down, maybe to get Avaline and Perido to stop.

"Don't stop, don't stop," I yelled, and my voice cracked to the point where I couldn't speak. "Don't stop," I mouthed noiselessly. "Don't stop." I wanted her out.

The goddess shook her shapeless body inside mine and tore at my hair. She tried to crack my bones and screamed in my ears to keep me awake.

But then my consciousness slipped away.

* Johnny *

I held onto Max's arm tightly, my other hand at the base of her neck. Her skin was hot then cold, rising and falling dramatically. Soaked by the rain and sweat, she yelled at the top of her lungs, now incoherent. "Hurry," I said to Avaline.

She nodded and motioned for the king of Valta to step forward, but as he did, King Kier Sylan, the king of the First Kingdom Alice, pressed into action. He dove forward and thrust a dagger into Max's shoulder. "For Alice! I will release you by blade goddess, remember us."

All became a blur as I leaped to the side, dragging Max with me, and Avaline went to extinguish the Alician with her fire. It blazed up into the sky with such force that she was knocked backward from the sudden blast and Kier was pushed forward. His dagger glinted briefly red and slipped from his hands as his body hit Perido's with a strength that sent both of them onto the ground.

I cradled Max in my arms; her visible hand was bloody and quivering, open to the sky. I mumbled to her in a soft voice while Avaline tried to dab away the blood from her shoulder and remedy the pain. The spikes were still driven into her flesh, neatly in place as if nothing had happened. I fingered them absently as I watched Avaline. Max was limp.

Nearby, Perido pushed the charred king off of him and stood up. Prince Hammond and the queen of Oslo were huddling where they had been the whole time, lucky to be off to one side. Father watched as King Kier Sylan of Alice was dragged away from our collision by four Valtan guards while the soldiers from Alice seemed to be ready to raise their white flag of surrender to the seizing force of Bortal and Oslo at the base of the hill. Their plan to gain all the reward of the goddess and fend off the other guards had gone horribly wrong. Guards from all the other kingdoms surrounded the Alician camp, kept the rebellious kingdom in check while we finished the ceremony.

I looked back to Max.

Avaline turned to me in haste. "Johnny, hold Max up while Perido and I finish this."

Max's shoulder twitched as the blood continued to pour out. The wound would not be fatal as long as she did not lose too much blood or get an infection.

She had begun laughing hysterically. Her trance was getting worse and it was evident that she was on the edge of reaching no return. I pulled her up to her feet. She slouched all of her weight on me and rambled on quietly to herself.

Avaline lifted two bags from the ground where Sylan had fallen. One was small and gold, the other had been Avaline's, knocked from her hands in the commotion. From her bag, she pulled out a small bottle. "Here, see if she'll drink this, it will help the pain and ease her mind a little," Avaline said.

"Dragon's blood and lily nectar," I said quietly. I lifted the liquid to her lips and poured it into her mouth. Her slurred words subsided for a moment while she swallowed and then started up again. "Okay," I said.

Avaline gave a signal and Father stepped forward. All his focus was here. "I, Cross Rowan, king of the Second Kingdom Valta, present these gifts to Adahlia. May she lift to the heavens renewed and in peace." Father handed the small bags to Avaline and stepped back with the queen and prince Hammond. Father had presented the Alician gift as well as Valta's and I knew very well that Alice's power would not survive long past this. She had lost much more than she would have expected.

I shifted Max's body against me. Father bowed his head. Before we had left, he had said that this ceremony was magic and therefore illegal, but there was no other doubt than that, no other questions. He had trusted in his sons, and that was all I could have asked for.

As Avaline approached, Max's body shook violently. Her head was limp, rolling on her shoulders. The spikes remained in place. Avaline tilted Max's head up and gently brushed the hair from her face. She opened the small Valtan-green bag.

"The second part of the final event: the Paint and Dust," Avaline announced. "This will encourage the goddess," she said to me. She pulled out the jar filled with a thick, shiny orange liquid. Also in the bag was the little brush, which she brought out and presented to now only the three of us. All the royals had stepped back to observe from a distance.

This was the last of it, but a knot of terror still rested in my stomach, one that would never subside until Max was safe and well. I wondered if it would ever settle.

Avaline opened the jar and dipped the brush in. The slow liquid glimmered and dripped on the grass, getting watered down by the rain as she raised the brush in front of her and drew a line across Max's forehead. The liquid ran down the bridge of her nose and along her cheeks until her face was streaked with the thick orange mess. Avaline dipped the brush in again and painted Max's lips, then gave the jar and brush to Perido. There was only one thing left. She opened the golden bag contributed by Alice and put her hand inside. When she pulled her hand out, a bit of golden dust was pinched between her fingers. She flicked it at Max's face and Max screamed like a child.

Max shook her head and heaved in big breathes of air and rain and golden dust. She coughed. The lightning cracked as Avaline poured the rest of the dust over Max's head. Hurriedly, Avaline dug into her own bag, pulled more herbs out and willed them into Max's mouth.

Adahlia was surely ready to leave, but would it work? I wasn't one to ask the gods for help, but I muttered to myself just then, "Let her be okay."

Max opened her hands to the sky, let her head fall back, and a dim glow illuminated her.

I stepped back, letting her carry her own weight.

Perido grabbed Avaline's arm in shock and I huddled with the two of them, only capable of watching at this point.

It was up to Max and Adahlia now.

* Max *

She hissed in my ears and I thrashed. Adahlia was leaving me behind, floating into the sky through my pours, through the mark. I could taste sweet liquid and rain on my lips as she yelled and taunted me with words in the language of the gods, so familiar to me now. She tore at my body, wriggled in its hold until she breached from the surface and lunged for the sky. She was a bright light, full of color and perfection, and great, tremendous flaw. She was forgiving as she flashed her brightness in my eyes, sorry as she caressed my cheek, and thankful as she left the earth behind. "You are blessed," she said to me, and I understood. She was finally free and she didn't pause when she spoke. She traveled fast and far and then all of a sudden I was alone on the earth, completely empty in my own body. And it felt very strange.

With no pull toward the sky anymore, my muscles gave in and I fell forward onto my knees. Rain pounded on my back. I could hear distant voices saying a familiar name as warm hands fumbled about me. A sharp pain in my shoulder arrived. I vomited over and over, retching out all the horrible things that I had swallowed. I ripped the spikes out of my neck and clenched my fists as my stomach contracted and quivered. I ran a hand over my face and it came back bloody and stained with a thick, orange liquid that now tasted more sour than sweet on my lips.

Adahlia was gone, but what she had left behind was something worn and weak. A shape with tears pouring from her eyes for reasons that weren't coherent anymore. Blood covered the very hands that were supposed to hold on; it came from my shoulder, my neck, dripping and lingering.

My rational mind distantly wandered above the rest of my mind, but soon only images and sounds entered my stream of thought. I could hear laughter, a name being called, warm hands touching my face and back. I saw a river and unimaginable colors and vivid faces of people I thought I knew.

And, finally, I saw my freedom.

* Johnny *

After laughing and vomiting, Max fell to the grass completely. The thunder and lightning had seemed to give up, but the rain still fell, unsubstantial now that we were soaked and didn't care. The royals of Oslo, Bortal, and Valta rushed around, helped Perido and me bring Max to her feet. We carried her only part way down the hill before a member of the Valtan guard took her from our arms. Prince Hammond and Queen Foe clung to each other as Father tried to comfort them. Avaline collected the items for the recipe and pushed them into the folds of her dress. Her red hair hung around her face, wet and quivering as she moved. She did not glow at all now, not even when she met Perido and me and walked with us back to our tent.

Not even when we rushed to Max, as the Valtan guard set her down on the bed, and blood poured out to stain the sheets.

* Max *

The shades were drawn over a little window and I rocked from side to side. That small, insignificant image of the window stayed in my mind, even as my vision failed again. The world went black.

I heard muffled voices speaking like before, only this time I recognized the syllables and sounds more clearly. But I tried not to listen. I didn't want to hear them. I could feel my fingers clench against soft sheets, and a dull pain came from my shoulder. And I ignored it.

Some things made sense and others didn't, and I did all I could to shut out my own questions. But they came anyway: Where am I? Who am I? Who is speaking? But the more I thought in the darkness of my head the more I started to remember. I remembered names, images, sounds. Max, Avaline, Perido, Johnny. Johnny. That name meant something more than the others.

I saw red, like blood, heard screams in the memories. I saw orange and smelled the clear scent of stormy air. I felt rain on my skin, pain in my neck, dryness in my throat. There were flashes of light, booms of angry voices, and a sudden emptiness.

I moved my head slightly and the image of the little window came back, tilted. I felt alone, but not abandoned. Safe, but not watched. Loved, but not heard.

Something was gone, if only I could figure out what it was.

I slipped away again, into a blackness that was sudden and inescapable. The next time I woke, I was in someone's arms and the sun was high and bright. I could hear waves, and the steady step of people walking across wooden planks. The person carrying me breathed heavily and spoke softly, as if I were listening. I clenched his shirt as he shifted me in his arms. My head pulsed and my neck stung with immense pain. My shoulder felt as though it had been crushed.

My mouth formed a name and whispered it hoarsely, "Johnny?"

The person carrying me stopped.

"Max," came the voice. It was tired, but relief filled the tones. "Max, you're awake. Are you alright? We'll get you to the palace soon. Perido's here and so is Avaline. Everyone is here. Max, don't speak, just hang in there."

I nodded against his shirt. More voices dipped in and out of my mind as I was jostled more and more. Horses whinnied, men shouted, and the sounds of the ocean retreated as the sounds of city streets entered my head and swirled around like bees.

But I swatted the noise away. I made it leave. And I fell back into my sleep, hoping that the next place I woke was somewhere quiet.

My head didn't need any more pain or voices. I needed my peace and I needed it for a long while.

The last thing I heard before it all went black was Johnny's voice again. "It'll be just fine Max, I promise you. I'll take care of you." That was enough encouragement to keep me awake a little longer, keep me on the path toward real healing again. That voice was good enough to bring me back from the darkness that slept so easily in my mind. It was what I hoped to hear again very soon.

Chapter 15

* Johnny *

Max slept for a week straight without speaking to me again. It was only that single time on the way home that she showed signs of improvement, but now she had us all concerned. A fever tested death's waters, hung deep in her chest and made her skin pale. Perido and Avaline had stayed with me in her room for that entire week, but none of us spoke much. We barely ate.

Avaline fed Max herbs for healing and mental repair, but none seemed to work. She lay still in her bed, not even willing to swallow some days. Others, she would scream in her sleep, waking the entire castle and causing guards and servants to rush in, ready for battle or action or change. But none was ever met when they opened the doors, just three tired pairs of eyes and a still patient.

She had vomited for hours in the stormy weather of that dreadful day. She shook from the chill of the rain, her clothes completely soaked, and mumbled between her stomach-clenches like a madwoman. That evening, the smells of sweat and the sour contents of her stomach were enough to keep the sickness coming and at times I had even left the small tent to breathe for a moment, feeling queasy myself. She had stopped out of pure exhaustion after going well into the third hour of her talking, twitching, and heaving episodes.

What had the goddess left behind?

The king of Alice was still alive, despite Avaline's fires, but he was very near death. He had been taken away to the dungeons of his own castle immediately, along with some of his guard, by the soldiers of the newest kingdom, Dela. The Fifth, with help from Oslo, was agreed by the other two kingdoms to hold temporary rule over the people and the army while order was restored, although Alice was still strong with rebels.

Besides her king, the rulers had all come by to check on Max in the Valtan tent, but they all saw the same case: a girl on the brink of insanity and possible death.

My father had given orders and kept people safe the rest of that day. The different kingdoms had fallen into chaos after the event was finished, and I could see on his face that night how hard the day had been.

Father did not hesitate to give Prince Hammond of Bortal a Valtan ship to take him home, along with his guard. Father knew things would change in Bortal, but for now, keeping her people safe was his priority. I knew that he had been happy to see a Bortalan step across the wall. All the Valtans were. Bortal was Valta's greatest ally.

On our sail home to Valta, Father told me he was proud of both his sons and that he was eager to pass the crown to Perido. "Today he proved to me the kind of king he will be. To see Perido take action, be responsible..." Father had trailed off. "He will be a great ruler."

We were all losing hope in the recovery of Max because we knew the trauma was great, but we stayed in her sickroom in Valta nonetheless. Perido, Avaline, and I were all determined to see her when she woke. It was as simple as that.

It was when she mumbled that we all startled. I could hear sheets crumple and a little moan escape her mouth and instantly the three of us were at her bedside.

"Max?" I whispered, although even then my voice sounded loud in the quiet room.

Perido nudged my arm, "She's just shifting in her sleep."

"But this is the first time she's made any sound," I insisted. But he was right.

I walked across the room and slumped down in one of the chairs by the window. Better to think of other things now, wait it out more enjoyably, as strange as that seemed. Closing my eyes, I basked a moment in the late springtime sun. It would be summer soon, and

Perido would be announced as the new heir to the kingdom in nearly three months. Then a year would pass and he'd be crowned king of the Second Kingdom Valta. And take a bride that very same day.

I looked over at him speaking softly to Avaline, the both of them leaning toward each other, engrossed in the conversation, and thought about how ready he was to be king. He had been overshadowed by tradition and my responsibility for so long that he had been blunted and humbled. Let down because of my immaturely forced absence, and the fact that Father still wanted to make me king even after such a large betrayal. He was belittled from the moment he came out of mother's womb behind me, and lived under the cloak of superiority all his life. It was his time to shine; his time to rule and show Father that he was the better choice. It was Perido's turn to show the king that for once Father was, in fact, wrong in his choosing. Perido would be the best Valtan ruler there ever was, and I was happy for my brother. He was ready for the weight of the kingdom, and I was ready for the absence of the burden.

"Johnny, Max is stirring again, I think she's waking," Perido said. I came out of my thoughts and was at her side in an instant. I placed my hands on the edge of the bed and looked down at her.

"Her face is more colored than it was this morning," Avaline said, placing a hand on Max's forehead. "Her fever is still high. But do you hear her breath? It's clearer on the inhale."

I nodded. "Max? You're safe. You can come back to us. You're here in Valta. I know you can hear me. Wake up. We're all waiting for you."

Her eyes fluttered, and down by her hip I could feel her fingers pulling at the sheets of the bed. Her lips moved for a moment, and then she spoke.

"Close...the drapes," she said weakly. Perido rushed to the task and soon the whole room was transformed into darkness. I stared down at her face and she opened her eyes and blinked. "I feel...like...Avaline," she stuttered.

I nodded again, grasping her hand, wincing at how hot it was. "Avaline?" I asked. "Why's that?"

"Fire...in my...veins," she said. Her lips cracked into a smile and Avaline laughed.

"Well, don't go practicing the art of fire in the daylight, people do not like magical women," Avaline said, patting Max's head.

"I...know," Max said. She licked her lips. "The goddess...nearly got...me killed with...her powers."

For what had happened, her spirits were light and enthused. I started to feel the same. The goddess had left behind a woman with amazing strength, astonishing purity.

"Well, we're working on getting that fever out of you, don't worry," Perido said.

"Perido," Max said, "You can be...so cruel."

I blinked, completely shocked, but saw a smile flicker across Max's face again.

"Am I?" Perido said, immediately sensing her playfulness.

It was hard to believe her sarcasm after being so delusional for so long.

She shook her head against the pillow, silently mouthed a pain stricken "ow," and then went on. "Quick to...deal out the...herbs...and spikes," she said. "You're diligent."

Perido laughed. "I knew what I was supposed to do."

She attempted a nod again. "Yes. You...were perfectly...brutal," she said. "Thank you." My brother grinned. "And you," Max went on, "Johnny, you...have a strong...grip when the...girl you...love is violently sick and...shaking."

"Love?" I whispered at Avaline.

She gestured at Max, "You heard her."

Perido launched his hands into the air, flailing them above his head. "Finally," he said, "what have I been saying this whole time?"

"Oh," Max said, "Johnny...never listens."

"True," Av and Perido said in unison.

"You need your rest," I told Max.

She looked as though she were about to tousle my hair. I doubted she would be able to lift her hand so easily at this point. Her eyes met mine a moment before she spoke again.

"I need...rationality. And...believe me, it's not inside...my head. I will...not go back to...sleep." We all laughed, even Max, who silently struggled for her breath.

She had changed somehow, a pearl built around grit and irritation. She was finally free, rid of the torment of being someone else's shackle.

But was it worse to be bound as the captive, or stressed as the captor? I thought briefly about how Adahlia had fared, if she was safe among the gods once again.

But this was no time to wonder more dark things. Max was back.

* Max *

A month passed slowly without much talk but with extreme healing. Johnny and Perido were both busy with their mysterious Princely duties, I was bed ridden even with my insisting that I was fine, and Avaline spent her days either reading in the Valtan library or taking walks in the garden. All was peaceful, if not a little monotonous in my case, until I was invited to walk in the gardens with Johnny.

It was now in the height of summer, blistering days withered anything that ventured outside besides Av, who had the heat in her veins already. I told the maid I would only go out in the evening, when it was cooler, and she catered to my wishes.

"This is becoming a regular thing," I said to Johnny when I saw him coming toward me in the garden.

The sun was already down, the air just starting to cool. The clouds had dimmed from pink to deep purple, and night was on the cusp of breaking.

He stretched his arms over his head tiredly and flexed. "I hope not," he said. "I'd hate to think that the only time we can go for a walk together is after you recover from an awful injury. This is twice now, I hope there will not be a third."

I shook my head. "This was not an injury, it was a battle. As for the recovery," I spread my hands, "that type of healing can't be done simply by sitting in a room for weeks. It's time that I need, not inaction. Lying in bed will not help mental damage."

Johnny laughed, "Then what is it you need, if not bed rest?"

"I need to live," I said. "It is torture to be cooped up in my head all day. I need to do things, I need to experience, I need to…" I trailed off and looked into Johnny's dark eyes. He stared back at me, not at all afraid of the intimacy of the lengthy gaze. "I need to be free, Johnny," I finished. "That's how I heal."

We began walking down the garden path, past withered flowers and dehydrated trees. I watched my feet scuffing over the stones.

When I looked up, Johnny was smiling widely, "Perido and I were talking today about this very topic," he said. "My brother spoke of how the kingdom is his freedom, that he can make decisions and care for people in a way that sets him free." Johnny looked as if he were going to place a hand on my shoulder, but then let his hand fall back to his side. "I don't understand that, but my idea of freedom is different. My idea does not include castle walls, it doesn't have room for rules and indoor politics, it is framed by the ability to travel and make a difference in the field. My idea of freedom is very much like yours, in that it is mental and it is physical.

"You were a slave for the first part of your life, and as you escaped it, Adahlia took over. I was trapped in the castle walls, forbidden to see the world I learned about every day. I had a duty, and it was here," he said. "Perido finds his freedom through his mind, through his power, as humble as it may be. His imagination carries him places I could never go on foot and his role as king will only release him more. It will open new possibilities." Johnny sighed, "I know exactly how you feel. Now, I know that you don't really like the palace, and you know I don't care for it either, but I hope you realize that I still need the connection. I need a connection to you and I need one to my home. I am lost without either, I have found lately. That is why I'm going to become a messenger for my brother, when he is king." He waited a moment and then went on, "I'll travel everywhere in Cavail, find out information, explore, and inform my brother. You have no obligation to serve either of us, but Max, I speak for both Perido and I when I say that it would be dreadful to leave you behind. So I'm asking you now if you'd like to accompany me in service to the new Valtan king. It'll be a year before he takes the crown but I'm asking you now, in hopes that when it is time for Perido to rule, you will stay by our side, stay with us brothers, and enjoy your freedom with us."

It took a moment for me to decide, but when I did, I knew I would never regret my choice. "Yes," I said. "Yes, of course I'll stay with you two, what else would I do? Where would I go? Who would I go to that I would need more than you?"

Johnny quieted and looked at me from under his eyebrows, as if he didn't believe me. But then in one smooth motion, he had me in a tight hug and was whispering, "I think Perido would have been crushed had you said no." When I pulled away, he was only grinning more.

"Yes, Perido would be lost without me. But you, you'd be fine," I added, waving a hand.

He caught my wrist in the air and pulled me to him again. "I would go after you before your hundredth step in that wrong direction."

Caught in his grip I wanted to shove him away and I wanted to rush into him even more. But I could do neither for Avaline appeared around the corner and came toward us.

"I hope I'm not interrupting," she said.

Johnny and I stood still a moment, then broke apart and turned to greet our friend.

"It's good to see you up, Max. Did you have to escape, or did the maid finally cast you away?"

I shrugged. "It was an even chance, but I managed to escape before she could get rid of me."

Avaline knew very well that I needed to be out and about to feel better, but the Valtan maids and services had insisted I stay in bed at least a month. My condition had been horrible when I came in after the releasing, after all.

Av turned to Johnny now. "So, have you told her the news?"

Johnny shrugged, his big shoulders rising and falling in the dim evening light. "Which news? There is much to tell."

"I'd guess, but I don't want to reveal any secrets..." Avaline said.

"No secrets that can, or should, be kept from Perido's newest messenger," he said, delight filling his voice.

"Ah, so she has heard of that deal," Av said, "but does she know that I will be with your little posse also?"

I clapped my hands together. "Avaline, you'll be staying?" I asked.

"As long as I am human," she said. "But as soon as I'm a phoenix again..."

"Oh I am so happy," I said.

Torches were being lit inside the castle, the dim windows filling up with sudden brightness. The gardens were cooling quickly and it felt wonderfully mild and breezy under the darkening sky. The first stars were starting to shine.

"Then does she know that she will have to be at Perido's Grand Party as a freshly chosen messenger? When his new title is celebrated, all of his new royal trustees will be expected there," Avaline said.

"A ball?" I asked.

Johnny smoothed the air with his hands. "You only have to attend, wear a dress, eat the food, then go back to your room," he said. "No dancing or mingling is required."

"I won't be formally introduced will I? In front of Valta?" I asked him. "I don't feel ready to be publicly announced. I'm already known among the royals as the girl who lived after Adahlia."

"Well, it's always possible you'll be recognized, but not as Adahlia's mortal," he said.

I nodded at him then turned to address Avaline. "So are there any more surprises I should know about?"

She cocked her head, sending a ripple through that beautiful hair. Even in the wavering light, she still looked magical. "He's to take a bride when he is crowned," Avaline said, "But I believe that is all."

"A bride? Oh, well I'll have to ask him about that," I said.

"And I'm sure he'd like your teasing," Johnny said.

"Is it an arranged marriage?" I asked. Johnny nodded.

"To the wife that was once expected to be hand in hand with Johnny," Avaline added.

"Poor woman," I said. Johnny went to protest but I went on, ignoring him. "Bouncing from one prince to the other, it must be hard being betrothed to someone you don't even know."

"I would have liked that sympathy when you first heard of *my* marriage," Johnny said.

"Ah, but see how that worked out?" I said, "It's very well that she didn't get married to you, that would have been a nightmare," I said, stressing the last word.

"Perido is just as bad. And yes, I'm sure it would be a nightmare to be my wife," Johnny said.

I laughed, but reached out and ran my hand through his hair. The short dark strands felt smooth between my fingers. I rested my hand on his neck a moment and then retreated it back to my pants pocket. "Only to a woman who can't keep up with you," I said.

"And you have me, a man to keep you in check, on your toes," Johnny said. "A daunting bunch of messengers to anyone who crosses our path," Avaline said.

"All the better," said Johnny.

"I look forward to this," I added.

"A feeling well earned, Max," Avaline said, casting a wide smile at me.

I felt a bond to Avaline, Perido, and Johnny now that they had saved my life so readily, without any question. I vowed to do the same for them, that moment. I would be just as loyal to them as they had already been to me. It was an easy gift to return. I knew now that I could trust the three of them with all my heart.

The sunlight had all drained from the sky, leaving behind a dark, empty bowl. The air was warm and teasing and a blanket of stars glittered brightly against its backdrop. As I looked up, I wondered if Adahlia was among them, and if she was looking down on us. I wondered how her journey to the heavens had gone, if I had helped her enough. And the strangest thing was, I sort of missed her voice inside my head.

Johnny sighed and placed a hand on the small of my back. "Come, shall we eat as a group this night? It's been a while since we all ate a dinner together. Perido will be inside waiting for us I'm sure, and this is just the night to celebrate."

Chapter 16

* Max *

Princess Sarah seemed delighted to do my hair for the ball, but I knew that few people would see me. I would eat, I would wear a dress, and I would go back up to my room. But she insisted on the ribbons and the autumn flowers, asking Avaline to help her. I never had that much attention to my appearance, and it was strange. Every once and a while Avaline would place her hand on my shoulder and tell me to relax. It was supposed to be an enjoyable thing.

The summer had died away slowly and it was finally autumn. Tonight Perido would be announced as the official heir to the Valtan crown. I had to be there for him, though I would be attending briefly. I might be among princes and living in a castle, but I still had the etiquette of a street girl. Balls weren't something in my expertise, and the thought of one made me nervous. Avaline was much calmer, and I knew she had been to other celebrations in her many years. I wondered briefly about all the things she had seen and been through. I would not want to live that long.

I caught her eye in the mirror and smiled at her. She held a length of ribbon for Sarah, but when she saw me looking at her, she bowed her head slightly. Her eyes creased when her cheeks tightened into a grin. She began to glow slightly, but when Sarah reached for the ribbon, her skin was normal again.

I turned to Sarah when she was finished. "I look beautiful, thank you," I said.

"Oh, I love to help," she said. "The maids and Mother all think that it's a disgrace to work like this, but I say, if my brothers can practice swords like their men, then I can practice dressing and styles like my women." Sarah placed her hands on her hips.

"I'm sure they'd hate me for telling you this, but do what you love, whatever makes you happy," I said.

She tipped her head. She was already styled for the party in a beautiful sapphire gown, her hair done up much similarly to the way mine was. "That is exactly what Johnny always tells me," she said. "No wonder he's so taken with you."

I laughed and started to speak, but she clapped her hands together and spun in a little circle. "Well, I must be going downstairs. I promised Mother I'd arrive early to greet the guests. I will see you later tonight, Max." She gave me a light, awkward hug and bounced out of the room.

I sighed and looked at Avaline. "How many balls have you been to?"

Avaline shrugged, her glow coming back. "Many," she said, "but only one in Valta." She paused. "Tonight will bring back old memories that I have pushed back for a long time."

"You do not look forward to it?" I asked.

She shook her head. "I am happy for Perido, and I look forward to being here for him." And with that, she left the room. I smiled to myself, thinking about the many possible celebrations I'd be attending in my life. Surely this was only the first.

When I finally entered the Great Dining Hall, I found that I wasn't at the same table as Johnny, Perido, or even Sarah. I hadn't seen either of the brothers that entire day, and longed for the company of my friends. I knew Avaline was already seated. She would not eat, obviously, but she would sit among the diners nonetheless and converse with the people at her table. I was away from her as well. Johnny had mentioned that Kye was attending the ball as well. I couldn't see him, either.

I was placed just off to the side of the head table, with many lower, but still very prestigious royals. Or so I was told. Everyone was attending but the highest rulers of the other kingdoms. All of the royals of Bortal were home as well, still trapped in a difficult situation regarding their freedom from being inside the Great Barrier.

I looked around, distancing myself from the conversation with the man at my left. The white walls of the hall were draped with the regal Valtan Green velvet drapes. The tables matched the white and green, with every piece of silver and napkin etched or stitched with the Valtan seal.

There were eight courses served and when the diners were mostly finished, the king rose from his chair and called attention to all of his guests.

Whispers still lingered when he started to speak, but soon everything was silent, all but the little chimes of silver clinking together.

"I have asked you here today to join me in celebration of the trading of power between my sons," he began. "Prince Jonathan, the original heir, has decided to pass the crown to his younger brother Prince Perido. Though it is against tradition, it is my very great honor to present you all with this news. I couldn't be prouder of my sons for their strength," he said, glancing down to his left at Johnny, "their courage," he said, glancing to the right at Perido, "and their astounding loyalty to the kingdom, their people, and all those that they hold very dear to their hearts." The king looked off into the crowd, possibly at Avaline. I was surprised when the king looked over to me with the very last of his words.

When it was Perido's time to speak, he stood, spread his hands, and pushed his shoulders back. He held a cup in one hand. The liquid inside it quivered as he addressed the entire room. He was like a crystal inside a stone, and now that the stone had been split open, he glittered and sparkled, bore his sharp edges and openly presented them to the world. "I, Prince Perido, new heir to the Valtan Crown, am truly grateful and honored to be named with this title. A year from today I will be your king, and there is no greater joy within me. I will strive to bring only happiness and comfort to my people, and I vow now that I will practice and learn and strive to be the best king I can be. Johnny," he paused and looked to his brother, who was smiling up at him, "you are the reason that I am here tonight, and I want to recognize you for all that you have done for me. You are not only my flesh, my blood, my brother, but you are my role model, my friend, my support, and my courage. I thank you, my twin." With that everyone broke out into more cheers, drinks, and clapping.

I ate the rest of the meal silently, hoping that was all I had to do, but when it was time for everyone to head to the ballroom, time for me to retire to my room, Perido found me and begged that I at least have one dance with him. By the time I agreed—because I certainly couldn't deny the new heir—the other guests had already swept him away into the ballroom. He waved to me as he left and I followed slowly through the double doors.

* Johnny *

I looked everywhere for Max once all the guests were in the ballroom, but I didn't see her. Surely she hadn't gone to her room that quickly, without even saying hello.

I tugged at my black and green vest, trying to make it more comfortable, but it didn't work. I tipped my new hat and glanced around the room again. Max was nowhere to be found and neither was Avaline. Perido was already dancing on the floor with a pretty young noblewoman, gliding in perfect step with the music. He would be dancing with his future wife tonight too, among all the other ladies who desired a dance with the new heir to the kingdom. I would not be as popular tonight as I had been in past balls; I was no longer poised to receive the kingdom.

Couples bounced all around, but I was fine watching from the edge of the room. Perido had always been a better dancer. He had always been the better choice for king.

As the music closed, rolling into a scale and lowering quickly in octave, I noticed Avaline walking onto the floor. She was magnificently dressed in a long gown, colored in the purest of gold. She radiated light and put to shame the styles of the other women, exploding with a color and boldness that made her take on a look of otherworldliness. Her hair hung undone over her shoulders in a wave of red and orange and gold. Perido was in front of her within the moment she came into sight, kissing her hand and smiling at his friend. I knew he was telling her she was beautiful, just like he did with all the other ladies, but this time he would mean what he said.

He was dazed by her beauty, his awe so easily noticeable on his face. As the musicians rose into another song, Perido took Avaline's hand and swept her onto the floor. It was wonderful seeing them dance, but halfway through the song came a distraction that tore me away from their elegant movement.

Max entered the room, a look of serenity on her face. She approached me directly, getting closer too fast for me to soak in her magnificence the way it deserved. My fingers started to tingle and the hairs on the back of my neck spiked. She wore an earthy crimson dress that made her green eyes look dark and mysterious. A square neckline wrapped itself around her breasts, cut off abruptly at the shoulders, giving her dimension. The rest trailed around her waist and then spilled thickly into a dark pool of blood red fabric. Her pendant hung squarely in the hollow of her neck and glittered the same color as Avaline's dress in a patchwork of warm, magical hues.

By the time she reached me, I was nearly speechless.

"Well hello," she said.

"Hi," I said, stumbling over the word. "You look..." I spread my hands as if that would explain better.

Max shook her head. "I feel awkward and bare. Dresses make it so difficult to move. And I miss my sword."

Her complaints were amusing. "No, you're beautiful. That dress, your pendant..." That *smell*, I thought. It was like being wrapped in the cozy air of autumn itself. She smelled of sweet squash, lavender, mint, sugar all rolled into one. "You look positively radiant," I said.

She blushed and touched my arm. "And you look very handsome," she said.

But then she was greeted by Perido. He kissed her hand and laughed like it was the silliest thing he could have done. "Will you grace me with a dance, my lady?" he asked, bowing in front of her in a flourish.

Avaline came up beside him. Her fiery glow wasn't so evident now, but her eyes still flickered with the intensity she had taken on when she had entered. The woman's cheeks were red from her dance with the heir.

"Avaline, you look amazing, very nice," I said. I could see her and Max exchange a look and then she beamed.

"Thank you, Johnny. It has been a long time since I danced like that," she said.

Perido was still grinning widely as he took Max's hand and guided her away onto the floor. "I can't dance Perido. You'll look like a fool if you dance with me," she was saying as they walked away.

"I'm used to looking foolish," he said, before he twirled her out of sight and I lost them to the moving crowd.

Avaline touched my arm. "You have made your brother truly happy," she said. "Look at him."

I did as he and Max spun into view again. He guided her with an ability and a simplicity that made her look very graceful for her first dance. He smiled broadly. Even his eyes and actions looked pleased, his senses more alert. He seemed to stand taller, look brighter.

"He doesn't seem to be so dissimilar and wild anymore, Avaline," I said.

"There's no reason to," she said. "He embraced being different because it was expected of him, because in a way, he was defying those who teased him and belittled him. Why would he do that now?"

I smiled. "I wish they all could have seen him like I did, from the very beginning."

"If they had, he would not have grown stronger, more passionate."

"He would have suffered less," I said.

"His suffering brought him to this happiness tonight," Avaline said. "You have given him a very significant gift."

"The same gift you gave Max," I told her.

She bowed her head. "But you were a part of that too. And for that, you are very noble Johnny. You have a good heart."

"And yours is pure," I said.

Avaline touched my arm briefly, her tattooed hand gentle on my sleeve. "No," she said. Her hair rippled. "Not pure, Johnny. I may be wise, but never pure. Not after living this many years."

I laughed slightly, though she seemed to have turned grave on the subject. I placed my hand on top of hers. "Avaline, when we met in the forest.... Thank you. You have been magnificent from the start."

Her smile returned and was warm. "You're welcome."

We stood a moment, silently, and then she turned and disappeared into the crowd, just as magically as she had arrived.

Kye came up beside me. "She loves you," he said. "I can see it in the way that she looks at you. And you feel the same I'm sure; she's brilliant."

"Do you feel—" I stopped speaking.

Kye nodded, not needing to hear the rest of my question. "Yes, but she's yours," he said, resting his gaze on me. "Max has always been yours. Keep her safe."

"You know I will," I said.

* Max *

I was dizzy as Perido spun me onto the edge of the floor, back to where Johnny was standing. I leaned on the elder prince for a moment and caught my breath. They both laughed lightly and Perido kissed my hand once again.

"A good dance, I take it?" Johnny asked.

"Very good," Perido said. "She's very, ah, teachable."

I laughed. "Teachable. Well thank you, Prince Perido," I said.

He bowed to me and then regarded his brother. "She would dance better in your arms, I'm sure."

I could feel my face go flush, but the thought of dancing with Johnny did pique my interest a little. "Oh, I don't know," I said. "I'm already out of breath from one prince."

"Nonsense. You want to, I know it," Perido said. "A waltz is next, Johnny's best dance. Show her how a true Prince dances, Brother."

Johnny laughed. "A true Prince? I don't think either of us fit that description," he said.

Perido cocked his head. "Well," he said, "then show her how a man in love would hold his woman in a waltz." And then the new heir of Valta, Prince Perido, my friend, bounded back into the chaos of the dance floor.

I turned to Johnny. "I can only handle one more dance."

He tipped his hat and placed his hand on the small of my back. "Then let it be a good one," he said, and then he directed me to the floor.

The music started quietly, fluttered on the sweetest of notes while the couples bowed and curtsied to each other. Johnny faced me and bowed, modestly, gallantly. His dark eyes stared at me with intensity as we waited. When the music dove into its real sound, Johnny pulled me to him, grasping my hand in his, placing his other on my back. I could feel his rough hands catching the fibers of my gown as he pressed into me and moved me through the waltz with open grace. With each step, I could feel his breath, steady with our movement and the music. He maintained the gaze on me throughout the whole dance, silently gliding over the floor. I had no idea he could dance so well, so flawlessly, but he had it mastered into an art. He pushed me away with a spin, drew me back in, stepped to the side and pulled me closer. Our faces nearly met at the end and I could feel his breath close on my skin, but the rush of people's voices and laughter drew us apart and back to the edge of the floor.

"Would you like to step outside?" Johnny asked as I fanned myself and breathed deeply.

"I would," I said.

He held my hand as we walked out, but when we reached the railing of the balcony he let go and leaned on the bars.

Colorful lanterns cast red, green, blue, and purple lights into the darkness. The balcony overlooked all of the Valta Canal, offered the stars and presented me with a chill. The moon was out, hung above the water as if it floated on the surface. I could see the ships bobbing in the harbor.

"You dance like you've been doing it all your life," Johnny said finally.

"You lead like you seem to love."

"And how's that?" he asked.

"Loyally," I said.

He laughed, but became very serious very quickly. "You are quite spectacular."

I knew I blushed then. "Thank you."

"But I have to know: do you feel for me like I do for you?"

I didn't answer for the moment that he waited, so he went on.

"Do you find it hard to be without me? Do you think of me during the day? Do you long for my touch like I long for yours?"

I looked out and up toward the stars over the canal and thought of the goddess. She would be looking down on us, peaceful now that she was returned to her home above the world. Set free herself, just like I had been.

"Yes," I heard myself say to him. And it was true. Yes to my very center, I thought, that's exactly how I feel.

"Well," Johnny said, pulling away from the rail to face me. He reached forward and brushed the strands of hair from my face, cupped my cheek. He stepped close, so our bodies were touching, but just barely. "That makes me very happy." Somehow, it seemed like he had already known.

We stood like that for only a moment, and then he dropped his hand and we parted. I leaned on the rail again and took a deep breath of cool autumn air. The scent of salt came up from the canal and I could hear a gull call in the distance.

"So," Johnny said, "how is it without the goddess? What is it like just to be Max?"

I leaned on the rail beside him and looked out over the Kingdom of Valta. Little lights lit the windows of the houses and taverns. They looked like suspended fireflies in the darkness, vastly spread over a great amount of land until they reached the water and dispersed.

"It's different," I said. He slid his hand along the rail to meet mine and I shivered. Our fingers intertwined, tightened around each other.

More Fantasy and Science Fiction from Booktrope:

Cathedral of Dreams
By Terry Persun

Unchecked emotions made the world outside dangerous and violent–at least, that's the official story in Newcity, where everyone is content. Otherwise, you will get a visit from the police....

Keith escapes from Newcity but outside pressure is building to revolt against the insidious regime of social control in the city. Leadership is thrust upon him, with only his visions for guidance, only a small band of friends for support–and the fates of both Newcity and the outside world at stake.

Cathedral of Dreams is a compelling tale of a dystopian future and personal heroism.

The Printer's Devil
By Chico Kidd

A tale of ghosts, magic, music and modern heroism, *The Printer's Devil* will delight fans of historical fantasy. A musician discovers a spell laid by a grieving lover in Cromwellian England, opening forbidden channels through time and unleashing a very dangerous demon. Now Kim must put an end to the sorcery – or lose her beloved Alan forever.

"This affectionate tale of supernatural suspense twines ghostly and diabolic forces with a love of art and scholarship to produce one of the most readable such yarns in quite some time." *Dragon*

CPSIA information can be obtained at www.ICGtesting.com
Printed in the USA
270664BV00001B/269/P